Praise for Breena Clarke's
ANGELS MAKE THEIR HOPE HERE

"Well worth your time.... Told throughout in language that gives us the verbal music of the period and the soulful reality of this little community of outliers."
—Alan Cheuse, National Public Radio

"Rich, readable, and full of authentic detail."
—Bethanne Patrick, *Washingtonian*

"Set in the years leading up to the Civil War, in settings from the wilds of New Jersey to the streets of New York during the draft riots, Clarke's novel offers fascinating characters coping with heritage, identity, and complicated relationships."
—Vanessa Bush, *Booklist*

"*Angels Make Their Hope Here* is a compelling story about conflicts between conscience, culture, and one's calling. The dialogue singes and tickles virgin ears, yet is essential to developing strong, memorable characters. Clarke expertly engages our senses as she weaves nature, dreams, and ancestors into each chapter."
—Robin R. Pendleton, *RT Book Reviews*

"Dossie Bird is the daughter of a slave, seemingly born to be worked to death, until Duncan Smoot liberates her and squires her to freedom. Both of those names are rich and unusual, and perfect indications of the story Breena Clarke weaves in *Angels Make Their Hope Here.*"
—Jacqueline Cutler, *Newark Star-Ledger*

"A tender historical novel."

— Natalie Beach, *O, The Oprah Magazine*

"Breena Clarke gives voice in her lyrical third novel to a group of proud and free African Americans. The inhabitants of Russell's Knob — a tight-knit outpost community of mixed-race people in the New Jersey highlands known as amalgamators for their interracial mingling — are a law unto themselves, willing to go to any length to protect their own. Though individuals, and not the sweep of history, are the focus, this coming-of-age story of Dossie — spirited into Russell's Knob via the Underground Railroad — illuminates the terrible reach that slavery laws had into the lives of free black people in American towns and cities of the time. As Dossie grows from a scared girl to a strong woman, learning from the people around her and the trials she endures, readers will feel the pull of the fictional community of Russell's Knob and have hope that Dossie will thrive there. Clarke's fans will want this book."

— Laurie Cavanaugh, *Library Journal*

"Clarke's third book is a page-turner. She skillfully illuminates both the grime and shine of the age (both moral and physical) as her characters come to life."

— Kristen Hannum, Historical Novel Society

"As a coming-of-age tale, the novel is effective and satisfying. More than that, though, *Angels Make Their Hope Here* is an empowering story about community, self-realization, and freedom of choice, something every person deserves."

— Sarah Johnson, *Reading the Past*

ANGELS MAKE
THEIR HOPE HERE

ALSO BY BREENA CLARKE

River, Cross My Heart

Stand the Storm

ANGELS MAKE
THEIR HOPE HERE

A NOVEL

Breena Clarke

BACK BAY BOOKS
Little, Brown and Company
New York Boston London

Back Bay Books / Little, Brown and Company
Hachette Book Group
1290 Avenue of the Americas, New York, NY 10104
littlebrown.com

Originally published in hardcover by Little, Brown and Company, July 2014
First Back Bay paperback edition, July 2015

Excerpt from *Appalachian Elegy* by bell hooks, copyright © 2012 by bell hooks. Used with permission from The University Press of Kentucky.

Back Bay Books is an imprint of Little, Brown and Company, a division of Hachette Book Group, Inc. The Back Bay Books name and logo are trademarks of Hachette Book Group, Inc.

The publisher is not responsible for websites (or their content) that are not owned by the publisher.

The Hachette Speakers Bureau provides a wide range of authors for speaking events. To find out more, go to hachettespeakersbureau.com or call (866) 376-6591.

ISBN 978-0-316-25400-7 (hc) / 978-0-316-25401-4 (pb)
LCCN 2014937385

10 9 8 7 6 5 4 3 2 1

RRD-C

Printed in the United States of America

listen little sister
angels make their hope here
in these hills
follow me
I will guide you
careful now
no trespass
I will guide you
word for word
mouth for mouth
all the holy ones
embracing us
all our kin
making home here
renegade marooned
lawless fugitives
grace these mountains
we have earth to bind us
the covenant
between us
can never be broken
vows to live and let live

— bell hooks,
APPALACHIAN ELEGY

PART ONE

SHOULD HE OR SHOULDN'T HE burn the lowlander's house? Was he a burner? Should he burn them people's house to free the girl? Did he know what way the wind was blowing? Was she safe in the barn?

Indians, Africans, and amalgamators! Always caught up in fire startin' is what the whites say. The lowland white farmers are scared of burnouts from hostiles. Ha! Well they ought to be. The People have redressed wrongs and prevented trouble by burning their enemies before.

Burning folk out—ruining what they built—is a serious thing, though. Maybe the slavery of one little girl ain't enough to make it justified? Ah, these people are not fit for their farm! Their enterprises have failed. They have brush near the house. The woman is lazy. They have no water trough close by. The man is stupid. They should abandon the place.

Maybe they will blame the boy who works for them? He is a white, but he's a motherless bastard they despise. That boy will be lighting out soon. He's putting things by. That boy will take a horse and head off as soon as he sees a chance. Is it horse stealing if you take a thing that is owed to you for the life you put into an enterprise? Duncan thought not!

Duncan Smoot has never honored a bargain that was breached

by carelessness, disregard, dishonor. The boy was doing what any sound man or boy would do under the current situation. But with him gone these folk will put more work onto the little bond child. They will likely run her down to her skeleton.

Duncan Smoot, a practiced hunter, kept himself concealed. He looked up into the sky—into the trees—and saw few birds. But bird sounds reached him. They were incongruous. He observed the girl's travails. Is she the one he'd missed taking up because of the arrest of the Evangelist? Was this the very same girl after so long a time? He knew what happened to the Evangelist. Word was passed. They said the young girl was traveling with her. They lost her on the road when the Evangelist was taken up. It was the policy of those who transported the secret cargo on the canals and rivers that they off-load their responsibilities at different and varied stops so that risks were shared and watchers were fooled. It was vital also that, at the busy docksides and way stations, the wayfarer not be lost to the hands of a profiteer. Stationmasters and other agents of the shadow network knew when to expect their packages as information traveled ahead. Is this the girl he was to have taken up? Had the Abingdon ring grabbed her instead? If so, these lowlanders—these so-called farmers—had bought her off the Abingdons and were using her like she's a slave.

Evangelist Zilpha Seabold was a clever, well-prepared wanderer, but she had been caught. There was no reliable information about the girl she was conducting when arrested. Duncan Smoot was to have been the next link—the next conductor. He was to have met her near the town of Peach Bottom and taken her on to other helpers. He was a happy cog. He was satisfied to be neither the first nor the last of the chain. But the failure of this endeavor stung him. It irked him being unable to find the girl and know she was freed.

Duncan canvassed the colored towns and the fringe settlements looking for her. If she'd been taken in or helped along, then he would be content. He would know. He looked and searched in the woods where the girl was separated from the Evangelist. He talked to like-minded folk. News of Evangelist Zilpha Seabold was troublingly consistent. The hooting and hollering preacher woman was said to have been put in stocks and, by all accounts, tortured. Duncan's informants said her face was pulpy and her legs broken when they last lay eyes on her. No word of the girl. Reports of the pitiful state of the Evangelist surely meant that she had not given up any names or hideouts. Bless her, she had suffered for her folk!

It is time for a bold action! Duncan thought. He knew himself to be a man consecrated to a cause and pledged to a purpose. Mostly he worked within the system and was one of a chain of folk who followed on the information of others. Now was time for him to act on his own gut.

"What you thinkin' 'bout, Duncan? You're a-ponderin'?" Mama would say when he was small and thoughtful. Duncan had been a ponderer when he was a young boy. Then when his sister, Hattie, came, his mama forgot to hold off his tormentors. His cousins, a few years older, were cruel boys. They toughened him up and turned him quickly from a ponderer to a plotter, a schemer, a burner, and an eye gouger.

New York! New Amsterdam! Ach! Grandmother spit when she say it. She say "since when is new?" Grandmother's spittle runs into our creeks. It sustains us. We won't die of thirst in these hills. Our Grandmother sleeps there up ahead. She is taking her well-earned nap. Her lips fall back. Spittle runs out of the side of her mouth while she sleeps. The hills, the outcroppings, the ridges, these are her misshapen teeth. Them sharp juts are what remain when flesh pulls back from bone.

It is no doubt that grabbing off this girl from the lowlanders is against some law. Thou shalt not steal off your neighbor's bond servant, your neighbor's slave, or your neighbor's wife. Can you steal off a girl who has already been stolen? Duncan knew he was taking a lot on himself, but surely these lowlanders were holding her by illegal and immoral means. It itched him. It bothered him.

The ring had been uncovered and verified in Philadelphia. They were nefarious. They worked by chicanery to take custody of their victims. Josiah Abingdon and his confederates were a clutch of despicable pirates of all colors who operated a shadow underground. Young escapees were lured or fell into their hands then were sold outright to a variety of work situations. Profit from the sale of children was good because they offered little resistance, and their fear and confusion made them easy to control.

This much Duncan knew for certain: the child he had been searching for had passed into unscrupulous hands, was sold and taken off by this derelict farmer named Logan and his wife.

Was he so fixed on it because of what had happened to Pippy?

As Duncan advanced his plan he mulled the man whose destiny he was changing. Logan was a fool with no neighbors. He'd not even made a dam to exploit the stream that ran in back of his place. If he had water and buckets to dip it, he might save some portion of the house. He is stupid and lazy and not one who would stick in this place.

Duncan watched. They had no dog to raise an alarm that an interloper was nearby? He wondered at a keen man being so careless. At his home in Russell's Knob no unknown man or animal could come so close unobserved.

She's a wisp of a child. She's a bit younger than the boys — than Jan and Pet. Oh! His sensitive insides were softening for her? Pinched and burdened with work, she is losing strength with each day. They feed her little — just bread and what she takes from the cow. Pet's dogs sleep closer to the fire.

She is kept punishingly busy with tasks. The farmer's wife seems only strong enough to force the girl to lift and haul and sweep and fetch. She misses no chance to beat and slap at the girl.

Duncan flushed with remorse remembering his chastisement of his nephew, Jan. He'd been so angry that he'd forgotten Jan was a child. He was a willful, irresponsible child who was a bad influence on his younger cousin. But he'd been too hard with him. The child had knelt all night, had listened to him rail, had collapsed in a faint at dawn. Later he had run off.

He resolved to grab the girl up. He resolved to burn the low-landers out. He figured they meant to use up the little girl, then sell her south. Neither of them was above it. They had a smell about them — an aroma of unconscionable avarice. They would sell her and have the money to go to fail in the farther west.

Duncan Smoot knew the house would burn as he meant it to. He resolved firmly to burn it for them.

He risked a lot of trouble for a little dross. No, no. No. They called her Dossie. Her name is Dossie. Was it for the little Dossie he did it? Was it on account of her that he did so grave a thing? Her tiny goodness and complete helplessness was what did it then—that convinced him? She has two eyes still! Take her up while she still has two eyes to see from. Dossie, Dossie, Dossie. Was it a chirrup from a bird he'd never before listened to?

Duncan attached a bundle of dry brush to the tail of a possum and lit it and chased the poor terrified animal into the yard that had more dry grass and brush. An untidy farmstead is a dangerous place. There is much fodder for flames. And because the wind came in from the northwest and Duncan Smoot knew that it would, it whipped the fire and pushed it toward the Logans' house and away from the barn.

Duncan knew there was time enough for Mister and Missus to run out of their beds and escape with their lives. They would be startled out. No dog to raise a ruckus! The boy would call out before he rode off. They would certainly rush for their clothes and their money.

And he could escape with the girl. Dossie. The name made him smile. He had heard them calling her in calloused voices. He knew it was a sound that sang and delighted the ear if the voice but said it right.

The girl had come to feel that the cow loved her—cared for her—was concerned with her fate. The animal responded kindly. She turned her head when her teats were touched, and her milk let down when the girl stroked her flank. Her tail brushed gently and distributed her smelly gases far and wide.

"You got a deliverer coming," the cow said with satisfaction. She moved her mouth in its customary circuit. "Stay alive until he comes," the cow exhorted upon an exhalation—a snort of breath that raised up chaff and dander. As the pressure in her udders eased under the girl's squeezes, she added brightly, "He's coming soon."

The girl was given only bread and the cow's milk. Since she was given no other thing—no meat or apple—to fill up, her stomach was stalled and queasy. The cow pitied her and wished she could nibble on grass. The cow swatted flies off her own ass and wondered what was taking the deliverer so long to come.

When in the morning the heavens were clear. Dossie opened the door to the barn a crack and peeped. The bright light startled her. It was the same as to open all the windows in a house and let the sunshine come in like streams of yellow glory. Dossie felt the hot air on her face and sang her morning birdcalls like Bil and Ooma would do when the day came bright. She stood in the doorway of the barn, looked back at the cow, smiled, and thanked her. Though she would leave off sleeping with cows, she was filled with a notion of kind regard for and heartfelt appreciation of cows. Dossie turned and walked off. She looked back again to see the boy leading a horse with a bundle tied to the saddle. She saw the unsteady, middling tree that stood aside the house fall in and crush what remained of the charred roof. Smoke smell was in the air. Feeling still in her head, she walked away to the clearing at the edge of the Logans' tract where their cries of alarm did not reach.

Duncan Smoot took the girl away from the Logan farm on foot uphill—her small hand buried completely in his much-larger one. They followed a trail cut by a stream and marked by slick boulders. Water ambled downstream and reflected sparkles of the sun. She walked behind him and troubled to keep step. Perhaps he lifted her from the ground? Yes, when they reached the tall marsh grass at the edge of the stream, he lifted her and carried her across it. Did he carry her through the dense cover that bordered the Logan farm? No. No. He put her down and her feet passed over the ground — over rocks, moss, through a dry streambed.

She felt herself borne along with the man as a mite in his pocket or a string on his sleeve. Her breath came ragged as they climbed. She was unused to the terrain. Her mind formed little or no idea about her fate. She ought perhaps to have been frightened, but she was not. She believed the cow. At every turn she was treated to a different wonder.

1

RUSSELL'S KNOB, THE VILLAGE he brought her to, was secreted. It was a hide, a hush-up, a keep-quiet-about spot, a conceal-and-bottle-up sanctuary, a curtain, a disguise, a dissemble place. The homesteads that formed it were laid so that they were encountered singly — knots along a string. If one homestead was set upon, folk could fall back and escape uphill to the next house and make a stand with their neighbor. Together they could push a flaming barrel down the cliff to discourage the interloper and, if they were overrun, they could retreat to the next place on the string. This arrangement resisted the possibility of a complete burnout as had happened once or twice in the early times at Russell's Knob.

The first building in the village was a small stone house that sat like a muddy brown bird hiding herself in dense foliage. Outsiders and casual climbers were meant to miss seeing the cleverly disguised house and the cut that led to the town. If you knew the cuts you could find the town.

The old stone house, built so the natural slope of the hill obscured it from view, was the last home of Russell Sitton, the village's founder. Old Ninevah Van Waganen, a great-granddaughter of Russell Sitton, lived there and kept a signal fire.

Russell's Knob — is it a town or a village or a country all to itself? Who is to say? They are what they have always been. They are refuge from bondage. Whosoever seeks to make them slaves will get a damn good fight. Whosoever starts trouble here will die here. So they survive by staying watchful, clever, secretive, and well armed.

Officially they began as Munsee. When others walked farther west, they laughed and spit and came to hide in the highlands. Warriors looted from their homes and shipped across the salt sea came to Russell's Knob when they could escape a mountain and find their way. Angolans brought from the sugar islands by their fat Dutch masters ran off to the highlands whenever they could. More black Africans and Caribs came when the patriots chased them and they couldn't keep their white gals in the lowlands and the white gals didn't want to go off to the cold in Nova Scotia or suffer heat in the West Indies. Coal-black and half-black gals came to the highlands after running off from white men, and some white men came chasing them and didn't go back. Black men and their black wives whom they would not be torn from came to escape. Fearful, unattached women of all colors came and were given sanctuary. Most of the women brought jumbled babies and, because they wouldn't give up their jumbled babies, they stayed alongside each other in the hills. The People of Russell's Knob were a blended soup of colors after a few generations and made their own circumstance. Amalgamators! Ach! It was a word that was hated here. To outside eyes they were an immoral mixture. Between themselves they were so tightly woven and bound up together that they were impenetrable by outsiders. They were staunch and strong.

Lowlanders who knew of their existence often said, "Oh,

those Indians? Smelly ol' women and bucks and amalgamators that can't come in town like civilized folks."

The People of Russell's Knob, snug in their hide, came into the nearby towns regularly to trade and buy but did not sleep in the towns. The People of Russell's Knob came in town for commerce, then went back to their own hidey-holes. They lived their lives many colored — they dared it! — where it was high and dry and safe. They were known — when they were known at all — for clinging to each other tightly, defending their homesteads with their lives, and being fierce and living free.

It felt to Dossie, who had only known lowland flats and tangled brush, as if the trees around Russell's Knob created a house by fanning themselves out and meeting high up in the middle to form a shelter in the woodland. At one rise she pulled at the man's hand to halt him but was too timid to lift her head and look at his face when he turned. She stood and trembled before him with her hand in front of her lower self.

"Gwan then," Duncan said and indicated with a nod that he would wait for her to attend to her wants. She scampered off into the forest and did as she wanted behind a bush, picked some berries, and filled her mouth. When she was done and rejoined him, he smiled to see her blue-tinged face.

The way of settling in a string made for an extreme of privacy for the people of Russell's Knob. The pattern — the necklace — could not be fully appreciated except by long familiarity. Each of the houses was well back in a copse, most of them with small brooks running by. Smoot and the girl encountered no one else on their journey to his homestead, though the smell of cook fires attested to other folk and their vittles nearby. When they had reached the place, he gave her drinking water from the fast-running stream that cut through the hill and spilled out at the edge of his homestead. He seated her on a wooden bench over which trailed a grape arbor. He then went ahead into the house and brought out a bowl of berries for her refreshment. Mountain blueberries, held to have the power of magic healing in these environs, benefited the girl immediately. She gorged on them in a bowl of milk. It was said by lowlanders who had seen the mountain folk that they grew long-tall and lanky for reaching so far above their heads to dine on blueberries on the bushy tufts in the crevices of the highlands. Through the summertime in Russell's Knob, few of the children's mouths were colored anything other than dark purple. Each one a contented and laughing face.

The man's homestead had a welcoming, charred-wood aroma. While Dossie consumed her berries, he watched her. He seemed pleased that she ate. When she had finished, he rose up and left her sitting again. She watched him attending to his animals and wondered that there was no wife bustling about and no young'uns running out to greet him. He built up his own fire in the hearth. He drew up his own water.

He told her his name. Duncan Smoot pronounced his name clearly and proudly but did not ask hers. He retrieved her from the grape arbor and led her by hand into the house. The smell of cooked coffee dominated the aromas. The man himself smelled of sweet ale—an aroma she'd caught as the two climbed and sweated that was very different from the smell of whiskey and retching and yellow water of other men. She had the notion then that he was not so old as his hair might say. His hair was gray mixed with dusty brown and was soft-woolly— was of a kind that was disposed to snag at dust and seeds and bits of fluff. His eyes were a color that was like a dark mustard seed. Drawn by hand into the kitchen, she was led to a table, and a seat was indicated. He placed a small cup of coffee before her. She sipped timidly, concerned not to displease him by refusing to drink what he had offered. After a while he took her to a room with a large wooden bed laid over with a fluffy feather mattress. He seemed to present the room to her. He said nothing, but held his face in a gentle, firm expression. He showed her the night pan. When he left the room, Dossie stretched out on the rag rug and waited for the arrival of the woman whose room this must be.

Mr. Smoot's wife must be a wonderful woman, Dossie assumed in a comfortable curl on the well-worn floor. After a short while her urgency would not let her sleep. She left the room and saw that Mr. Smoot still sat at his kitchen table. He looked at her and pointed out in the yard to the privy. Now the smell of whiskey in the room dominated that of coffee.

No woman came that night.

Dossie knew 'twas a young'un's job to sweep a yard. As soon as it was light she found the bound-up stick broom and set to. She did not want Mr. Smoot to think she was a lazy gal.

Where is his woman? Dossie thought as she worked and looked around. She had peeped in the bed when she rose from the floor. There were many possessions about the house all set in good order, though many things were notable for their absence from this room. The bedroom of this woman was free of dust and belongings. She is got no hair that needs tending? She needs no rag to tie it? She need no shawl? Mr. Duncan's wife must've took his children and gone visiting with her people, Dossie thought to herself.

The solid house had good plank floors that cried softly from being stepped upon many times and worn in gentle ruts. It had wooden shutters and some glass panes in the windows like the house of Mr. Abingdon, though it was not nearly so big. It sat in the center of a clearing on a point of land higher than the surround. The house was ringed with a sitting porch on three of its sides and was ringed at the outer edges of the swept and pebbled yard with a low stone wall. Near to the house was a growing patch protected with a short wooden fence, and at back was the chicken coop, a small, well-built barn, and an outhouse.

After a day had passed in this idyll—abundant food and water to drink—Dossie wondered and questioned herself to know why she had come so quietly when Duncan Smoot took her by the hand. Was his hand the hand of God? Was this deliverer the answer—the consequence of her fervent prayers? Was this the know-everything God that Evangelist Zilpha had hollered about? Dossie was not troubled by her thoughts. She was only puzzled. When she slept on the first night she'd cried for Evangelist Zilpha not because she wanted help from the woman, but that she saw the horrible collar on her neck when she closed her eyes and saw the Evangelist's poor tongue hung nearly to her chin. In her dream she asked the Evangelist who was this man. The Evangelist could not answer because of the tightening of the horrible thing. Spittle and blood and small, hard white chips flew out of the Evangelist's mouth as she tried to speak. Only her eyes had spoken. "Gwan, gwan with him!" The collar came to be upon Dossie's own neck and she screamed.

Duncan Smoot was kind when her cries startled him. She leaped up like a small animal flushed out of its nest and ran smack into him standing in the passage. The sound of the wind shushing through the trees ringing his house lulled her back to sleep.

"Aw, Hattie, don't come here a-barkin'," Duncan Smoot said to a woman who stood on his porch when Dossie entered his kitchen from the chicken yard on the second day. The woman advanced on him with her knuckles pushed against her waist.

"Aye, Rooster, what kind of thing are you doin' in yer house!" She stood toe to toe with him. Her voice rose in volume.

"You're a good lookout," Duncan said and patted the woman's cheek. Her face was flushed with indignation, and he grinned to cool her. "You got it wrong. Come on in and meet the girl."

Dossie saw the woman's stormy face and heard her angry voice with alarm. At last the woman of this house had come! Dossie froze still, bowed her head, and braced herself. The woman was on a boil!

Harriet Smoot Wilhelm's cap fell back from her head in her excitement. Her hair, curled and napped like sheep's wool, fell well below her shoulders. She was Duncan Smoot done softer, smaller, more delicately turned. And she was as straight-back-up in this house as he was. She walked in boldly when he stood aside the doorway, and she came up to Dossie and ran her eyes all over her.

"This here is my sister, little gal. Hattie—Hat—is her name," Duncan said. He followed his sister into the house carrying the basket he'd relieved her of when she walked up. "Don't be scared of her. She don't always come in making a big blow," he finished and pecked his sister on her cheek. "Hattie, this is the little bird you heard about. This is Dossie."

Ah, the magic in his manner! Dossie's heart, which she thought of as so tiny in her chest, began to expand and swell. She feared that her senses would leave her. His voice was so lovely, and he spoke with so much fancy! Why she didn't even know that he knew her call.

"How do. Are you treated bad?"

Dossie, whose eyes became wide when Hat approached her, answered, "Oh, no, ma'am. How do, ma'am." Dossie tucked her chin with deference.

Harriet — called Hat, Hattie, or Pippy by her brother — screwed up her brow and folded her arms across her chest, then dropped her arms before speaking again. "Let's us have a cup of coffee," she said, finally smiling, and went to the stove. "You drink coffee before, girl?"

Dossie answered, "Yes, ma'am."

"Lesser stuff than this, I bet you. The lowlanders don't know 'bout coffee. We got the good Carib beans — mountain beans. Coffee is best the closer it grows to God. Duncan gets them beans down at the canal boats. He thiefs 'em," she declared breezily. "Like he thiefed you."

"Hattie," Duncan cautioned.

"She ought to know who she's taken up with," Hat teased. "'Tis only fair. And 'tis the best coffee. Our water is sweet, too. Put cream in your brew, though. You're a little girl. You're too young to have your coffee black."

Dossie watched Miz Hat put her shawl on a hook familiarly — without glancing — and go to the stove to pour a cup of coffee. Dossie knew then that this kitchen was her kitchen. Hat walked into the cook room and lay out the things she'd brought in her basket. She set a pan of biscuits near the fire to restore their warmth and put jars of jam on the shelf. She examined a basket of eggs that Dossie had gathered.

"These are good eggs, Brother," Hat called out, walking a circuit between the two rooms. "Shall I build you a cake? Let's us have a cake, little girl," she said in a manner of merriment. "Brother, you're not caring for your chickens good. Your henhouse needs tending. Maybe you got some help now?"

"Is nothin' wrong with my henhouse, Pippy, except that your son is lazy and won't do what I tell him. And the other one is spoiled and lazy, too. That's what is wrong with my henhouse," Duncan said. Hat heard the tone and, for the sake of her son and her nephew, said no more.

Dossie realized then, when Hat tied on her apron, that it was the sole piece of woman's clothes that she had seen in the house.

Watching Hat spin up a cake was like watching a sudden flush of butterflies or a swarm of lightning bugs in the dark. She was so pretty, Dossie thought. Miz Hat picked up one thing and another with such grace and skill! She flew through the steps and got the cake up to hang on the cookstove before one's head could turn.

Hat left the house while her cake was cooking and returned some time later with a bundle.

"The People of Russell's Knob are lawless," she said in a wryly humorous manner as she put a large piece of fluffy cake covered in a thick berry sauce before her brother. "We're a spurned people in a spurned town. This is where you're at, little girl. You not jus' in Duncan Smoot's back pocket. We're a town of people. We're not much wanted in the surrounding towns and we keep away from them."

"Aw, Hattie, hush. Give the little girl a piece of your cake,"

Duncan said. Hattie's cake was the most delectable thing he'd ever tasted. In fact, Hattie could well be considered the finest cook for miles around. Duncan laughed to himself that he might never marry as long as he could eat at Hattie's table. He wanted to fuss at her, but instead he asked for more cake.

"The girl can come with me — for good lookout," Hat said as she stood up to take leave. She twisted up her loose hair and pushed it under her cap, which had fallen lopsided when she took off her apron. Tidying up her loosened hair was her favorite and well-known habit. She gathered it and twisted it, then undid it in the next gesture. The final was that she pushed it under her cap.

"Mind your business, Hattie," Duncan countered. His tone had a warning, though it was still sweet.

"Do what is . . . proper, Duncan," Hat insisted. She wanted to stamp her foot at him to drive her point but hesitated. Duncan might toss her onto the kitchen floor with a slap if she did that. He might. She calmed herself. Let it remain just a tiff. Hat backed away from Duncan and crossed to the door. At the last moment before leaving, she marched back toward Dossie and reached for her wrist.

"Come with me, girl."

"No, ma'am," Dossie asserted and drew back. She then added in a small, clear voice, "I will stay here with Mr. Duncan, ma'am. I can be a good chicken girl. There is things to do."

Hat cut her eyes at her brother, then turned to Dossie with a pleasanter face. "You need some things then," she said and handed over the bundle she'd gone to fetch.

Later while Dossie scraped ashes from the fireplace, and Mr. Duncan Smoot salted down some fish, he said, "Yonder bed is for you to lie in." Dossie dropped her eyes to the floor before his feet. Duncan was perplexed. He'd expected a naïve smile. He hoped he hadn't frightened or shamed her. Ah, Dossie had not been raised here, where children laugh and frolic! It wasn't in her nature to be carefree or to be saucy or to ask for what she wanted.

"Thanks, sir," Dossie mumbled.

She'd made a choice for herself. It made her scared. But recollecting how Mr. Duncan had spoken of her earlier made her thrill.

Miz Hat's bundled gift was an apron wrapped around a calico dress and a white chemise that had been pounded and wrung to softness. There was also a pair of slipper shoes, two head scarves, and some soft, ragged strips.

Though Dossie was uncertain of herself in the things that Miz Hat brought, she made a good fit in the new clothes. The dress was big on her but had ties. The apron fit exactly to her size in all points. The waist seemed just her own, and the strings tied came to a pretty, jaunty bow. There was a decorated edge along the bodice of the apron, though it had lost its bright color. She had never worn a thing so prettily decorated. Ah, has Miz Hat got a daughter who has given up her things?

"Ha! Pippy's apron," Mr. Duncan said. He chuckled when he saw Dossie in the new clothes. He smiled full at her for the first time. The radiance of it bedazzled her.

Dossie took up the job of chicken gal, fetching gal, cook, and cleaner. She did not ask questions of Mr. Duncan because he anticipated her needs and directed her to this, that, or the other. He told her when to do certain things and made it plain when his expectations had not quite been met. She continued to be quiet and self-effacing in his presence.

*   *   *

On many an early morning in the highlands, misty rings that look like distant cook fires appear in the mountains. With the advance of the sun, mist burns off, and the colors blend with full sunrise. Jan Smoot, a younger version of his uncle, strode up just after sunrise on such a morning and ever after caused Dossie to think that he was called Son for that reason. But he was occasionally called Son by his uncle to mark the baby title he was given at his birth. Dossie looked out from her peeking perch when she heard their voices. The two had an exchange in the clearing. The young one, head-bowed-humble and paying Duncan Smoot a requisite obeisance, listened, then departed. When he returned hours later, he unhooked a large dead bird from his saddle's pommel and came in the house.

He, too, was comfortable in the house. On entering the kitchen, he crossed directly to the table and slapped the bird down. Dossie jumped with a start. The large gaudy-colored thing seemed more a tithe or a toll than a meal.

"Uncle, there are five other ducks," Jan said. He stood erect and kept his eyes on the floor in a slightly insincere manner of deference.

"Leave another here, take two to Noelle and two to Hattie," Duncan said sternly.

"He won't harm you, little girl. He's for the dinner pot," Jan added and smiled full out at Dossie.

"This is my sister's boy, Jan." The sound he gave the name was a short, crisp sound that was half of "John"—a thud, a thump.

"How do, sir," Dossie answered timidly.

"He ain't no—"

"I ain't no 'sir.' How do," Jan said pleasantly. "What is your name? Are we to call you girl and nothin' else?"

"Shut up, boy," Duncan barked. "Her name is Dossie." Duncan felt a tick of embarrassment for his lack of proper manners. Jan had come to be very much like his mother. Cissy would notice if someone's bread was not buttered or if some timid voice could not be heard in the hurly-burly.

"Yes, sir," Dossie said. "I always been called Dossie. I can take your duck's feathers off. I ain't scared of a duck. He is got a pretty head." Dossie took up the bird, trilled happily, and began pulling tail feathers. It might have been the presence of Jan that brought out her liveliness, but by the time her pot of water was heated to bubbling, Dossie was humming, meticulously creating piles for the different types of feathers she'd pulled from the bird, and so completely involved in her pursuit that she did not pay much attention to Duncan or Jan. She sang snatches of the wood duck's calls softly as if in dialogue with it but handled the evisceration expertly, dispassionately — cracking the wings and breastbone with the heel of her bare hand.

"Sir, is there meal to make a hoecake?" Dossie asked Duncan, who looked at her with surprise, noting flecks of the duck's flesh on her apron. When had she come with a question, a request? The duck had emboldened her. It was peculiar.

Duncan kicked the sole of his nephew's foot and commanded, "Fetch up the meal, boy."

Jan sprang up to do Duncan's bidding, and his chair scraped on the floor planks. He'd torn his coat with his uncle and was anxious to regain Duncan's affection. Jan had been put out of Duncan's house for the mischief he'd caused, and he felt adrift. If he had it to do again, he probably wouldn't feed soap to a stray dog and, when its vomit came forth in white foam, would not have chased it through the village yelling that it was a mad dog. Maybe then Old Miz Ninevah would not have fainted in the panic and needed teas and cakes to revive her.

"I hope your mama ain't mad at me," Dossie spoke up to Jan when he returned to the cook room.

He snorted gently as if answering a horse rather than her. "She don't get mad," Jan said, paused, then continued, "My mama is dead. You met An' Hat. My mama was the old man's other sister. She was called Cissy. My papa killed her when I was still little. The old man run him off and kept me. An' Hat's got a boy, too, called Pet. He's got a papa, but me and him both still b'long to Duncan. It's the ol' People's way. Uncle got a right to claim us, to teach us, to punish us. Our mamas are part of the Smoots so it matters less who our papa is." Jan finished speaking and cut open the sack of meal.

"Who is Pippy? Is she Miz Hat's little girl?"

"Naw, she's An' Hat herself. Is what the old man calls An' Hat for her sweet name."

"Oh," Dossie said.

"I los' my sweet name, I guess. Give me a mug of ale, girl." Jan spoke as if he were suddenly greatly annoyed with her.

Dossie brought him an ale and said, "Sir."

"I told you I ain't no 'sir.' I'm Jan. And, Miss Dossie, you can give us our duck anytime," Jan said and smiled. There was something in that radiant smile that was an antidote to his uncle's anger. The three of them had a pleasant duck feast.

"Make a pallet on the floor, boy," Duncan said when the three had eaten.

"I'm not no dog, Uncle. I got a bed," Jan replied, saucily aware that whiskey had made the older man drowsy. Duncan's stomach was full of the duck, and he was content. He had soft-ened and would confer absolution. Duncan's invitation to stay was proof that Jan was forgiven, and no more need be said about the prank or the punishment.

When Jan left the house, he had planned to head up onto the next ridge to Noelle's place. Her house was his house, too. Instead he headed down.

The descent was quiet and dark. Jan's feet were sure of the way — were always confident in buckskin. Their bottoms were intimate with this ground, and all that could be known could be felt through the balls of his feet. The people of Russell's Knob were clever in their twisting and turning. On their circu-itous pathways they never risked slipping off or being caught on spirit paths or being discovered by outsiders. In this pre-cinct, Jan Smoot could keep his head in darkness or in light of day.

When he was in smelling distance, two figures burst through rustling understory to meet him and nuzzle his hands. Portzl and Friedl, his cousin's mastiffs, came to accompany Jan to the porch. They were waiting for him. Doubtless they had heard him make up his mind to come and had listened for his footfalls.

Pet slept on his back with his mouth open and gassed the place with ale breath. Jan pushed him toward the wall with his foot and came beneath the covers beside him. Pet had warmed the bed but not yet soaked it with sweating. Jan was comfort-able at once. Pet moved about in adjusting to Jan's presence, but he never woke.

Pet woke before sun up, moved close to Jan, put his hand on Jan's member, and stroked it.

"Leave off, Pet," Jan whispered and shifted himself.

"Is a wonder you didn't stay to watch the old man with his new gal," Pet said and giggled.

"She's a little girl. He ain't doing it," Jan said.

"How you know if you ain't stay to watch," Pet asked.

Jan punched him in the side and laughed.

"What she look like, Jan?" Pet asked.

"A pretty little dark plum. Ah, but she's skinny and ain't got no tits. She's a little girl."

"Uncle likes 'em grown. He likes 'em big." Pet snickered and drew his hands to illustrate bulbous breasts.

"The old man ain't gettin' so much pussy lately. He's living like a papist since Noelle got mad at him. She's the only one that'll take my part, Pet," Jan said.

"Jan . . . I," Pet stammered.

"Oh, shut it, Pet. No point you gettin' a beatin', too. An' Hat could have took my part with Uncle, but she ain't ever going to do that. He's thrown me out. The little girl is sleeping in my bed, Pet," Jan said in a plucky voice tinged with hurt.

Two happy, chattering voices burst out of the surround when Dossie came from the chicken house the next day with a basket of eggs. As the two chatterers approached, Dossie saw an oddly dressed woman accompanying Jan. She was clothed in a tunic of softened deerskin and a skirt of the same and skin boots decorated with quills and feathers.

The woman's face was trained on Jan's. He carried her baskets and pouches and tried to hold her around the waist as well.

"Hey, little nanny goat!" Duncan burst from the house and startled Dossie, calling out from the porch in a voice and manner that she had not yet ever heard. "Hey! Where you been wanderin'?" Duncan yelled. He hurried toward the woman, swept her up, swung her around, and squeezed her waist. He set her back on her feet and swatted her backside. Jan stepped away to allow his uncle this prerogative, but he didn't completely give up the woman. He raised his hand to her cheek, and she held it while she looked at Duncan. For one blessed moment Jan was exhilarated.

Dossie stopped and stared openly at the three. Oh! At last the woman of Duncan Smoot's house had come back. But it was clear when she walked onto the porch and entered that this was not her house. She was comfortable but exuded no air of ownership. Her bundles and baskets were left on the porch, and both Jan and Duncan treated her as a guest. She nodded her head toward Dossie.

"Girl, bring me some of tha' coffee I smell," she said. Dossie continued to stare, taking in the woman's striking countenance. For it was her altogether rather than some piercing, pretty eyes or one lovely nose or spongy soft, smooth skin or her thick braided hair singly.

Duncan, who'd been wholly engaged by the woman's arrival, came back to himself. "Dossie, this here is Noelle. Miz Noelle Beaulieu," he said with a charming and humorous emphasis that made the woman smile broadly and show all of her teeth.

"Noelle, this here is Dossie. Boy, take off Noelle's boots," Duncan ordered Jan. Dossie realized she'd never seen Jan so happy as he now seemed. His face was split wide across with smiling. He sat before the woman in the cross-legged fashion and pulled away her boots. When Dossie brought the coffee, Jan took the cup from her and gave it to Noelle.

Duncan looked like an embarrassed hound dog in Noelle Beaulieu's presence. He drank in the woman throughout supper.

She traded looks and smiles with him so that Jan knew she had forgiven Duncan and was as itchy for him as he was for her.

Jan knew them best after all. After supper, he gathered up Noelle's things from the porch and took them to her place. He knew she'd stay the night with Uncle.

Jan considered his relations with the two of them. Noelle would have made a perfect wife for his uncle. But she would not — could not — be obedient to him. You can't tie a Spirit Woman up in the kitchen and expect her to cook and clean and tend to young'uns. She has got to be out and about her healing. She can't be expected to let herself be told what to do and not do by a man.

She would have made a good mother for him, though. Jan's mama had been Noelle's dearest friend. Her death had only taken her body away from them is what Noelle always told him. As much as his mama loved him, she was surely still watching and guiding, Noelle explained, and so they must keep a place for her. Jan reflected that his fervent little prayers had simply never been answered. Nobody's god listened to him! He'd wanted his mama's body, and he couldn't have it. He wanted them — Uncle, Noelle, and him — to stay together around a hearth, under one roof. He could not have that either.

At daybreak Dossie woke to see Noelle's back as she walked away from the house. The woman in doeskin was carrying her boots and picking her way out of the yard. Her eyes were trained on the path. Her hips moved with energy like potatoes in a sack. What kind of a wild circumstance was this woman who looked so different and acted so different? The surprise was that Mr. Duncan seemed smitten with her. He'd looked at her and listened to her with rapt attention throughout supper. Dossie had to admit she was annoyed. It didn't suit with him being God. This woman's sudden appearance had messed up her cloud of imagination. She'd conjured up a whole circumstance with herself at the middle of it holding on to Mr. Duncan. Here come this woman! Dossie kept up her sulky reverie throughout the early morning until Duncan Smoot came into the kitchen for his repast. "I want my coffee, little girl," Duncan said sharply. Dossie came back to herself quickly. His face was freshly splashed with water, but he did not smile at her as he'd become accustomed to doing when his first cup of coffee was brought to the table.

"Hey, Dossie gal, gwan in and help Hattie with our supper," Duncan said as soon as they reached the Wilhelms' porch. Dossie's head bobbed in response like a puppy's. She quickly looked down at her feet when Jan, Pet, and Ernst Wilhelm, seated for their morning repast at the Wilhelms' kitchen table, turned in her direction. "Tell Hat to sen' me some sour milk and bread 'cause I'm hungry!" Duncan called loudly, then sat. When Dossie bowed her head in automatic concession to his command, a small cloud of shame passed over him. Though perfect obedience was what was wanted and expected in a young female, Duncan did not like to see Dossie cringe. If anyone would ask, it is why he'd brought her here. He could not stomach what he'd seen of her treatment at the hands of the lowlanders.

The boys, too, had learned to obey. Perfect obedience or suffer the punishment was what all of the People observed. Though, for Jan and Pet, it was not always clear whom to obey.

"Petrus has work to do here, Duncan. I need him at the brewery. He cannot go today," Ernst Wilhelm said and started the tug-of-war. The cousins exchanged a glance, then continued with their mush and bread and coffee. This argument would not be settled by them. "Petrus must stay here today."

"That big oaf there is worth two men, and I need him. We're negotiating for a string of mules. Jan can't handle them alone," Duncan said.

"My son ain't no oaf, and he ain't born to do your bidding!" They were bald faced in their scrapping about who should tell the boys what to do. But Wilhelm was the more exercised because his wife ceded authority for her son completely to her brother.

"Calm down, Wilhelm. I ain't stealing yer boy. I'm just borrying him. What say you, Hat?" Duncan asked, asserting his authority with his sister. The boys hung their heads and waited for the answer.

"Let him go, Mr. Wilhelm. The three banded together is better," Hat pronounced.

"Squaw!" Wilhelm snarled at his wife. "You would side with Duncan against daylight. Your brother don't own my son!"

Petrus Wilhelm and his father frightened Dossie. It was not solely on account of the fuss and tussle that erupted when Duncan and Ernst Wilhelm spoke but because they were so pale. Neither of them was brown tinted by sun or circumstance. Petrus Wilhelm did not, at first sight, look anything at all like his mother. More's the pity, Dossie thought, for she believed Miz Hat was the prettiest woman she had ever seen. Pet had his father's lank brown hair and, though his body was modeled on his father's, it was not yet as hard and fat. Pet had the same small sky-blue eyes, the identical long, bony nose, the same blushing complexion as his father, and the similarity was often remarked upon. Though Mr. Wilhelm raised his voice in shouts, Duncan Smoot did not cower before him. And though Petrus Wilhelm was the image of his papa, he was obedient to his uncle.

Pet wanted to rebuke his father for insulting his mother, but he did not. No boy in these hills rises against his father unless he is prepared to hurt him. This was Pet's eternal turmoil, because he loved Papa, though he would defend his mother with his life. That, too, is the mountain boy's code.

"Papa," Pet said, pushing back the empty bowl of mush. His youthful appetite satisfied, he was eager for riding and raiding and adventure with Duncan and Jan. They were a band.

"I got to go and look after Jan. He's soft and liable to get hurt," Pet said and slapped playfully at Jan's head. "It's only a day gone. Me an' Jan'll work like beasts when we get back. Uncle needs an ox. That's me." He spoke in the self-deprecating tone of voice that always succeeded in extricating him from a fuss with Hat and Duncan and his papa, but pissed Jan.

"Don't let your uncle get you killed," Ernst Wilhelm said. He rolled his eyes at Hat, though she had cast her eyes to her lap. "And take care of Jan. Your mama will be inconsolable if he gets hurt."

Duncan and the boys returned at suppertime. The band had cajoled three jacks and a jenny from the landing after driving a bargain with a boat boy who had swiped them off a westbound barge. Ever the clever bargainer, Duncan skinned the boy — giving him half what the animals were worth even on the fast market — and the three were jocular, pleased with their adventure.

Dossie nodded to Duncan when he walked onto the Wilhelms' porch behind Jan. She wanted to rush up and hug Duncan because he'd returned. Dossie restrained herself at some effort, and he rewarded her by holding her chin high, asking her to bring him a repast.

"Mr. Duncan wants a glass of sour milk, ma'am — an' some bread for it, he said."

"Well, he gon' wait for his supper jus' like Mr. Wilhelm!" Hat retorted with some humor in her fussing.

A look of grave discomfort crossed Dossie's face. Hat noted it and was some bit alarmed. Was this girl so scared of Duncan that she dared not jump to do his bidding?

"He hasn't been layin' a hand on you, has he?" Hat asked, feeling guilty that she hadn't marked the relations between this little gal and Duncan.

Affronted at the question, Dossie spoke up like she'd done that first time Hat had seen her. "No, ma'am. He does no such thing! I only wan' him to have what he ask for," she answered plain and simple.

Hat chuckled and remembered that she had once been absolutely obedient to her brother. "Pippy, go fetch me . . . ," Duncan would say, and she would run off to get string and small knives and glasses of buttermilk.

"Yonder," Hat said and pointed toward a crock. "Give him sour milk and some of tha' stale bread and tell him I say to stop up his mouth with it!" she said with a guffaw.

Dossie knew that it wasn't proper for her to sit at Duncan's side on the porch with Mr. Wilhelm and Jan and Pet. She wanted to listen to his banter, though, and feel his domination of the other men. This was the part of seeing him in company with the others that she most enjoyed. She liked crediting that

Duncan was chief among the others, and that all of the others, including her, lived in his heaven. His voice cut through the others' talk when he expressed an opinion or told a tale or rebuked one of the boys. She presented the buttermilk and bread to him in the midst of banter and withdrew to the kitchen.

Later Hat gave her a pot to hoist, and she did and carried the dinner stew to the table.

"Sirs, your dinner is down," Dossie mumbled shyly. Jan and Pet laughed stupidly, and Duncan cut his eyes.

Still worried that she ought not to be seated among the others in God's heaven, Dossie sat on the edge of her chair ready to leap up to answer Duncan's slightest wish. The boys snickered at her and hunched each other's ribs when their uncle was not watching.

After eating themselves to founder, Ernst Wilhelm and Duncan went to the porch to smoke cigars and drink whiskey. Jan and Pet followed them, and Jan began to dance — raising his arms and shuffling his feet in soft moccasins. A cloud of smoke was soon so thick around them that Dossie stood back in the doorway and watched and listened. She was transfixed at the sight of Jan's dancing and got woozy from the aroma of liquor and the smoke. Hat did not let her linger long.

"Come away," she said and led Dossie to her own bedroom.

Dossie stopped just inside the doorway and, as before, she marveled. She was still unsure that Duncan was not God and these others his minions. Their places — their houses, their beds, the chairs at their hearths — had the atmosphere of a heaven. The People of Russell's Knob were, no doubt, caught in tangles and angry fusses, but they had plenty and they were lusty and loyal and celebratory. Yes, she had indeed been rescued by God and brought to Canaan Land.

The room was a large one and was divided in the middle by the large bed. All of Hat's wardrobe and her many adornments were placed to the left of the bed, and Ernst Wilhelm's clothes and sundry were to the right of the great bed. Once inside the room Hat began to loosen her clothes as if to slough off her great and many duties, placating and providing for her titans. She stooped to pick up her husband's clothes from the floor and snorted with annoyance. She was a fortunate, privileged woman in Russell's Knob, but Harriet Smoot Wilhelm was not self-indulgent. She was busy. She was a woman of industry and so was weary at the end of the day. Hat sat in her high-backed rocker and set to brushing her voluminous hair with a large fancy-handled brush. She twisted up her hair in thick ropes and further wound and pinned the ropes to her head. She covered up her head with a cloth.

Miz Hat was changed when she came into this precinct — this part of this fine room that had her chair was nearby the window facing east, that had her accoutrement, that had her embroidery on a small table beside her chair, that was a cozy within a cozy home and hearth. If you did not see her in this room, you might think she was stingy with smiles. Oh, but here, unfurling her hair ribbons and looking at her combs, she was animated and cheerful as a kitten, a laughing girl. When she'd done up her own hair, she went to a drawer in her chest and took out a sleeve of red cloth.

The sleeve was tied with a fancy ribbon and, when Hat opened it and lay it out, revealed pockets for combs in a bed of deep green color. The inside of the wrapping was further embellished with stitched pictures of birds and flowers. Hat smiled gleefully when she spread the breathtaking array of bone and wooden combs. Dossie caught up her breath at the sight of them.

"Ah, Miz Hat." Dossie was dumb and overwhelmed with wonder. "Where they come from?" she asked.

Hat snickered behind her hand and hugged her hands over her stomach. "Mr. Wilhelm brought me a fancy present when he behaved badly and I stung him, you see," she said and executed an intricate set of eye movements. "I wearied him. I fussed. I cried constantly until he went to the city and bought me this. Then I was sweet again, you see." Hat giggled. "Whore's tricks! We all learn them. But are they not a delight?"

Her words were thrilling, they seemed uncertain waters, a grown woman's secrets. Ah, she knew Miz Hat suffered her husband. Dossie disliked him herself.

Hat pulled off her headcloth and applied firm but gentle fingers to her hair. "I'm glad of you, girl," she said massaging. "Cissy and Noelle fought over fixing up my hair. They played with me like I was a doll. I was a very spoiled dolly before Cissy died," Hat said, letting her levity fade.

Hat's nut-colored hands were beautiful on the white sheets when she pulled back the counterpanes and exposed her bed. Ah, in God's house they are flush in bed linens! Hat's hands amazed! She had nails so clean and smooth shaped a baby could suck her fingers like a tit.

To have a warmth beside you in your family is not a prize or a privilege; it is a necessary. So surely God would have a necessary, because God would have all that was necessary. God wouldn't go without. God must have a family.

Invited into the bed, Dossie lay awake beside Hat and listened to the drunken talkers for a time after Hat had fallen asleep, disappearing beneath her covers. Had she escaped and landed next to God and his family of folk? Dossie still believed they were her divine deliverers. She slipped out of the bed onto the floor, drew up her knees, and sat back against the four-poster. Miz Hat was a wonder! She was so sweet when the men weren't around. Well, sometimes she was sweet with Jan, but with Mr. Duncan most of all. It seemed she never wanted her husband or son to see her smile.

Dossie was too nervous to sleep deeply in case Mr. Duncan wanted her to fetch or to follow. She listened and was certain she'd identified his snoring. She rested and drowsed against the bedpost listening to Jan whistling. He was the last to be awake. Pet had long since ceased playing his spoons. Mr. Ernst Wilhelm must be the one who was snorting snores every so often. It was a rude sound, and Dossie attributed it to him without proof. She listened to Jan make up music with his own mouth and mark the cadence of his dances. There were trills in Jan's sounds that put Dossie in mind of some birds and, though the dancing was unavailable to her, she heard the shushing of Jan's soft moccasins on the wood. Was that the flapping of wings? What was this boy? Was't possible he took the air when all was quiet and all the others slept? Only her fear of waking Hat kept her in the bedroom away from peeping at him.

Jan Smoot was the most handsome of all God's people. Jan was dark eyed like his uncle, deep tan skinned, fluffy haired beautiful in an aloof, unself-conscious way. It was as if he knew very well how beguiling his face was but didn't care to take advantage by calling attention to it. How could he help smiling, though, for his soul was sweet. When he smiled he drew all eyes, and even the blind woman at the well would know that he was beautiful, for she would hear the sharp sigh of delight that passed the lips of folk who could see him. It fitted together to Dossie. Jan was very much like his uncle.

Finally it became completely quiet in the Wilhelm house except for snores. God's people were noisy when they slept, Dossie thought. It was a measure of their happiness, their peaceful and unguarded ways, that they lay themselves down and closed their eyes with little care when they were spent from the day. And they sucked air and made sounds that must have carried for miles. But no one heard and found them. Their mountains kept their sounds from giving them up. Birds were their confederates, everywhere masking their voices with singing and chattering.

Dossie did not know it, but not everyone slept at once in Russell's Knob. There was vigorous defense of their perimeter. Folk in Russell's Knob liked to say they had learned to sleep deeply without care because no one ventured up so high but the bears. Truth was they posted lookouts.

They kept and built their own fires at their own hearths. They slept in pretty places. Their beds were sturdy and covered with quilts. They dressed up fine. They had the mastery of their beasts — their donkeys, horses, hogs, chickens, and cows. Their chickens gave good eggs. They freely killed what ducks they wanted, fished the streams, and ate the catch. They planted the crops they ate and sold.

Dossie had listened to the drunken barbs between the men and heard wisps of Hat's discontent. She knew that Duncan was very harsh with Jan for his mischief-making. But though they fussed and upbraided each other, they were tightly woven.

They pushed berries into their mouths from bushes at the

back of their own porches and went about openly with blue-stained faces — unabashed.

They sang if they cared to. They were as unconscious of it as warblers. They fiddled and worked their feet to entertain themselves. They drank ale and whiskey and smoked tobacco. The People were beautiful in all their aspects and saw it in each other. She thought of herself as come all this way and here she sits on a promontory among these wonderful folk — all of God's family.

And she — Dossie — was delivered here by Mr. Duncan Smoot just like Evangelist Zilpha had said God would do. The Evangelist had been so sure! She said it with a heat that chased off any kind of doubt. She said Dossie child was going to be swept up by a strong, kind, powerful God who would answer a girl's little voice raised in prayer.

"You woke, Dossie?" Duncan called under the window before it was full seeing light. She was awake — poised to hear him and to answer. "Yes, sir," she said quietly.

"Come on then. Let's us go."

He had his donkeys tied together and ready except for the jenny who stood apart. Hat woke, too, and wanted to fix coffee. Duncan refused, saying that Dossie would fix coffee when she got home. The sound of his words thrilled Dossie. He had named her and given her a purpose and told of his satisfaction — all in the few words he spoke. Hat packed a basket of stale biscuits, buttermilk, and quince jam and gave it to Dossie. The girl hoisted it and followed Duncan. He hung her basket on the pommel and lifted her into the saddle to ride the little way up to their home — God's promontory. Dossie was careful to pull herself tall in the saddle like he said and tuck her skirt and leave her legs onto one side of the horse. "Make yourself a good seat," Duncan had told her the first time he put Dossie on horseback. "Spread your butt out and settle. No fidgetin'."

He brought the she-donkey's reins to where she could handle them. "Click an' cluck at her. See if she'll follow," he said. Then he went back to string up the other two donkeys. Dossie ran through some sounds and came to a tongue-sucking call for the beast. Her ears fanned back and forth and brought some energy to her haunches. Duncan came around and took the horse's reins with one hand and the other donkeys' in the other. He clicked to the horse to set them all off in a parade.

Jan let cold water over his head and came around the side of the house to see his uncle and the girl setting off home. A completely undignified and unbidden thought crossed his mind. He was green jealous her — of Dossie. Uncle had pushed him off! Uncle pretended to love him still, but something had changed. And Jan thought it was unseemly that the girl followed Uncle like a puppy dog — so obedient. It bothered him to feel like a visitor at Uncle's hearth. Hadn't he grown up at Uncle's feet and tied his flies and fetched his nails? It stung him that Uncle walked off with the girl riding his horse and him not saying one word to Jan. Uncle did not tell him a single thing to do.

"Do this for me, boy," Duncan would say all day every day. Him and Pet competed to please Uncle. Early on it was sugar tits in his pockets for the fastest one or the strongest. Then they competed not to be punished by him or to earn his grudging compliments. And now he had the little girl to fetch for him.

Ah, let him go then! Jan sighed and looked around to see what chores he would do for An' Hat to earn his seat at her breakfast table. He was hungry and regretted eating so little at last night's supper and drinking so much.

Jan Smoot had been Charlie Tougle Jr. when he'd witnessed his cousin's birth. He was called Son then. Only after his mother's death did he get the name Jan Smoot. Uncle had given him the venerated name of the youngest son of Lucy Smoot to save him the pain of being called by the name of his mother's killer.

It had caused Jan some confusion and discomfort losing his earliest name. The name belonged to the time that contained his mother and, though Duncan tried to erase the ugly memories of the killing, he was unable to stop talking about Jan's mother. So she remained a part of his uncle's memories and An' Hat's and Noelle's, but not his. Jan had no clear recollections of her unless he strained and wished and sweated and invoked magic.

2

WHEN DUNCAN RETURNED FROM his winter work, he wondered momentarily who was the beautiful woman sitting on his porch step. Indeed he rubbed at his eyes to clear them and look. The woman saw him lift his arm and she waved excitedly. Dossie! He hadn't expected her here. He'd wanted to come up and clean himself and see her and the others at Hat's dinner table. He hadn't expected her to be here. The pretty one is not responsible for her own prettiness, he thought. It is an accident of nature. She can't be credited or blamed for it. So Dossie could not help that she was pretty. And Duncan could not help that he wanted to gaze on her. If the horse had not been impatient, he'd have sat and looked at her for an hour's time. Could she stand and hold her arm aloft for that long? The sight of the girl's right arm high above her head, hoisting her right breast and mashing its nipple against her bodice, might have been the one vision that would change his life.

Nervous to peruse Dossie's body, Duncan could see that she had flourished in his absence. She was taller and plumper. She was robust. She was exuberant. She stood on the porch and giggled.

She ambushed him. She wanted to see him first — touch him first. She wanted to be the first one to hang on his arm and ask him how he'd been keeping. She wanted to receive the first smile of paternal pride when he looked around and saw the winter accomplishments.

She wanted to draw water and warm it for him to clean up. She'd spent winter with Noelle and Hat, as before, but she'd been coming to Duncan's house each day since the Flower Moon — since the streams had started to run. She rose in the morning looking for him — preparing for him. She threw open the windows each day to clean out dull odors, but as the air was still cool, for three days running, she'd made up a fire and cozied the place with wood Jan chopped. At dusk when he hadn't come, she extinguished the fire and went back to Noelle's house to sleep.

He arrived at midday, and she thought it was inappropriate to run at him and grab on to him, though this was what she wanted to do. She wanted to press her body flat against him and have him feel the beautiful breasts that Hat had been trying to make her conceal under an apron. Dossie knew Duncan's tastes — what things Jan and Pet laughed about. She stood on the porch and waved furiously. Oh, she was so glad to see him that she could have bitten off his ear and chewed it and swallowed it for love of him! It was a tribute to her new maturity that she remained on the porch until he and his horse rode up to greet her.

"The most a woman can gain is what I want for you, little one." Duncan Smoot had announced his decision to Dossie with unabashed earnestness at the conclusion of all the harvest festivals in the first season of her life in Russell's Knob. "I want you to learn to read and write and to be clever," Duncan said in a voice that surprised even himself. Dossie was to understand that he was thinking of her the way he thought of his nephews, as one of his children, as a stone needing polish and embellishment.

"Noelle and Hattie will look after you for the wintertime," Duncan had said, explaining that she would stay with Noelle and have winter lessons with her at the longhouse. His sister had agreed, Duncan said, to instruct Dossie in sewing, cooking, and other womanly sciences such as canning, jam making, cheese making, soap- and candlemaking. Duncan went further to recommend that Dossie learn beadwork from Noelle. He said it was certain Dossie's cooking would improve if she had the chance to closely study Miz Hat. It would be a time for useful instruction.

It was clear Duncan was pleased with the plan he'd devised. He did not expect Dossie's face to fall. He was prompted to add that, in the cold months, there were others who depended on him elsewhere. Some folk left bondage after the harvesttime, he lectured her, for they had some provision then and, though the weather may be cold and their foot coverings sparse, they took the risks. Shouldn't he go to help them, he'd asked. She was stung. She'd believed that, as he was all of the world to her, she was all of the world's concerns to him.

She fought to squelch tears, as she knew he would be displeased at such a show. But the list of deficiencies and duties and skills to be mastered was so long!

"Must I have winter lessons, sir? I can keep your house. I can stay in your house while you're gone and keep it clean. I can learn all about cooking from Miz Hat. I don't need to learn no reading, Mr. Duncan," Dossie blurted, having lost complete control of herself. Could she not go with him on his travels? She wanted to say that she could not bear to be anywhere else but with him and that she was frightened of Noelle. She would gladly follow Miz Hat, she wanted to plead. She could work hard, but why must she have winter lessons in reading and writing? Perhaps she was too thick for it and would fail badly. Miz Noelle would be pleased then to show her up to be a dunce.

"Yes, of course you must," Duncan answered without equivocation. Dossie had not asserted a contrary opinion since the first day when she'd piped up to say she would stay with him. She was obedient and deferential as was proper. But just as on that first day, Duncan felt a shiver of presentiment. It felt like the young girl had a soul's mission despite him.

"You are not my servant girl," he said. "You are a ward in my house and I must look to your instructions and your circumstance. Yes, you must learn to read and write."

Dossie knew that she had made a mistake to question Duncan. She would take her winter lessons and do all else that he said, or she must go away from his house.

Dossie's plan was crumpled some. She must go to live with her rival? For now she did think of Noelle Beaulieu as her rival. She was an obstacle. She'd have to learn all of Noelle's lessons and then move her out of the path.

Ah, this is what Dossie wanted! She knew it. She wanted to find a place of permanence with Mr. Duncan Smoot.

"You must learn a lot, little girl," Duncan had said to her when he mounted his horse the first winter he went away. "Mind yourself." He'd left her sitting on Noelle's porch without lingering further or looking back. He revived the funny, delightful feeling she'd had before Noelle had come into the picture.

He cared for her. He reckoned her—Dossie. He sounded like he was saying he would miss her.

A circuitous path wound between the houses on the western chain of the town and was well traveled. Dossie learned her own cuts between Noelle's longhouse and Duncan's and the Wilhelms' houses. Her winter responsibilities were considerable, as Mr. Duncan's chickens required daily attention, and she was a hand at the soap- and candlemaking, as well as being required to learn letters and figures and the history of the town.

The very largest homestead occupying the pinnacle of Russell's Knob was the Van Waganen place. The Van Waganens were prominent, purely African-looking people who had been in Russell's Knob since early days. Their ancestors were people who had come from disparate places in Africa but had been acculturated to their enslavement in the sugar islands. They came to belong to Cornelius Van Waganen, a Dutch farmer who purchased them in Barbados, then died intestate in New Jersey. Van Waganen's former slaves left and hid out in Russell's Knob. In those days, if you reached the hideout, you had reached your refuge. Russell Sitton and his band would not let them take you back. Russell Sitton had cut a border—had set a mark—had said, "Here I stay and I will kill a man who comes here for trouble." He punctuated his declarations with skirmishes. Most of the families, like the Van Waganens, had come without clear title to themselves. None was relinquished, and none was taken back.

The Barlows, Gin and his wife, Sarah, and their children, worked hard on land leased from the Van Waganens on the eastern chain of the town. The Vanders—Honey; her daughters,

Sally, Mary, Tilly, and Anna; and Paul, her husband; the Bells, who were Honey Vander's people, as well as the Hovens, who were the part of the Vander family that broke off, moved away, and came back after the race riot in Cincinnati, all lived and farmed on the eastern chain.

The numerous DeGroots in Russell's Knob were all descendants of Jan DeGroot, who came a mountain after breaking from his brother over the decision to bring his jumble children back with him from the sugar islands. Made unwelcome in the lowlands by his white family, Jan DeGroot and his wife and children departed and came to the highlands.

The Paul and Siscoe families had ancestors who were runaways and stayaways. The stayaways were those of the Delaware and Munsee who had stayed away from white towns when others of their nation left for west. The Pauls and Siscoes had passed down British land titles near Russell Sitton's holdings, and all of these titles, contested after the War of American Independence, were later ruled legal. It was said by the older folk with reverence that Russell's Knob was truly Grandmother's town — ancient ancestor Grandmother. For the true knob — the core navel of the town — was these British deeds.

The Sitton family, closely related to the Smoots, was directly descended from a woman called Grandmother Sitton, a Munsee woman who bore children for a British army officer. In lieu of marriage, she was given title to land for her children. She passed the title forward. She convinced the other women thus situated to accept the British view that the land was theirs if they meant to die to keep others from taking it. They raised their children to think the same. They fed them courage with their milk and mush, and they built up a settlement that became a town. And the Smoots became blood related to the founding Sitton family through their revered ancestor Lucy the Angolan, who became a Sitton wife.

The Tougle family—Charlie Tougle's people, Jan's father's people—were now spurned in Russell's Knob. They'd been stayaways like the Pauls and the Siscoes, but left the town after Cissy Smoot Tougle's murder by her husband because the Smoots swore oaths, and the Tougles' shame overwhelmed their grit.

The Beaulieu, Noelle's people, were a curious group whose numbers had dwindled to only the one. The "Boo-loo" was what folk sometimes called them, though most of the inhabitants of Russell's Knob were facile with languages and found little about the European tongues difficult. It was a way to tease the family because their fortunes had fallen precipitously over the recent decades. They were disesteemed because Noelle's grandfather, son of a French rich-boy adventurer and an Angolan girl he bought from a coffle, had once been very haughty. He escaped from his father, lit out with a wagonload of silver and most of his father's library. He came into the highlands to stay free after he'd sold half the books to a pair of westward-bound Jesuits he met in Trenton. The rest of the library—several hundred volumes in English and French—he displayed in his house. He built a separate cabin for the books off to its own for fear of a hearth fire, then joined the cabin to the house, which made it appear to be an old Algonquin longhouse. He sold the silver pieces over two decades in New York City and was well set. In Russell's Knob, Jacques Beaulieu married a relative of the Sittons and had several children. All of his children except two daughters died in a harsh, pestilential winter when he was away. The two daughters left were idolized by Jacques Beaulieu and his wife. He aspired to educate them and marry them off to special candidates. Some folk would have it that the common tradition of calling the mixed-race mountain folk "Jacks" had some connection to the flamboyant Jacques Beaulieu, though others believed it sprang from Jack-in-the-Green fests and the Jamaicans.

Duncan Smoot's house was on the site of the original Smoot homestead. Rebuilt after a big burnout, it nestled on a ridge on the western chain just south of the Beaulieu house. On the next southerly ridge were the house and brewery of Ernst Wilhelm and his wife. Their land came as Hat's inheritance and was much improved by her husband's industry. The pretty farm-land on the next ridge south of the Wilhelms was also Smoot land—that part belonging to Cissy Smoot and her son, Jan. Until Jan was considered ready to manage it, this farm was administered by Duncan and leased to Mensah Paul.

Noelle's home was as peculiar in Dossie's eyes as the woman herself. Most noticeable were the strong odors that emanated. Questions arose as to what was being boiled—what concocted. The aromas were complex and confusing. In fact, the interior air was thick with smoke at most times as pots of heated unguents created clouds of steam. The fireplace, at the median point of the large rectangular room, kept fire and was attended to throughout the day. An opening to the sky, governed by a long pole, was opened so that some smoke escaped. A shelf of stones at the back of the pit formed the place for cooking food, and a further, hotter place was used for boiling and rendering.

On the first chilly evening in Miz Noelle's longhouse, the fire high and hot, Dossie sat close beside the woman and thought, with some displeasure, that she smelled like Mr. Duncan. Dossie recalled his stern last words. "You must learn to read and write, girl. Surely, it is what your mama would want for you."

Dossie's head still spun from seeing Miz Noelle's grandfather's room for his books, the place for winter book studies. This had been Noelle's mama's schoolroom and was adjoined to the cooking rooms and storerooms by a breezeway. Here the Smoots, Noelle, and other children in Russell's Knob had learned lessons from Madame Beaulieu, had smelled Madame's patisserie, and had become beguiled by her mysterious domain. A central feature of Noelle's and her mother's instructions involved the books of plants and their descriptions of the uses of herbs and fruits. Noelle's grandfather's library included many texts of the drawings of naturalists. Both Jan and Pet liked to peruse the books of animals and plants that occupied an entire shelf of the room, and Noelle spurred them to gather herbs with challenges to find a tree, a plant, or a rock depicted. Both were much less the mischief-makers in Noelle's domain of fascination.

The boys welcomed their forays into the woods for kindling and aromatics for the women's industry because it was lighter work than the winter chores at the brewery. They came as often as Ernst Wilhelm would allow. After supper, Noelle tackled Jan's hair with her combs, tugging and pulling out detritus and plucking him about the ears because he resisted her. She loped off his tufts haphazardly when his chatter began to annoy her, though he was still handsome when she'd done.

Warm near the fire and worn out, Pet leaned on his mother and slipped to sleep. When he was roused for his turn wth Noelle, his pale face had become very red.

"Is he ill, Hattie? Has he caught a chill, you think?" Noelle asked solicitously when she pulled the drowsy boy close.

"No. He's likely been very naughty in his sleep is all. He is like his father when he misbehaves," Hat replied.

When Noelle's brushing caused Pet's hair to crackle and Jan refused mulled ale for himself and Pet, the boys left to sleep elsewhere. Hat and Noelle pulled out mats and pelts and arranged them around the fireplace. Ah, winter candlemaking time was the time for stories, too! Hadn't Noelle confessed her dalliance with Edgar Vander one winter and admitted that she'd gone with him to Phillipsburg? Hadn't she smiled and gloated and related all of the salacious details? Hadn't Hat told Noelle the tale of her rescue and the things she'd done so that Mr. Wilhelm would bring her home? What a pity the boys had left before Noelle spun a story for them all.

"Who brung you?" Noelle asked and pulled Dossie into her lap. Noelle gently pushed and tugged on Dossie, handling her head. It was a prerogative—a social habit of the mature women. They groomed young girls in their laps and exchanged palaver. The girls didn't balk. Hairbrushes were applied with vigor, and youngsters were accustomed to be stung but relished their time between an auntie's or a mama's or a sister's knees.

Noelle used her comb to separate sections of Dossie's hair down to the scalp. Grease she applied to the hair was pungent, and it traveled up into the girl's nostrils and caused a lethargy—a calm and trusting feeling.

"Mr. Duncan brung me here," Dossie said timidly. She answered the woman politely but was puzzled that she'd asked so obvious a question.

"No, little one, you were brought. You were rescued here. Where Duncan pluck you from?" Noelle continued.

Dossie sat cross-legged with her head fully forward at rest on her chest. Well—how was she to answer? She decided to stare downward and hold her mouth closed like butter would not melt in it. Maybe the woman thought she had beguiled Mr. Duncan—put a spell on him? No, no. She couldn't think that.

"Young one, go and get that bag yonder," Noelle ordered and gently pushed Dossie to her feet. "Where he pluck you out of?" the woman repeated when she came back. She took the skin bag and used a sharper bone comb from it to cut through Dossie's thick fluff and reach her scalp.

Fond of a range of hair dressings, women in Russell's Knob exchanged ribbons and trinkets merrily. It was frequently a point of erotic humor that the men of Russell's Knob enjoyed undoing and stealing hair ribbons. Noelle's own braids, gathered into beaded thongs and hanging like horse tails, were a source of fascination for their thickness and their length.

"What god do you follow, child?" Noelle asked as though seeking an orientation, some guidance. "No matter. All gods are welcome here. Your god must b'lieve in you. You're here aren't you?"

Puzzled, unable to raise her head and study the woman's face for clues to her meaning, Dossie spoke tentatively, with her head clamped forward onto her chest, with all of the sincerity in her small, untutored soul, "God love a turtle."

"Dossie," Noelle asked in a beckoning, facilitating, prodding voice. She used her fingers on Dossie's head to reach and coerce her. "Where you came from? Whose baby child are you?"

Was it a song? Was it a question? Dossie began to speak before she really knew she had.

I don't have to show wet on my face to weep. Ooma know that. She not looking at my eyes. Every bone in me is shaking, trembling. I bite my own tongue and I taste blood in my mouth. Ooma will crush my heart with squeezing me between her hands. She pinch and twist my jaws. She grind me soft and pummel me like a round of dough. She buss me close and fill her nose with the smell of me. I bury my face in her shift for I know I must remember her this way. I must learn her good 'cause I will tear away. Me and my Ooma part from each other. My heart los'. It sink to the bottom of me. I feel sick and I lose the few little bits in mah stomach. I think bad at leaving mah Ooma. Would no child leave her mama and go forth alone what the kingfisher call. She talk loud in her rattling caw-caw. She know the surround.

Is this the place that Ooma's prayers had sent her? Yes, it was Ooma and Bil who had fanned her to this place. Maybe they would leave the island one day and come here?

"Give her off to the protection of the Lord," Bil said to Ooma.

"We'uns on a spit of groun' floating in the surround of water, little girl. You know it?" Dossie shook her head to say she understood, but she was uncertain. Dossie had no way of knowin' the wide world. Bil knew that. He was putting the baby in a bulrush basket and setting it off to its fate the way Moses's mama had done.

Bil loaded the chest and put the crates and boxes 'board his punt. Dossie squatted on the straw—her knees hugged up to herself—chewing on a biscuit. The furniture was lashed to the boat so it would not cause the craft to heel, and other crates were pressed beside it to make a tight cargo. Bil told Dossie to let her body fall and sway with the movement of the boat and not to cry out no matter what. Bil hummed to settle to a rhythm. Dossie was steady enough on a small boat—been born at the Island Plantation. The sound of rushing and receding water lulls babies to sleep there.

Bil poled away from Kenworthy's island—steady and sure—headed for Havre de Grace, the beautiful harbor at the crux of the Big River and the Bay. Sweat rolled down his body, and his fear added an odor. He stewed in his own trepidation.

At the helm of the shallop, Bil urged it to be fast and careful and single-minded in reaching Havre de Grace. With shushing and sighs the boat responded, and Bil and little Dossie and all of the new wife's inherited furniture bore off to the port.

Bil was well known as one of Master Perry's people from the island. The regular patrollers on the river knew him and knew he had leave to go about in his shallop. These men had to consider what they'd do if Peregrine Kenworthy found them messing with his property. Dossie stayed out of sight, though. There were plenty of people who would train a scope on the water to note the passage of who or what and when on the river. Looking, looting, and salvage were big occupations for inhabitants in the spits and coves of the surround. And sometimes salvage meant bond people. Fishing a runner out of the water and taking that catch back to its master or to an auction stage was lucrative commerce.

She has Ooma's face, Bil thought sadly as he rowed. Between the eyes and down her nose and to the top of her lips, it is Ooma's pretty face. Naw. It is what Ooma's face once was before so many ordeals stamped it. Ah, Ooma's face too had once been soft like little Dossie's. To honor this softness Bil fanned Dossie like so many seeds—scattered her to the wind. Yes, it was time to let the breeze take her to a better dirt. Cast her out to the unknown. Master Perry's world is a knowable horror. Save her from it!

At Havre de Grace the raucous bargemen went off to their jolly times in the taverns and left the hours between sunset and full dark to runners, sneak-thiefs, and stowaways. Bil walked along the dockside tugging the girl by her hand, looking for the signal. At the two blinks of a lamp he recognized the help-meet and the steamboat. Bil tangled their hands up and savored the last sight of Dossie.

He must walk off from her now and go back. It was the plan—his pact with Ooma. He would not bear off by himself as well he might—and might succeed. He'd sworn he would return to cover Dossie's escape and to wait with Ooma. If she gained back her strength, they would both try to run. Then they could scour to find Dossie.

Gone, gone, gone. Ooma and him would grieve like hound dogs—moaning and whining to themselves. They would cry out loud as if Dossie had died in the water surround, but they would secretly reckon her gone to freedom. After crying for all to see and hear, in the deep dark they would rejoice. And then they will whine and whimper when they sleep for wanting to see the little girl gone on.

"They brung us up here from 'Napolis. Don't 'low nobody to take you back to 'Napolis," Bil said. "Bear off to north, girl, and ne'er return." Bil then gave Dossie's hand to a grease-covered, loose-limbed figure with cunning eyes who shoved her onto a pile of dirty rags.

"Stay shut—quiet!" he ordered.

*   *   *

When Noelle and Hat decided there was soap enough and candles aplenty, only mending and letters were left for winter work. Dossie was pressed harder to accomplish and given lap work and Ernst Wilhelm's honey-mulled winter ale in the evening. Hat and Noelle solicited more of her tale.

Though now Dossie fully believed that she had been destined to come to Duncan Smoot's heaven all along, she mused and remembered Mutt, the ragged deck boy whose foul mouth spewed water with every word he said. She recollected the smell of the numerous small cook fires in corners of the vessel and the engine itself that put out noxious clouds of smoke. The husky smell of the dockside at Havre de Grace was nothing to the stench of the steamboat. The air was almost firm enough to hold on to. As smelly as the gassy atmosphere of the boat was, the wiry figure who brought her aboard the boat had a stronger, more startling odor coming from his mouth. Spittle dribbled onto his chin in a steady wave. He reached to remove Dossie's shift and whispered reassuringly through a flume of water. She understood finally that he was called Mutt and that she must put on a ragged costume. Then Mutt smeared her face with greasy dirt and loudly declared her the worrisome old hag that bore him. He burlesqued a foolish, cursing manner and represented the "old" woman as addlepated and harboring lice. He thus accomplished the disguise by which Dossie began her travel on the river. At dawn she sat topside and watched the water. The river was a lovely blue band, and they coursed it at a good clip. With her knees drawn up to her chin, Dossie faced the dark horizon beyond which, as Bil said, was her freedom.

The next day the boat reached the thronged landing at Port

Deposit, Maryland, a place of fast-moving rapids and busy people. This was the destination for the goods aboard their vessel, and the crew set to lifting hogsheads of tobacco and molasses onto the dock. Mutt roused his passenger, shoved a bundle into her arms, pulled her off the steamboat, and shouted loud curses at her for the entertainment of his shipmates. Mutt then leaned down to whisper that she must wait at the spot to be taken up by the next conductor on the chain.

The wait was not long. "Take shelter in yon barn," a woman said sharply yet maternally. She had the voice of a disciplinarian, not a cruel driver. And as she spoke she clapped her hand on Dossie's left shoulder and pulled away a mote of thread. The child followed the woman's instructions without hesitation, though shivering in her fears. In the barn Dossie was hurried into another costume. Molly Cropsey operated a boat that hauled farm goods along the Susquehanna with a crew of her own children. Dossie was taken aboard the barge, mixed in with the other children, and fed. "What they tell you to say if somebody ast' you?" Molly questioned.

"God love a turtle," Dossie said.

On the morning of the second day out of Port Deposit the Cropseys' barge came to the snaggletooth rapids at Conowingo.

"You are to stop off here and be carried onward by another," Molly said stiffly as they approached a landing. "Do not wave us off. Be big, little one." She punctuated her words with a kiss on the girl's cheek, and once again Dossie's face was baptized with the well meaning spittle of her conductor.

Dossie wondered now what had become of the Cropseys. Hat and Noelle watched her face in silence. Even if Mr. Duncan and the people of Russell's Knob had taken her in and saved her, Dossie could not forget what life had come before. Under the influence of ale, she was unsure if she told her tale or dreamed it. She lay back on her pallet and closed her eyes.

That place, the place at Conowingo, had a clean, pleasantly fragrant straw aroma, and little Dossie, tossed and handled and frightened, lay down in complete surrender to what will — sleep, abandonment, capture, pain, or death. The smell of timothy grass and the concert of breathing lulled her.

She heard a voice. A tremulous and uncertain repetition of prayers. It was a pleading, supplicating tone that became swollen with confidence and became very loud. The voice filled up the animal stalls.

Dossie left her hide and crept to a place where she could see without being seen. To her astonishment, the exhortations were being produced by a kneeling female figure, who yelled at her God and asked him to help her and guide her and hear her. The woman stood up finally, pulled ever straighter, and opened her arms as if to encircle a congregation of listeners.

Was no one nearby to hear? Was none other than Dossie fearful of this torrent of prayer and barking? Was the woman scalded or whipped? Why had no one come to see what the great noise was?

The woman brought herself to an ever-wilder pitch, then fell to her knees in collapse. She murmured prayers and sobbed quietly for some minutes, then went to sleep in the straw. She was long, tall, and her hands were like water dippers.

Dossie's own throat became parched in sympathy or in concert with the woman's outpouring. She became terribly, almost desperately thirsty, but also frightened. She retreated to her corner and listened to the woman's audible slumber.

Dossie continued to be startled by Evangelist Zilpha Seabold. The woman was the next conductor on the railroad, and she spewed many, many words out of herself in bursts and she barked and stuttered and her eyes blinked and swirled in their sockets.

The two travelers set out at next sunrise, and the Evangelist took command of their congress along the path. They reached a ferry landing at midmorning. They were to make way to the town of Lancaster, where little Dossie would, to her relief when she heard the Evangelist say it, pass into the hands of another conductor. Around the town of Millersville, Dossie and the Evangelist accepted shelter in the stall of a nervous believer's barn. Zilpha Seabold slept soundly until a sheriff and two deputies broke in upon her. The girl heard their noisy call to purpose and scattered to the corner of another stall when the men burst into the barn. Fear took her senses—made her eyes dim to blindness and compromised her hearing. She could not understand their words. She felt the first blow that landed on the Evangelist as though it had landed on her own shoulder. There was a loud cracking noise, but no outcry from Zilpha. They hog-tied the Evangelist and took her into their custody.

She endured the darkness in the stall. At sunrise she saw a man at work in the straw. He had gathered Evangelist Zilpha's belongings into a burlap.

"Gwan away from here. Go on before they remember you was wid her," he said harshly when Dossie opened her eyes and took in the scene. "Do your cryin' on the road out of here!" he said. "Yonder is the track to some a the colored towns." He shook her to rouse her up and off. He hoisted the belongings on her back and gave her a hickory stick and a biscuit.

Dossie flew off. She left the town of Millersville on foot—on flying foot—alone and leaving a whirl of dust.

The Kingfisher Woman say it all the time: One look, one deep breath, set out eastward with determination.

*   *   *

The next evening, at Noelle's request, Dossie ran through some birdcalls. Hat and Noelle allowed themselves more mulled ale now that their winter tasks were mostly done. They became giddy, boisterous, and chatty. Hat wondered if Noelle was worried, and embarrassed to be so, about her relation with Duncan since this girl had come—since he had brought her. Noelle was self-possessed, but Hat had seen her crying into her hand when Duncan left. His eyes had been on Dossie's face only—not carnally, but caught, held. Hat knew Noelle believed in auguries, had taken them and seen a change in her circumstance. Hat unraveled Noelle's braids, brushed her hair, parted it at the middle of her scalp, and kissed the part at the back of her head as she had done when they were children and dressed each other's hair for fun. The kindness thrilled Noelle.

"Papa asks you to come home, Mama," Pet stammered to his mother. "He says his stomach is sour, and he needs your cooking." Pet, on direct orders from his father, whose patience with his wife's absence had worn down to the rails, presented himself to his mother hoping she would come home without a fuss.

"I'll be home when I get home," Hat answered without smiling, then felt a little ashamed of her abruptness with the boy. "Go back an' get a cart for my things and one of your dogs to pull it and carry me home, boy." Pet's face brightened immediately, and Hat was touched to notice it.

Hat was fussy busy when she returned home. Pet helped her reorganize her kitchen and bring in her stores. Ernst Wilhelm came into the cook room as she was putting a stew on the stove and caught his first sight of her with her hair mussed up and her dress with damp spots under the arms. Hat turned, saw his lustful glance, and tidied her hair, surprised at feeling aroused by his presence. He sat down at the table and looked at her as if she were a phantasm.

"You are not well, Mr. Wilhelm? Noelle sent some powders for your stomach." Hat brought him a glass of milk.

"Ah, Hattie, now you've come home I won't need Noelle's powders. Petrus will be better, too. He's cried every day since you were away. Now I won't have to hear the awful wailing," Ernst Wilhelm said and guffawed.

Pet, who was stacking up his mother's soaps, became excruciatingly red when Hat glanced at him. Of course he had missed her. But it was Papa's pillow that was wet with longing.

Hat set a meal of her husband's favorites and cautioned him to take care for his stomach. Later he dressed himself in the clean nightshirt that she put beside his pillow, leaving off his pants, underpants, and blouse in a pile on the floor. Ah, his wifely comforts had returned!

Hat knelt to retrieve his clothes and felt his eyes on her. She busied herself about the room—restoring order to his sundry. Ernst Wilhelm eased beneath his covers. It was a comfortable bed when Hattie was there to make it warm. There was no woman who knew more tricks for making a bed cozy on chilly nights. Ernst Wilhelm chuckled to himself unkindly that her tricks ended with placing bed warmers, though. Pretty as she was—as stimulating as she was to gaze on—she rarely responded to him with any sexual enthusiasm. And, he sighed, she had no art for the act. Hattie just let herself be fucked most times. His little mistress had much more fun with her lovemaking. She hadn't forgotten how to be playful. Only after a long absence did Hattie liven up at all, and her appetite for touching was quickly satisfied. She was obedient to her vows, though. Ernst Wilhelm lay back and pictured Arminty and imagined her tickles and pinches while Hat wound around the room straightening things. The warm bed nearly coaxed him to sleep. When Hat raised her arms to her head to twist her hair, his patience came to an end.

"Come, have a glass of ale, Hattie," he said in a soft-spoken command. "Did you make me some candles, wife?"

"Oh, yes." Hat bustled about and brought out a box lined with grass and filled with slim, bright red bayberry candles. These were the highest pinnacle of her candle craft, and he knew it. He knew her excitement for making candles.

"Oh, the color is so bright — *herrliche!*"

"I have a secret," Hat said and smiled as if she meant to make a game of finding out. She knew the bayberry candles were his favorite. She watched his face and enjoyed his smile.

"You are very sweet, Hattie."

To cover her emotion, Hat drew out a taper, trimmed its wick, lit it, and placed it at his bedside. When she came close he undid the knots from her head and tangled his fingers in the hair at the nape of her neck. He stroked the side of her face with the back of his hand, and she kissed at his fingers when they came near her lips. "My pretty pearl!" he said then and worked his fingers beneath her bodice. He passed her a mug of ale, and she drank it while he fingered her tits. She allowed herself to be pulled into his arms.

As he'd climbed past the watch house and toward his porch on that early spring morning, Duncan Smoot nearly wept for wanting to be at home. How had little Dossie fared without him? It was his first thought. How had they all fared? He reflected that it had been a hard thing to set out from the comfortable hearth and know that cold weather and privation were ahead. He'd gone because there were those who needed his guidance. Oh, but how he wished he'd stayed this winter around the fire in his home. Hattie and Noelle were a delight in winter—were both like little squirrels boiling herbs, putting away the harvest, and stocking the cellars. He had missed these pleasures.

Duncan returned to the Wilhelms' to find the others hale and hearty. Jan and Pet seemed taller and broader and more manly. They greeted him warmly when he and Dossie came up. They hurried to relieve him and the horse of their packs and provisions, and he was moved to see them happy at his return. He was glad that he'd brought gifts for them.

He was the one who had come back bedraggled. Out in back beside her washing closet, Hat looked him over critically, took away his soiled clothes, and gave him clean things of Pet's. Hominy, pemican, and a fruit pit that he had sucked on spilled from his pockets.

"Your winter gal don't cook much. You look thin," she said.

"Aw, Pippy," Duncan answered.

"You look like you been drinkin' hard and sleepin' in a bear's cave. What kind of whore don't take better care of you," Hat continued saucily. Duncan would not dare be ill tempered in the circumstances.

"Aw, hush, little hen, stop cluckin' at me. You look plump and pretty. What you been doin' all winter?"

"Makin' soap," Hat snapped. "And is a damn good thing. Your clothes stink!" She pushed his dirty things along the ground with her foot and laughed merrily. Duncan laughed, too. Hattie's gentle fussing was a winter pleasure sorely missed.

This spring, nearly sick with anticipation of Mr. Duncan's

return, Dossie had come alive, had grown and come forth with promise. She had improved after each winter's study with Noelle and Miz Hat. She had acquired competency in the womanly sciences, and she had learned to read well. She was anxious to show off her recitations of verse. She could show Duncan where Annapolis was on Noelle's map and where on the map was Paterson, where was New York City, and where was the Canada border. She could assure him, with the same wry, defiant smirk that Noelle used, that Russell's Knob was not to be found on any white man's map.

She had improved the chicken house and the birds. The hens she'd coddled produced enough eggs for his appetite and her own with some left to trade. She had not spent her time lolling about preening herself, though she knew that lovely things had happened to her face and figure as well. In these winters that he'd left her to learn from Noelle and Hat, she had improved. She had grown up.

Her time had come, too, and she knew the import of it. She'd had her monthly miseries regularly for all of this past year. Ah, she had put herself on that porch to greet him, to be the one who gave him the very first homecoming smile.

3

HAT WALKED OUT TO her plant garden unnoticed. At the far reaches of her plot she looked away from the house. She rubbed at her breasts and felt their tenderness. She ground her palm against her left nipple and rubbed and pinched it until she could no longer stand the discomfort. Her head had got full of the foolish notion that causing herself pain would dislodge the comer and cause it to flush itself away. She stomped her foot in disgust. She had a baby! It was most certainly true. She had not felt this way since — how old is Pet? Fifteen? Or sixteen? Ach! He is seventeen at least. How had the time winged away? Nevertheless she had been a girl then, waiting on her husband and waiting for a baby to take up her life. It is embarrassing now. A woman like her. Damnation, damnation!

It was a cruel shock! Her sauces had betrayed her. She'd become careless with Ernst. Perhaps she'd become smitten again with wanting to be touched and held.

"He's clever!" Hat said and kicked at pebbles all the way to Noelle's house.

"You're a pretty sow these days," Noelle said with a chuckle as she walked up behind Hat dangling a string of possums.

"Eh?" Hat questioned.

"They're a pretty picture. Your tits — so plumped up. From your husband's attention?"

"Is it so plain to see?"

"It's that I know you well. With you it's the first sign, and I haven't seen you boiling your drawers lately."

"I've come to see you about it," Hat said and sat on the porch step.

It was the thing that made Noelle Beaulieu a pariah to some. She was a fix-up woman, though her reputation as a Spirit Woman mitigated the negative associations.

"I've been careless, Noelle," Hat said.

"Does it matter, girl?"

"It matters to me if I want a child. I ain't a brood sow."

"Yes, but you have only the one yet. A small brood!"

"I love my Pet, but I don't want no 'nother child now. You know what a time I had. I . . ." Hat stood and walked a few steps, bent, pulled up a few weeds, and put them in her apron pocket. She turned back and faced Noelle. "He keeps a girl in town. I don't want to be a fool. I don't want people to think I'm a fool."

"Yes, Hattie, it's well known."

"Eh?"

"What difference does it make now?" Noelle continued. "You always say you don't care what he does. You say you don't mind him being gone off with his women."

"Still it ain't right and it pisses me. An example for his son!"

"Hmm. Looks like you're in a weir, Hattie. The pretty trout has got caught this time! How come you forgot your safety?" Noelle said and swiped familiarly at Hat's cheek.

"I admit to tempting him," Hat said and giggled. "Him

acting like he's got such an appetite for me when I come home from candlemaking. But I've seen the girl he's keeping in town. She spends his money on ribbons and trinkets and sweets. I'm still a young woman, Noelle. I made him wish he was a better man." Both women laughed heartily, though Hat knew it was bluster.

"He's always ardent when you come home from candlemaking," Noelle put in.

"Hunh? Aye, you're right. I should have been prepared. I should not have let him feed me whiskey either. I've come to see if you have a salve for my tits. He is mauling me nightly." Hat went in the house ahead of Noelle and removed her blouse, loosed her camisole. Noelle came in the kitchen behind her and stared at Hat's cinnamon-colored back. Still, the only blemish upon it was a scar from a childhood scrape on an iron hook. Hat turned.

"You are swollen up," Noelle said at first glance of Hat's breasts, then dipped her chin and looked away. "No blood either then, eh?" Hat shook her head. Noelle went into her stores and handed Hat a large dollop of grease on a leaf.

Hat handed back the salve, raised her arms above her head, clasped her hands, and submitted her painful nipples to Noelle's fingers. When the salve had been applied, she dropped her arms and sat without speaking.

"You thought of making your husband promise to give up his girl in town? You can make him stay at home tellin' him about the baby. He'll behave for a while. You're his wife. You can get him back for good if you want him, girl."

"His mouth may promise, but his jasper won't."

"Wilhelm is a greedy man." Noelle dropped her eyes again.

Hat sat pondering for a long while. Several times she began

to form up her lips to speak and did not. Finally she looked down at her breasts, seemed surprised to see them bare. She put on her blouse and camisole again, tucked herself, and restored the bib of her apron.

"Pet was born after a battle, as the old women say. I was hours and hours pushing him out! I remember my husband made you stay away because you were too much a conjurer for his taste. He got a white doctor from town and brought him. The white doctor frightened me. When he went onto the porch to smoke a cheroot, Cissy said, 'Come on, Hattie, let's have it.' She leaned down and called to Pet and said, 'You come out of there, baby. Come on now.' She chirped and coaxed until it felt like she reached in and handed him out, but I couldn't see. I just saw Jan's pretty little encouraging eyes looking at me over her shoulder because he was strapped to Cissy. She didn't leave me for all of the day, and she fed and cared for Jan at my side.

"I became more ill after Pet was born and I gave up my milk because it was meager. I took the granny powders Mr. Wilhelm gave me and, when my milk dried up completely, I was able to build my strength. I grew up quick after Cissy died. I learned to take care of both of them boys." Hat finished speaking in a teary voice. "I don't want that hurt again."

"You're no coward, Hattie. What's your reason?" Noelle asked. She was willing do anything for Hat, but she wanted them both to know why they were doing it. Sending a child back to the ancestors was not a small thing.

"He shouldn't win out. Mr. Wilhelm has too many sins on his soul. He doesn't deserve any more gifts. He wants to fill up the porches with children, but I've always thwarted that purpose," Hattie asserted, finally aware of her own motives.

"When your mind is firmly made, come in a day or so and stay a day or so."

Noelle and Hat arranged to do what needed doing — saying to the others that they were off to gather. They made up jam so the story would hold.

When the first color emerges on the distant ridges and frothy mist is just beginning to be visible, it is the time of the first chatterers — those birds that herald dawn. On most mornings they are in a keen and noisy competition. Hat got up and always did, as did most all of the women of Russell's Knob also, with the first of the bird banter. She did nothing to her hair but shake it. It loosened about her and rested on her neck and shoulders. The hair cloud followed her to dip up water, build a quick, hot stove fire, and make her coffee.

Only Dossie noticed that Hat's skin was ashy and her eyes dull when she took up her kitchen work on returning home from making jam.

By the end of the first day back, standing at the stove became unbearable. Hat sat in the accommodation and packed, lit, and smoked the pipe Noelle had given her to relieve her discomfort. Her womb ached and rightly so. She intended to bear the pain stoically because she believed she deserved some discomfort.

Hat felt dog tired. How much more tired other women must be — Sarah Cooper or Honey Vander. These women had a yard full of young'uns. These women deserved to be tired. Did Hat deserve a calm and unruffled day with no noisy young'uns? What kind of selfish woman was she?

She had raised Pet, her baby. And she had raised Jan. These were her babies, and they were grown. Until they brought up some children for her to spoil, she was a free woman. She had given her greenest years to Mr. Wilhelm, and she had paid him off. She didn't owe him any more of herself. It had always been about commerce between them. Didn't she deserve her jams and soaps and candles now? Didn't she deserve her commerce?

The effect of the tobacco and its aromatic cloud was that she felt herself go dull in her loins, and the throb subsided.

She — Hattie — was the spoiled one, had always been. She knew it well. The others had got into scrapes for looking after her or indulging her whims. She was the baby among them, had sat on her moss tuffet and been queen! She felt sorry for them — for Cissy, of course, and for Duncan and Noelle. Noelle had always been willing to imperil her own soul to help the Smoots. And here again she had helped the brat, Hattie. And Duncan. He had taken real pain on her account — looking after her, protecting her. Even greedy, voracious Ernst Wilhelm had brought her home at some risk to himself when she pleaded with him. And now she silently begged the Grandmothers not to punish her too harshly nor chastise Noelle for sending a child back to the ancestors. Feeling sorry for herself for the pain she'd endured all day, she decided she alone was responsible for what had happened. It had been her fault from the beginning. She was the cause of the big rift that divided the Smoot family. She was responsible for all that had come after it.

Duncan styled himself their protector — her and Cissy. He was the great warrior. All the boys played at war and warriors then, when they were little chaps. Sam, an older cousin, was Duncan's nemesis. Hat knew her brother hated Sam, wanted to hurt him. She should never have run to Duncan tattling on Sam. She and Noelle had both been flirting with Sam in the silly, innocent way of little girls who bat their eyes and drop handkerchiefs. Sam grabbed at her. Sam frightened her, and she ran and told Duncan. Sam Smoot lost an eye in the fight that followed. Duncan was sent off to work at the iron mines to compensate his uncle for Sam's lost eye. The old men of the family decided it, but did not know what hell they sent Duncan to. He went to the Black Rocks, not much more than a day's journey from his home, and was lost to himself below the ground and was lost to the People for some years. All of what happened could be laid before the feet of spoiled little Hattie Smoot.

She cried herself into illness when her brother was sent away—Cissy, too, and Noelle. They counted every day he was gone. Papa got tired of Hattie's weeping and agreed very quickly for her to marry a distant cousin of Noelle called Pierre Petit Ourson.

The boy who had been Duncan Smoot never came back to Russell's Knob. A man called Duncan Smoot returned and took up the boy's life. And then Hattie returned with Ernst Wilhelm.

What had she done now and why? Was she still being selfish—not wanting another of Mr. Wilhelm's babies? She was lucky that Ernst Wilhelm had rescued her and brought her home. Duncan said so—had said she ought to embrace her marriage to Wilhelm because he was completely smitten with her. He had been. He was rough and demanding, but he was fixed on her. To keep her family and her dignity she had married Ernst Wilhelm, and she had endured him.

"I'll do your washing in the mornin', Miz Hat," Dossie said, coming out back to where Hat was sitting. "You sleep in and get your color back." Dossie smiled as she spoke. She was slightly alarmed to see Hat sitting so still, so given over to her thoughts as she sat on the stump.

"My husband is gone off to town?" Hat asked, coming back from her reverie.

"They all left," Dossie replied.

"Stay then," Hat said.

"Yes."

"I have my miseries. Pardon me for not being merry."

Dossie made up a pallet on the kitchen floor. She insisted on the floor, though Hat invited her to sleep in her bed. She lay down in the kitchen so as not to obstruct Mr. Wilhelm if he returned to his bedroom in the night. Once he had been quite annoyed to find her lying next to Hat. And from the kitchen she was ready to follow if Mr. Duncan returned and called to her.

At summer's end, when Ernst Wilhelm had the boys working long days at harvesting, drying, and baling hops for the brewery, Duncan won their hearts by offering a trip toward the Canada border to shoot game with new guns. He proposed the adventure to harry his brother-in-law, too. Duncan knew it would make him nervous to be gone away. The boys were exhilarated. They laughed and purred like kittens as soon as they were told.

Now was the time for Duncan to be certain of Pet forever. If what he'd heard was true, Pet might be getting ready to have some trouble. He was sneaking around some white farm girl from New Barbados and could end up living in a white people's town. And his father might encourage him to do it. But Pet was Hattie's boy, and Duncan meant to fight for him just as he'd done with Jan.

Duncan had had to court and bribe three Munsee-Delaware so-called leaders in order to keep Cissy's child. Charlie Tougle's mother belonged to these people, and she said the child belonged with their clan after his mother died and his father ran off. Duncan would not relinquish him and sat before the old men and proffered gifts of cigars, whiskey, and pelts. They accepted Duncan's bribes and gave up claim to the child. Whenever he was especially angry with Jan, Duncan would say he'd traded a good box of cigars for him and now felt cheated.

At their first-night camp, Jan and Pet tended the horses and built a fire. Ernst Wilhelm brought out whiskey. To the great delight of the boys, Duncan passed cigars. For the first time he could remember, Duncan was more gratified to see their pleasure than to feel the excitement himself.

The boys were like the twin bear cubs he'd seen two moons past when they gamboled on a ridge at the full moon and their mother stood on a ledge above them to watch, allowing them the fun of scrapping and tumbling yet alert and protective. Fat, lively, and full of promise these boys and bear cubs.

"Jan's a sweet dancer," Wilhelm said when Jan began to step a jig. Hours on horseback had made them all feel tight and drawn up, and Jan moved to unwind himself. "But is he soft, Duncan?" Ernst Wilhelm challenged, an age-old custom in the mountains, insulting a favorite. This banter was an art, a conversation, a game of baiting the one who has trained and nurtured a child so they will rise in spirited defense.

"He's not soft. He is tough and clever. He can throw you on your ass, big belly. 'Tain't his fault he's pretty. Blame Cissy. She was pretty," Duncan said.

"Ja, 'tis a fact — a beautiful woman!" Wilhelm replied.

Jan looked up from his feet and got warm. He kept up stepping and whirling in his own jigs and shaking his left ankle as if trying to toss something off his foot.

"That oaf of yours and Hattie's is pretty, too. He's like a stallion growing up in a grass meadow. But is he tough?" Duncan slung out.

"Aye, he is that," Wilhelm replied.

"Oh, he's a proven dog, your son is," Duncan continued. He realized he would tattle. It was, of course, a cruelty to Pet, but he wanted to stick it to Wilhelm. "He's sneakin' off down to New Barbados pretty regular. He's got a girl — a white farm girl. I heard she's working on a stomach, and Pet's the cause of it," Duncan said to stun Ernst Wilhelm. He stunned Pet, too, who didn't know that Duncan had found out.

Pet turned to his father red and stammering, "Papa, I . . ."

"Alle und alles auf einmal gewachsen, mein Sohn," Ernst Wilhelm said and thumped his son in the center of his back.

"Papa . . . ," Pet repeated.

Jan piped up, "He ain't sneakin', Uncle. He can see a girl, can't he? Pet ain't no baby."

"Maybe when 'em lowlanders fin' out Pet is only half a white man, they'll come an' crack his balls," Duncan answered. "We'd better be careful with your boy, Wilhelm. What you gonna do when her papa comes looking for him?" Duncan fed hot words to his brother-in-law's anxiety.

"Petrus can marry her. I'll build him a place and he can bring her here."

"No, Papa!" Pet exploded. "I ain't gettin' married!" He and Jan guffawed.

"You will get married, boy, if I say so. You ain' got to do

nothin' but just behave a little bit. You bring her here and settle down."

"Papa, I ain't gonna do it," Pet said.

"Now, Pet, I think you ought to do like your papa says,"
Duncan said.

"No, Uncle, I can't get married! I don't want to."

"You tell him, Wilhelm. Being married don't mean he have
to stop being free with the women. Your papa intends to build
this white girl a house, and you and her will build him an
empire."

"No, Papa! No, Uncle, I don't want Emma as a wife!"

"Emma, is it? Is a nice name, eh, Wilhelm?"

"You ain't got to get married, Pet — just 'cause you're down
there plowing her rows," Jan put in and exploded with more
laughing. He punched at his cousin's ribs until he caused Pet to
laugh as well.

"But, boy, you got to do what your papa says," Duncan
insisted, driving the idea.

"Papa," Pet pleaded.

Duncan chuckled to himself that, of course, Pet was too
young to marry. This was a battle between him and Wilhelm.
Wilhelm was still a Europe. He was still thinking he ought to
be king because he's a white man. He's never wanted the
Smoots to claim Pet.

"Your papa is a slave buyer, Pet. Did you know it?" Duncan
said suddenly. "I s'pose you got to do what he tell you. Him a
white man, he got the final say."

"Aw, everybody's free in the highlands," Ernst Wilhelm said.

"Ask Dossie about free. Some lowlanders would say she was
free, but some won't — they'd treat her worse than a dog,"
Duncan answered.

"Then you brung her here to make her free. Is that so?"

"I have done it. She's as bright as a swallow and as free as a lark." The boys noticed Duncan's heat, his passion, and perked up their ears and tensed.

Ernst Wilhelm snorted disdainfully but said nothing more.

Each man held the other's glance, and the boys looked away. "Your papa is a slave buyer, boy." Duncan was gambling for Pet's soul, his inside stuffing. It was perverse, because he knew it would cause the boy some discomfort. But if he left Russell's Knob to take up in another town, he'd live as a white man. He had to know it all. And Wilhelm would not tell him the truth unless he was forced.

"Your ma left these hills as the virgin wife of a pretty man that held himself high and mighty — not your papa," Duncan continued, looking straight into his nephew's eyes. He couldn't remember ever having looked at Pet — Petrus — this way. Wilhelm was right that he ought not to be called Pet always. Ah, it was his name, though. It was adhered to him. It was Cissy's gift, and if they stopped calling it, they'd lose more of Cissy. How often this boy bowed his head in his uncle's presence. Now looking full into his face, Duncan saw that, though he greatly favored his father, he had the Smoots about him, too. *He is Hattie's boy child, and so he belongs to Duncan.*

"A sly boy convinced my papa that he loved Hattie and would take good care of her. Papa was drunk and fooled, and the boy took her down to Perth Amboy and sold her as a slave to your papa there. Is't not true, Ernst? Did you not buy your wife in a slave market?"

Only Duncan breathed. Ernst Wilhelm lost his breath. He could not answer. His chest commenced heaving, and puffs of air came back into his body, then left again in gasps. He kept himself from shouting and lunging at Duncan only because his anger and panic had made him nearly blind. Duncan Smoot, goddamn it, was a shameless provocateur! Wilhelm wanted to kill Duncan then, but he knew that decision would leave Pet without a father.

Duncan continued to provoke. "Isn't it so, Ernst? Tell the boy about the bill of sale that your wife won't let you tear up and throw away."

"I married my Hattie. Your mother is my wife, Petrus," he sputtered to his son. "I've got a marriage license," Wilhelm shouted at Duncan.

"That rounder that first took her off from here had some kind of paper, too," Duncan countered.

Ernst Wilhelm struggled to keep his voice down in volume and so began to growl. "That bastard had his new wife upon an auction stage within a day of his wedding," he answered. "She had on a blue dress and a pained look when I first saw her."

Wilhelm quaked to consider what he risked in telling all of Hat's and his story to their son. The boy's love could be lost, and Hattie might like him less, a privation he didn't think he could bear. But he kept forward, since he had begun. "Ah, he is right. You're fucking women and maybe making babies, so you ought to have the whole truth." The son stared at his father's face. Absolutely silent, absolutely still, Petrus Wilhelm became keener as his father recounted a story he knew nothing about.

"What parts of the story that came before I saw her, I have from her lips. I don't know what her husband told her, but she did not know what was going to happen. She believed they were stopping at a tavern. When the men in the room started to discuss her, she came to realize what place she was in. It was a pitiful shame — her so trusting and innocent and him wanting to book passage on a riverboat. He wanted to get aboard a boat with a stake and be off on his adventure. He touted her.

"I paid some above what I had allotted." Wilhelm lowered his voice further. "Was a market at Perth Amboy at the time. I venture it still is there. They're not legal, but they're known and they're open. I came to purchase a woman to nurse my first wife and fix up the food. My first wife was sick unto death and I knew it. We lived way out and I needed a helper. I decided to buy an African slave woman. I couldn't hire a white woman to travel such a distance for nursing work. I had cash from selling my beer at Perth Amboy. They had illegal slave auctions in all the port towns. So I went in flush with money. I had as well one more barrel put by. A man told me about a place that featured young and pretty girls, and I could not resist. I bid high and quick and shut off any other bidders because I wanted to stop them looking at her. It was mostly because I wanted her for myself," Wilhelm said and clamped his hand over his son's arm. "I was a lusty, young man.

"'Sight unseen. Sight unseen,' I shouted out loud. I stepped forward to stop the auctioneer from tearing her bodice.

"It was her face specially. She was so stunned at the way her husband had treated her. Ah, the gal was still a virgin was how he touted her." Both father and son colored up, and Wilhelm's watery eyes went back to Duncan. He wondered what the People had intended when they sent Hat off with the pretty boy.

"I was sore at her people," Wilhelm continued. "They should have looked at this dandy more close. I brought her back up here as much to show them fools what they'd let to happen as anything. And then the lowlanders wouldn't let us stay. For I took Hattie as my wife after Anna Beth succumbed to her conditions."

Wilhelm knew that what he said next would not be understood quite right by Petrus, but Petrus must hear it. His son ought to understand. He is a man who could make a child now. He is grown. "I thought of Hattie when I first saw her like she was a pretty bitch — a soft, pretty puppy that was going to be harmed with rough handling. I mean to say I didn't think of her so much as I wanted her to touch and look at and nuzzle on. Was the same as if I was to buy a mare or some other beast. That is how a dark woman like your mother was looked at whether she was a slave of yours or not. You didn't have to court her or ask her leave. You just could take as you wanted. That was the attitude. Or you could buy what you wanted if you had the money. I needed to have a nursing gal. I needed a gal to tend to my wife who was nearly dead in the bed. That is why I came there. I was in a place where men were buying young gals that had been snatched. All of them were young gals — some butter colored, some brown, some black, some white-colored. There was plenty of purchasers."

Pet and Jan were stunned, mute. Wilhelm started crying out loud. It was not unheard of. They'd seen him cry before. Tonight, filled with liquor and remorse, he hung his head down between his legs. Pet wanted to reach out to him to keep him from falling over, but his arms felt frozen.

Wilhelm cried and said a string of things in his old language. Finally, Pet reached toward his father. "Papa," he said.

"I had come to watch, too. It was a known entertainment. It

had many aspects." After pausing for some minutes, he continued, "Birds were flying withershins over our heads when we
came up the crest of the hill to my farm. I feared my wife was
dead, but she was not. She was low — filled with carbuncles. I
made Hattie look after Anna Beth and help me put things in
order on my farm. It was not easy, but she went about it. Owning women is a different thing than owning a man. I owned a
slave man once, but I was scared to keep him in hand. I let him
run off. But you can make a woman too scared to misbehave or
run off. I reckon, on looking back, that Hattie was very afraid
of me. She'd have done anything not to be put on a coffle going
south. Hattie helped me bury Anna Beth. We came here married, and you came to us, Pet. I give Hattie a soft life and I figure that's as happy as I can make her. Sometimes she don't like
me all that much. I recognize it isn't her fault. I've been harsh
at times, and she had no choice but take me," Wilhelm said
and squeezed his son's hand.

"You could sell Mama and me?" Pet asked and laughed. It
was the silly, only question that came to him.

"Naw, boy. Don't talk fool talk!" his father barked back.

"You could put a chain on her and me and take us down
south, Papa? You could make money on us?" Pet chuckled
again. "I reckon I better do what you say ... or run off."

"I saved your mama. That's what I did!" Wilhelm shouted,
then groaned.

"It don't matter, does it, Uncle?" Pet asked.

"Naw, Pet. We wouldn't never let 'em take you off."

For some reason, what Duncan said had sounded more cruel
than kind. Inexplicably, Pet wanted to go home and grab up
his mama and kiss her face. He wanted to touch her. He

suddenly remembered a night when he was very small that he'd clung to her like a little possum. She took him up from his bed. He could not now remember why. He was frightened, his arms were wrapped around her neck, she ran around the house holding him against her chest, and her skin was hot and very moist. He'd have thought it was a game except that her thumping heart said she was scared. He felt Papa pry him out of her arms and toss him onto the floor. Mama crouched over him and kissed his ear to soothe him. Papa came at her again and grabbed her, and Pet heard his mother say, "Don't." But he never knew what she was asking Papa not to do.

"Ernst, is it true Petrus has a child down in the town?" Hat asked while working a dough. Ernst Wilhelm sat at the table with his account book and did not lift his eyes.

"Ernst, does my Pet have a child in town?" she repeated.

"Yonder is a girl that loves him."

"Is there a child, Ernst?" Hat raised her voice and stamped her foot. Ernst Wilhelm looked up at her coolly.

"There is a girl who says it is Petrus who fathered the child she is carrying. He doesn't deny it," Wilhelm explained. "The girl wants him down there to stay, but your brother thinks otherwise. He wants to tie the boy up in his enterprises."

"What kind of girl is she?"

"This girl is no slut, Hattie," he said. "She is sweet on Petrus. This Emma reckons your son is white — white enough to live with her in her town."

Only momentous events ever halted Hat in the middle of kneading a bread dough. She stopped her fingers and wiped her hands and stood back from the nascent bread.

"A white man — because some little white whore wants him to be!" Hat squealed with indignation.

"Ah, he's one of your jumble boys because you want him to be!" Wilhelm sneered. Usually he did not bristle if Hat railed against his race. But it pissed him that she had wrinkled her nose and curled her lips in disgust.

PART TWO

SHE DARED NOT SAY she was frightened of the photographer. With Duncan at her side, she knew she was not supposed to fear anything, and Duncan would be peeved if she behaved like a rabbit. Nothing made him more annoyed with Dossie than for her to appear frightened of a white person.

"As we discussed. I want a photograph made of my wife," Duncan said.

He'd pulled himself taller than his usual tall and straighter than his usual straight; had handed her down from the wagon with a formal grace; had guided her, arm entwined, knotted with his; had ushered her into the photographer's office with a dancer's demeanor and now spoke with a careful, authoritative voice. Dossie knew she was simply to do as she was told. She was to be looked at, to be gazed at, to be captured so that she would always be as perfectly pretty as she was on this day. Duncan had said this with his first cup of coffee that morning. He'd chuckled at her embarrassed smile, her lips hidden by her hand, her eyes startled by his words. He'd repeated it on the ride to town in order to make her smile again and not be dumb with shyness, but also so that she'd know what he wanted.

He teased her saying that one day way far off, when she was forced to give up her claim to the crown of beauty, he'd have this to remind him of her glory. And, long after he had passed away, when her grandchildren asked her, she could show them she was not always bent and gray. Her face was taken over so quickly with expressions of dismay, with unconsidered consequences, with bewilderment, that he regretted joshing. Duncan vowed he would not show his treasure to anyone. He said he would not even show the photograph to her for fear she would become too taken with herself. He'd tapped her nose then and said, "Yes, that is a danger!" Yes, the ear jewels were her wedding present, and this portrait of her was his.

The photographer was smelly, and Dossie wanted to squeeze tight on her nose and hide behind Duncan to avoid him. The man touched her elbow lightly, and she was startled. He led her across the room, placed her arm upon a pedestal, and commanded her to stand perfectly still. Dossie glanced at Duncan, and he reassured her with a pleasant yet formal look in his eyes. *Accede. You are safe. I alone am watching you.* Dossie saw that Duncan watched the photographer's movements closely. He said he'd visited the studio and taken a measure of this man who fashioned photographs. He said he did not want a charlatan or bungler to capture his beloved's photograph.

The photographer was careful with his own face. He didn't give away much surprise when he saw Dossie, though clearly Dossie was not what he had expected.

He had never seen a real colored gal before and quite frankly had thought Smoot would bring in an ugly old crone whose sagging, wrinkled, hairy face he'd wanted to enshrine in memory. But Smoot entered the shop with a veritable doll on his arm. Carefully and stylishly dressed from head to toe, she moved across the floor with such grace that it appeared Duncan Smoot piloted her and that her feet did not touch the ground.

When Smoot unhanded her finally — finally relinquishing her to be posed beside the pedestal — the photographer thought she might not be able to stand alone. But she stood erect on feet that, unshod, must look like two small loaves of Christmas cake if they were the same color as her hands and face and neck above the dress collar of shockingly white, stiff lace.

Not until Duncan Smoot reiterated his request for a formal portrait of his wife did the doll raise her head, setting her earrings sparkling and illuminating the room with her arresting, piercing eyes. Her cap of hair aroused the photographer's curiosity. How odd that a Negress wore no head scarf or hat! Her hair was pressed to the sides of her head, pulled away from her face and caught in ropelike strands that did not escape her arrangement at any place along her face or neck. It was, he imagined, held in place with some fragrant gloss and hidden device that was most likely bear grease and bone, though she had absolutely no aroma of bear about her.

When he could break his eyes free of her face, the man observed that she was not so small in stature as he'd first thought. She was small, demure for a pure Negress, and she made him think of all kinds of edible delights. Perhaps his anticipation of the fee and the dinner he intended to buy with it accounted for his thoughts of cakes and compotes. He noticed with disdain that she was finely, carefully groomed. He decided she must be a working gal who'd hoodwinked an old man to make her honest. There was simply no such a thing as a true, honest matron so black as tar. He controlled his gaze and chuckled to himself when he operated his lenses.

He posed her delicately. His fingertips never actually touched her. He hadn't realized that a pure Negress smelled like Christmas cakes, like sacks of spice, or like flowers found in deep

4

DOSSIE REMOVED HER APRON before sitting on the step near Duncan's porch chair. He called her to sit close by him so that her voice could be soft. Likewise the soft fabric of her dress delighted him. Dossie ran through a set of birdcalls as the day faded, and Duncan sharpened his small knives. He seemed to like having her sit in a quiet, beautiful composure, though she was, on this evening, wearied from a long day's work at tasks he had given her. Duncan asked her to read out passages from the Bible, and he queried her about the habits of certain animals, the attributes of specific plants, and the cycles of the moon.

Dossie knew Duncan watched her and her body. It is important to note that he did both. She knew he watched her demeanor especially — the way she conducted herself about her work duties. She knew he had spoken to Noelle about her abilities at reading and writing and to Hat about her sewing and cooking instruction. He seemed to judge her diligence or deficiency at tasks and to be asking more questions and listening more closely than ever. This back and forth gave Duncan chances to look down at her, and Dossie felt the heat in his glances. There was a change, subtle yet verifiable. He no longer behaved like an indulgent father.

She judged him, too. Perhaps Duncan knew it? Dossie watched him. He was a well-formed man in his face. The high regard in which he held himself was etched across his forehead. He never shied from looking at just what he wanted to gaze on. And to follow his gaze in a group of talking folk was to know what was what and what and who was important. His dark, piercing eyes validated, recognized. His body was formed handsomely also. His waist seemed to be the base of him as if it were a pedestal upon which the upper part of his body rested. He was well built — all above his waist was muscled and strong without being coarse and brutish. His legs, though, gave him the height — the vantage over the heads of others. This was what picture Dossie liked: Duncan standing straight up tall and looking over the heads of others.

When she was a child she had considered her own body and wondered — considering herself as against Miz Hat or even Noelle Beaulieu — if she was up to scratch for a woman in Russell's Knob. The women were so beautifully arranged, and Dossie worried that she wouldn't come up to the snuff of that and would end up being just Duncan's servant girl.

His sausage and its biscuits were lovely, too. Dossie had seen them. One afternoon when he went for swimming and soaking in the stream she had followed unobserved. Dossie had been left in the kitchen at her duties when Duncan had sauntered off. A devilish tingle of adventure and shame had coursed through her. She found a place to hide that gave a clear view. She watched. It was a quirk that Duncan Smoot was fond of bathing. He enjoyed it, though it was not a habit of most men to dip themselves fully into a barrel or a stream. "You stink, boy. Take a wash," Dossie had heard Duncan admonish Jan often, for the boy hated to wash himself all over. Jan boasted that it was unmanly to bathe and was chiefly the reason that women were so fragile. Their reliance on bathing themselves undermined their health. Duncan Smoot, neither fragile nor unhealthy, was an anomaly.

That Duncan was unaware of her could only mean that he lost himself to his everyday when he came here. He plunged into the stream and cavorted in the water before returning to the rocks. He rubbed his skin to mash away pimples caused by chill air on his wet nakedness. His jasper did not emerge until he rubbed on it. He walked around with his head down, rubbing absently at himself, then squatted and lit a cigar. When it caught he smoked it languidly. Leaning his back against a rock—sitting on the rock ledge in a place worn soft for naked sitting—he rubbed and stroked himself.

Dossie felt the invisible ants of cold excitement. She put her fingers in her mouth to stop it up—so that she could make no sound. She pulled back farther from view and ducked her head. But she went back to watching him, and soon enough she worked her fingers inside her mouth in concert with the picture before her. She watched Duncan through it all until he climaxed himself, slipped back into the stream, swam about, then pulled himself to the rock ledge to doze with his hand over his groin. When she realized he was very deeply asleep, she slipped away.

The next time she peeped on him her fingers wove under her chemise and she touched her breasts. Duncan Smoot was so beautiful, be it shameful or not to say so, it was so. His body was a nut of loveliness! Though Dossie remained a virgin, after weeks of watching, peeping on, tailing Duncan, and touching herself, she was no longer chaste.

*   *   *

Duncan opened the window on the idea of Dossie being his woman by saying that he guessed her pretty nipples must be like two blueberries upon a bush waiting to be touched.

"What you say? Are they ripe yet?"

Dossie's mouth came open in surprise. She dropped the pan of beans she held and bolted out the door.

When she returned, Duncan was seated at the table with his coffee. He looked up at her as if he were puzzled about where and why she'd gone off. He worked at rolling a cigar. "You get los' on the way to the shit hole?" He laughed as if genuinely tickled by his own jest. "I know you been pinching those blueberries lately. Maybe I'm better at it than you."

Later Duncan stood in the doorway of her bedroom. She saw him and was shocked and turned away. His hammer jutted out before him, and he stood and rubbed on it and looked in at her. Dossie closed her eyes and pretended to be asleep. He did nothing more than stand and watch her.

Later he said that he simply crossed the stream. He saw a flower whose beauty startled him and he crossed to it. Its beauty drew him. In this way Dossie came to think that she was responsible for all that came of the seduction.

Duncan surprised Dossie when he came to her bed in the early morning. His mouth was sour and scratchy and he put it all over her. He said, "My blueberries," when he pulled up her gown and put his lips on her breasts. Dossie giggled. He moved her into his arms and held her like he needed the warmth from her body. But he didn't need it because his skin was hot enough to boil, and his sweat made moisture on her nightdress.

"Do you want me, Dossie?" Duncan asked. She was puzzled —

caught by surprise. She remained quiet. She said nothing to him, nor did she move from the bed.

It seemed like a silly question. Dossie had never shrunk from Duncan. She had only wanted him; had attended upon his wants since she had come to his heaven; had always and only been waiting for his call. So it only mattered now if he wanted her.

And here he came into her bed without any of his clothes on and she didn't scream out or tell him to stop it and he asked her if she wanted him. His swollen hammer was making his head swim, Dossie thought. Duncan was certainly silly-talking this morning! Animals were making their morning noises and she wanted to laugh out loud.

"Yes," Dossie said in a urgent whisper because she got frightened that he would be put off by silence. "What mus' I do, Duncan?"

Duncan took a turn at surprise. He was flummoxed to hear his name called so intimately.

Dossie tried to wiggle away from him because she got to thinking that she was not clean and wanted to get up and wash.

"Come here an' be tol' wha' to do," Duncan said and straightened Dossie's nightgown. He fixed coffee with a shot of whiskey for them both, though she could drink very little of hers, and he finished it as well as his own. He brought her a shawl and her moccasins and walked off. He turned only once to see that she followed.

When the day's sun got higher and was getting ever hotter on the rocks of his bathing place, Duncan patted Dossie's hind parts. "Go to the henhouse and get some eggs and fix me a good breakfast, woman." He stood, stretched his long, naked body, and went into the water.

When his heat was taken away and only the sweat and sauces of their bodies were left, Dossie was cool. She watched Duncan's face to gauge his mood. Yes, he was pleased! She felt a tick of triumph in that. She smiled up at him when he left the water, and he leaned down and planted kisses on her shoulders and her back. She sucked in her breath and shivered under the drops of water. He chucked her under the chin, nudged her with another pat to her butt.

"Gwan," he said.

In late afternoon Duncan walked away from the house at a sauntering pace. He wore soft shoes and took no shotgun or fishing pole. He held his arms behind his back and let them dangle unoccupied. He looked like an odd bird, one who is uncomfortable walking along the ground.

He felt peculiar in himself as he left the house. He'd fucked Dossie because he couldn't resist it no more. But he hadn't thought it through. Ha! Think about it? His jasper had done all of the ruminating. What was he going to make of it? Had he trespassed? He had asked her. Ha! She wanted him, she had said, and seemed to. He knew damned well he had a sway with her. He'd counted on that. Little Bird was so obedient to him now that he was afraid of himself. What was a man s'posed to do when a lucky coin cross his path? He will close his hand around it. He will praise his good fortune.

But still in all, this ain' the same as triflin' with a grown woman, Duncan argued with himself. He was looking at a responsibility with Dossie. If it were Jan or Pet who had done this — started fucking Dossie — Duncan would have chastised her and beaten the boy and made them marry and built them a house. Now what would he do?

He wanted to run off. Perhaps he would drop a line and fish

and think. But he'd left the house with empty hands. He wanted to sweat some and ponder it. Dossie bird! Dossie flower! Dossie girl that is as sweet as a berry! Oh, touching her had pleased him so deeply that he, a practiced fucker, had been quaked. He could still feel his own excitement. He went off to a sweat lodge kept by some old men and sweated, then ended by drinking with them and bragging on his conquest.

When Duncan came back he stood at the stone wall. He held three rabbits and looked at his house from a distance. Dossie watched him from her always place on the porch. Duncan had come to notice that she stood in the same spot whenever she waited. She positioned herself where she could grab the porch post and wave and hold as if a storm might come to sweep her off. Duncan smiled to think there was so much naïve joy in her. He raised his arm, showed her the string of rabbits, and she made gleeful noises.

After supper Dossie smiled expectantly and asked, "What mus' I do?"

"Gwan to sleep," Duncan replied out of confusion. She stood still, hesitating. The sweating had made Duncan's skin soft, and all of his hairs were slicked from the oils the old men slathered on him. Dossie was curious about the feel of the hair pressed to his head and face. She wanted to put her hands on him. She wanted to continue what had begun, and her face fell at his words.

Yes, it was trespass, Duncan thought. But he hadn't been able to govern himself. "Quiet, old man," he whispered. He wanted to go for another sweat. Noelle kept a sweat lodge, but he didn't want to be in a tangle with her just now. Duncan did not sleep much.

Dossie woke and listened for Duncan. He was not about the immediate area. There was no smell of coffee or tobacco. She lay still. The bird chatter became very loud. Dossie got up from her bed and built up the fire, made up the day's coffee, and visited the chickens. She was surprised to feel that she was glad he was not about. She enjoyed the absolute privacy to think about him — to thoroughly enjoy revisiting the events.

Some days later Dossie chose a call — a name for her mouth for him. She began to call him Uncle like Jan and Pet did, but with a certain turn that changed the word. It came upon a happy expulsion of her breath when he put his hand between her legs. "Uncle," she whispered in surprise at first, then with satisfaction. "Uncle," she said, meaning man to whom all things belong. She caught at his hand and slowed it and looked up into his face. She whispered, "Uncle."

Was it the women's or the men's blather that would be worse? Duncan did not want Dossie to be discussed. He couldn't decide if he wanted to keep secret about his loving her up or not. The boys knew, that was certain. If they hadn't smelled it on him they could tell by the look on Dossie's face. Duncan wanted to brag to them, to show off. He wanted to tell them in detail just how sweet it was to fuck her. But if one of them started to talk about her like they usually talked about their girls, then Duncan might not be able to say what he'd do next.

"I'm stuck on her, Pippy," Duncan declared when he confessed it to Hat. "I don't want no other gal than her."

"Ha," she replied and stood with her arms folded across her breasts, looking into her brother's face. Yes, the People believe a loud, frank confession of sin mitigates it. Proclaim yourself, own up to your weakness, and who but a churl will not forgive you? Who but God has not already been there?

"Punkin, what possessed you?" Hat exclaimed and stuck her fists into her sides.

When Hat broke the news to Noelle she served her sweet cakes and coffee and honey. For Noelle, Duncan was a love habit of long standing. Ever since he'd convinced her not to leave for the West with her family, she had been his tuck-up woman. But a woman who does not seal the bargain with marriage or children or land can't expect permanence.

"Well, she's a fine woman then. She's clipped the old turkey's feathers," was all that Noelle said. Clearly, Noelle had missed the point all these years, Hat thought. Punkin was a man and not a turkey or a rooster or a wolf, and Noelle, for all her spells and conjures, hadn't handled him deftly.

"She adores him," Hat said solemnly, "I've told him that to caution him." She remembered that she, too, was stuck on Duncan and had always simply adored him. All of them, her and Cissy and Noelle, had been enthralled.

When Cissy had fussed and fumed and had said that Hattie could not be Punkin's wife no matter how much she wanted to be, Hattie had been prepared to ride off and search out another big, wonderful man like Punkin. A little girl who wanted to mount a horse and ride off into the wooded terrain to find a man like her brother to marry! Hat had been a silly little chap when it came to her brother. She was a fine one to call Noelle willful. But Noelle had always balked at being obedient to Duncan, and Hattie never had.

Hat also knew that Duncan had filled Dossie's head with tales of wood witches, enchanted purposes, and destiny. It was no wonder that she desired him and was exhilarated that he desired her.

*   *   *

Dossie, the new woman—the man's delight—agreed very quickly when he asked her about driving her own jenny and wagon and traveling with Hat and the other women to market at Paterson. Ah, she tried to disguise her self-satisfaction, but she'd been planning with Hat all along. Her nascent maturity, he thought, was nearly as appealing as her naïveté.

Hat presented a strategy. Dossie could have an occupation as an egg seller at market in Paterson and in Russell's Knob and show the women that she had a slot with them. She could show, with a quiet industry, that she was more than Duncan Smoot's concubine.

"Give her a calling. She can come in with me. Get her some good laying hens so we can take more eggs to market," Hat said brightly. "I need the help."

"Tell Wilhelm to hire you a servant girl then," Duncan answered with annoyance. "Dossie ain't got to work."

"Folks will say she's working on your pleasure then. I don't need the help, Brother. But a woman doesn't want to think of herself as just a man's comfort, Duncan, even if she does love him. You scared for Dossie to go down to the town? You scared somebody can grab her up," Hat questioned him pointedly. Ale made her impudent, and when she reached to refill her cup, Duncan took her hand from the pitcher.

"No, girl. Hush," he said.

"Make it permanent if you do love her," she said with a look of challenge.

"Gwan home and do your drinking in your own kitchen, Pippy," Duncan answered.

"You're the one who has fixed her situation, Duncan. What are you gonna do?"

Hat left Duncan's kitchen feeling satisfied. She knew her idea had flown. With Duncan socially set, the Smoots and Wilhelms would build up. She was not sure why that mattered, but she was convinced that it did. She chuckled to think that it was Cissy pushing her and making her take control of them. *Take them in hand, Hattie, Cissy demanded in Hat's head. Her voice was as clear as the midnight sky at harvesttime. Settle them down. Make them behave. Make them be good, Hattie.*

Hat loved Noelle like a sister, but Dossie made a perfect wife for Duncan.

Duncan said Dossie must be able to handle the jenny and the wagon and the crates in order to take eggs to market. She dropped her eyes and said she would take his lessons and do everything just as he directed. Then, with her head still bowed, she asked for a few more chickens and a younger rooster. Duncan laughed and acquiesced. At first he considered buying the chickens from a wag who would thief them from a supply boat heading away from the falls. But he decided instead to treat Dossie to a trip to the town to buy her own birds.

She wore her nicest dress, her shawl, and her bonnet. Hat dressed her hair and wound it up prettily. "Ask him to buy cloth, and we can sew up some more dresses," Hat whispered. She wiped biscuit crumbs from Dossie's face with a corner of her apron and inspected her mouth for chapping.

Dossie's pleasure on the road down to Paterson was sublime. The seat beneath her hummed, and she linked her arm in

Duncan's as the jenny ambled. Close touching — nearness to him — was invigorating to them both. Duncan's muscles quickened on some turns and twists, and she loosed her grasp to free his movement. He pulled her back to his side into a pocket close to his body. It was a measure of Dossie's new confidence with Duncan that she chattered on the trip about her plans for the eggs. The idea had been attested to by Hat, but it was Dossie's suggestion that they trade eggs for deluxe honey from the Van Waganens and sell the honey in Paterson. It was well known that the Van Waganens never went into town, and so they did not sell their very highly considered honey at market. And it was often said by the other trading women that honey was much wanted in Paterson and could bring a bright price. And, Dossie assured Duncan, she was quite strong enough to handle the crates, the crocks, the ropes and straps, the jenny, and the wagon.

Duncan's only tick of displeasure in listening to Dossie spinning the plans was that she may become too opinionated like Noelle and like Hattie. Though it pleased him that Dossie was smart, he hoped she'd stay sweet, stay naïve.

The main thing to see at Paterson was the cataract, the place where the water fell down from a great height and rushed and whorled and ran away headlong downstream. When Dossie heard the tremendous roaring she wondered why they could not hear this great noise from their porch post. It was a strange and beguiling sound of rush and thunder. Though the cataract was the source of the tumultuous sound, its noise was embellished by the din of the great turbines. Tolling clocks and factory whistles and train whistles and boat-signal cries and the cacophony of yammering people speaking different tongues added more.

The cataract was the draw to the town, though. Noelle had taught them that it was the reason the lowlander whites had come so far a mountain and settled at this spot. They wanted the rushing water. Nay, any and all of everybody wanted that rushing water for something. That is how it had always been. All around this place folk had built millraces and coaxed water into sluices and rushes for it to do their work. Folk had always set their weir and snagged a copious dinner where the water flux sent turtles and fish headlong to their destiny in the People's stomachs.

There was much startling beauty to be seen. The city built by the whites was a marvel of sound and movement. The place was a hive! There were throngs of folk. Everything in the place whirred and turned and belched forth. It was such as Philadelphia had been to Dossie's recollection. Sitting up in the wagon beside Duncan, Dossie recalled her panic at being pulled through the streets of Philadelphia by Mr. Abingdon's lookout boy. My, but there were a lot of bedraggled boys hereabouts, too, running back and forth and toting great loads! Crowds of folk hailing and calling to each other queued up near the large machine houses. Duncan told her they were going inside to labor. Europes! There was abundant work in Paterson for a strong back and a white skin no matter what language was spoken. But the work inside was for the Europes only. "An able colored man can starve in this town that is full of work 'cause they won't take him on," Duncan said bitterly.

Though fearful, as always, of a rise in Duncan's anger, Dossie felt an exhilaration, too, at being his companion, his tuck-up and his fancy, his confidante. Duncan wouldn't say these things to just any silly girl. She knew if she was quiet and listened she'd learn more about him and the town than even the boys knew. Duncan was a big man in Russell's Knob. He was not boastful at home, though one might gloat that he was a powerful man. In Paterson, he was more quietly and fiercely dignified. Yes, fierce, like a wolf is fierce and fearless.

Duncan acknowledged folk, hailing some and nodding to others, along the road and in the environs of town. Dossie worried about her dress. She wanted to preen so that he would be as proud of her as she was of him, but she was concerned not to fidget about on the wagon seat.

They went first to a hen man who sold prime birds. The purveyor had a dazzling array of stacked cages of different-colored hens. Duncan showed Dossie some likely candidates and, though her head swirled in the stinking air of the enclosure, she selected five gray-and-red hens. They were beautiful! They were fancy! The man touted them as excellent layers. Dossie left it to Duncan to select the rooster, and he chose two. "'Tis your choice, ma'am," Duncan said and smiled at her. Dossie pointed to one, and the purveyor put the very fancy, very spirited rooster in a separate crate than the hens.

By some measures, it was immodest for a decent young girl to laugh openly in public with great pleasure, pulling her lips back and showing her dark gums, revealing rows of smooth, butter-white teeth. Oh, but Dossie was overwhelmed with childlike delight at the birds. She pulled her lips back and showed the widening gap between her two most front teeth and the tiny meat that hung there in an open display of joy that made small depressions in her cheeks and wrinkled the skin across her nose.

"What you need now, Dossie Blossom, is some dressmaking cloth," Duncan said cheerfully when they'd handled their birds into the wagon. "Pippy said we must not forget." Oh, he was using sweet names, a sign that he was pleased and free of care. Dossie was delighted to have earned a new sweet name. Dossie Blossom! It made her want to giggle and touch his face. But she rewarded Duncan with a happy, demure smile instead as he drew up in front of a store on a street that seemed to have colored folk milling about. Duncan tied up the wagon, held out his hand, and steadied Dossie down from the wagon seat.

They entered a store for ladies' goods. The pretty girls who showed the cloth tittered and smiled sneakily at Duncan and perused Dossie from head to toe. Dossie remembered to be very proud and slightly haughty like Hat was when she came into town. Hat was, like her brother, able to assume a stately demeanor that caught admiring glances. Dossie remembered also that Hat said, "With a shape like yours, if they're lookin', they're admirin'. Stand up straight." Dossie did that and chose several bolts of dressmaking cloth under the envious cat eyes of the shopgirls.

Dossie knew that some precincts in Paterson were avoided by folk from Russell's Knob. Duncan cut a wide berth around such places that a colored person dared not to be. The price for being unguarded was far too high outside of Russell's Knob. And by now Dossie knew what the folk in town — the white people — said about folk who lived in Russell's Knob. Duncan, Dossie, Jan, Hat, and Noelle were the Indians or mountain niggers, and Ernst Wilhelm and Pet and some others were called white niggers. At the market some women slyly called the women from Russell's Knob mountain monkeys or mountain whores because the People were known to mix colors freely, a practice despised in the other towns. Russell's Knob folk were also known for being proud and for having commerce and for being around these parts since the beginning.

Duncan drove them uphill, then down a street, around a few bends, and came upon a house near the waterside. He tossed a coin to a scampering, aggressive boy who greeted them as they tied up their wagon.

"Look after my wagon, boy," Duncan called, paused, then chuckled as he ushered Dossie into the tavern. "Was a time I'd leave Jan and Pet to stand guard. They could've been stolen off. They was little then." Duncan broke from his recollection and said, "You stay nex' to me, you hear?"

"Yes," Dossie answered as she stepped on the threshold of the place. Duncan did not hear. His attention was taken up immediately with greeting some of the people already seated at their food. The room was well lit, the air was abundantly aromatic, their stomachs rumbled in anticipation.

A bosomy woman hurried toward them as they entered.

"Mr. Smoot. Mr. Smoot. Will you have a bowl of vittles and some ale, Mr. Smoot?" she asked.

"Yes, ma'am, Miz Minnie. We will both have your stew and some ale and a whiskey for me," Duncan said in an expansive, self-satisfied way that caused Minnie Stewart to giggle like a small child.

"Mr. Duncan Smoot, how you do?" she cried through her laughter. Minnie Stewart sidled up to Duncan on one of her passes to deliver bread throughout the room. "If I'd known you was wantin' a constant gal I would have spoke to you about my Pearl."

"Miz Minnie, this here is Dossie," Duncan said cavalierly, hoping to disguise his slight ill-ease at not having a surname to add. He cleared his throat and pronounced with formality. "This here is my wife, Miz Dossie Smoot." Minnie Stewart smiled with genuine delight, and Dossie's face came alight like she had swallowed a candle. For the second time that day Duncan had brought forth a face of complete happiness. To the credit of Dossie's courage and self-control, she did not run out to the sanitary and toss up, nor did she smile too broadly for modesty. She sat still and felt very warm. Folk at other tables about the room nodded their heads politely and smiled. Dossie succumbed to the itch to smooth her dress and pat at the hair near her nape. Then she remembered she must answer the woman's introduction. She didn't want Duncan to be sorry he'd given her the honor of his name.

"How do, ma'am," Dossie said.

"Miz Smoot, ma'am, I am fine and happy to know you. You take a res' and eat a bowl of my stew," she said. It seemed that all the folk in the room smiled. Dossie smiled and thought that Miz Minnie was funny looking but very, very nice. Her breasts were like a cupboard shelf. They protruded so far before her that she could have used them to rest a pan of biscuits. Perhaps it was the influence of the ale or the profound happiness in her vitals, but everything said or heard or seen in this tavern was like a dream. Duncan stared at Dossie across the table, though he was well aware that it made her fidget.

The night was bright and starry when they left the tavern. Both of them were cozy with ale. Duncan was additionally mellowed with whiskey. Dossie wanted to lean her head on his shoulder but didn't want to embarrass him while still in town. When they were out of the town proper, out past the cataract and out past the play gardens for white people, and were climbing the long, dark road to their homestead, she did rest her head on Duncan's shoulder. He didn't mind. He was pleased with her and she knew it.

Suddenly he pushed her with his elbow and said, "Dossie,

make a nightjar call." She called and chirped at his command but thought that his voice saying her name was the prettiest sound she'd ever heard. She wanted to disobey him so that she could hear him say her name that way again and again.

"Dossie," he said, "do it again. Make the nightjar call." The new hens in the back of the wagon made coo-coo sounds. The sound of Duncan's voice was changed.

Dossie attempted the call, then felt Duncan's body tense up. He made the donkey move faster. They jostled in their seat, and she gripped her side of the wagon. Two riders came up on one side and the other. One of the men pointed a rifle next to Duncan's ear and yelled, "Pull up, nigger!" Duncan pulled up and squeezed hard on Dossie's knee to tell her to hold still and be brave.

"Where you steal them chickens from?" one of the men yelled.

The other man spoke and kept his gun right next to Duncan's ear.

"Where you steal that gal from? She a runaway? We was watchin' you down in the town. You was takin' her aroun' like a lady."

They knew she was a runaway! They knew she was hiding out? Instantly Dossie felt herself filling up with dread that they would tear her away from Duncan. Dossie looked around at the man next to her. Was his voice familiar? She jumped when she saw his red face.

"Yeah, you know me. You recollec' me, don't ya?" he said. Dossie did. It was the boy, Owen Needham.

"I know you, too, gal. You the one that left off from the Logans. I was s'prised to see you in these parts. I woulda thought somebody had caught you an' sol' you south. Those people that you was 'scape from, they lookin' hard for you. Yeah. They lookin' for ya. They post an advert and a reward and I'ma get it. They sayin' you burnt their barn 'fore you run off. I b'lieve the law is lookin' for you."

Dossie quaked. She didn't remember setting any fire. She remembered the smell of burning and the sight of Owen Needham packing up. She thought he was the one had burnt the place. They were looking for her? Her clothes began to feel clammy against her.

Any Negro could be accused of burning. And any opportunistic rowdy who could scare somebody who'd been running and hiding could make a bit of money capturing them or threatening to. A certain type of people didn't care whether the right one was caught up — one less was one less, and all to the good.

Duncan sat still like he was waiting for a signal. He seemed to be smelling the man who was menacing him because he made a shushing noise in his nose. He didn't shake with trepidation. He drew up tight and seemed to twist down in his gut like a rope setting itself in a coil. His coil seemed to get tighter with each thing Owen Needham said.

The man holding the gun began to tire. It often happened just so when a contest reached an impasse. The man had pulled the gun too soon. He ought to have used it, and now he wanted to rest his arm. The arm shook visibly. Perhaps if he faltered he would make a mistake and shoot Duncan, Dossie thought. Perhaps he would falter and shoot himself, Duncan thought. Dossie remembered then what Noelle said about the people of Russell's Knob. They would always come and help one of their number. Dossie figured they were close to home — close enough maybe for the crow call to be heard. "You give out the crow's call and they will come on the run," Noelle had said. She'd led a practice with Dossie and the boys, and Dossie had, of course, been the best at the call. She looked from the corner of her eyes, and Duncan seemed like he was saying, *Gwan and sing out.* So she did it! Before the men had a chance to tie her hands, Dossie stood and called out a crow call very loud. She cupped her hands to send the sound far and to make it perfect. She repeated it quickly again and again so the People would know it was not the true crow.

The men jumped in fear. Dossie's call was loud and thrilling. They might have shot her, but they were not confirmed outlaws, and they lacked the killing instinct. Duncan drew his arm back and cracked his elbow on the nose of the man holding the gun on him. That man's blood shot forth, and his gun arm dropped. Owen Needham raised up his arm to strike Dossie with his fist, but he dropped his hands when he saw Pet's mastiffs come running out of the brush. Those two sloppy pusses that drooled spittle and nuzzled the hands of their friends burst forth from the wooded surround like hellhounds. The barking and growling spooked the horse that Needham's confederate was mounted to, and his gun went off in the air. Two more rifle reports sounded, and Jan and Pet came out of the dark followed by Mr. Gin Barlow. Barlow had on his "hiding-out" clothes and could hardly be distinguished from the deep surround. Two other men came out of the dark with rifles. One of these was Ernst Wilhelm with soot smeared on his face.

Duncan grabbed the weapon that had fired, but the man stayed on his horse. He rode off holding frantically to the fleeing animal with blood from his nose flying behind. Pet's dogs chased him and ran him and his horse off a high drop.

The hollering and shooting upset Dossie's fowl, and she got down from the wagon to settle them. The fowl quieted quickly. They had all been brave, Dossie thought, though all she craved now was to grab on to Duncan and bury her face.

Pet's dogs trained on Owen Needham when they were done chasing the other man. They sat up next to him and had the smug look of good hunting dogs that will not bruise or harry their game.

Jan and Pet tied up Owen Needham, who was too scared to talk now. Dossie felt a pull of sympathy. She knew he'd had a hard time of it with the Logans, too. And she felt scared about Jan and Pet doing something to Owen Needham — whatever Duncan might tell them to do.

The men began to whisper, throwing around what they thought ought to be done.

"Take him in han'," Duncan said finally to his nephews. "Make sure he don't come here lookin' for nobody again." He clapped both boys on the back and shook their hands. Ernst Wilhelm scowled, and his sweat created sooty streaks on his face. He didn't like that the boys went off to do what Duncan wanted.

"Duncan, how you let these stumbles follow you from town?" Ernst Wilhelm demanded.

Duncan was himself unclear how these obvious amateurs had got the drop on him. He hadn't been careful. He'd been distracted with so much satisfaction. The presence of Dossie. Her small butt, a lovely lump of coal giving off heat on the wagon seat next to him, was a cause for distraction. He had moved closer to her and ignored the tingles of danger.

"My wife entranced me, Wilhelm," Duncan said softly. His words were caught by the boys as they made to ride off with

Owen Needham. Jan lifted his head suddenly, dropped his jaw, and looked at Dossie. Pet looked at Jan and prepared to make a noise to cover any words his cousin might utter.

"Come get in the wagon, Dossie," Duncan said. "We got to take 'em hens home."

He turned his back on the boys and left the finish to them.

Dossie knew Duncan was slightly shaken. He was uneasy, though he knew the boys could settle his scores with Owen Needham.

As soon as they reached home, Dossie changed out of her town dress, installed the new birds in the chicken house, and petted the old ones despite the late hour.

"Dossie, you a bold gal," Duncan said when he came to see how things were with the birds. "Maybe you're scared, but you don't falter. You call us out of danger. I'll never forget that. You're like my far-grandmama, girl." Duncan continued to praise Dossie's bravery, likening her to his heroic ancestor. "Lucy Smoot walked away from a Dutchman that aimed his gun at her. She walked off with her eight children and brought 'em here. You know who Russell Sitton is?"

"Yes," Dossie answered. She had learned—as all of the Knob's young'uns did—the stories about Russell Sitton and the founders. Yes, she knew Lucy Smoot's story. She knew that Lucy Smoot was Duncan's and Hat's forebear. To be compared to Lucy Smoot was a badge of honor.

"Russell Sitton took them wayfarers in and fed 'em and pro-tected 'em. When the Dutchman came to claim 'em and take 'em back, Russell Sitton and his band gave a show. They vowed they would not let no runaway be grabbed up and taken away from this place. A big part of it was that Russell Sitton admired Lucy and was insulted by the Dutchman. How dare an outsider come here and say who was who and who belonged where?" Duncan said with true vehemence, as if he was confronting the Dutchman himself, and spat on the ground.

"I'm proud to say I ain' gon' let no man take you off." Duncan pulled her into his arms and bussed her, his mustache and the chicken feathers tickling her face. She felt the wind squeeze out of her but felt the magic. She was well protected by him. Duncan was the brave one.

The boys were brave, too, and bloodthirsty. In the morning, Jan gleefully recounted the rest of the night's doings. He and Pet pulled Needham's clothes off and chased him through a maze of holly bushes. They used the dogs and leather crops to run him around on the rocky ground all of the rest of the night. Needham cut and slashed himself in the bushes. When the sun came up, they let him run off home naked and cut. Jan assured Dossie—as he stroked one of the new hens with his middle finger—Owen Needham won't come back to Russell's Knob. She supposed she ought to be pleased.

5

THE THING BETWEEN THEM was new and unruly. For Dossie, managing the new relations between Duncan and her was the same as taking the reins of a new donkey. She hadn't learned the ticks and clicks of the animal.

"You got to go, Duncan?" Dossie asked. Duncan was a little startled. He'd never heard her use this seductive tone, and she was pleased at his surprise.

"Yes, Dossie. I am goin'," he answered.

Then Dossie asked Duncan point-blank if he had another woman. "Another woman what, Little Bird?" He stopped cinching his horse and looked at her.

"Who you been listenin' to? I'm makin' a run. Then I'm going down to Paterson to see a woman. She's a businesswoman, Dossie. She runs a business of women that sell themselves— prostitutes. Prostitute is what happens to a gal who is too willful." Duncan pinned Dossie with his lecturing scowl. "I sell her liquor and cigars and oysters that I get from the boats and barges. I don't screw no other gal since I been screwin' you if that's what you askin'. And don't you fuss at me now 'cause you ain't my real wife in front of the law." He looked at her with a hot, angry glance that melted to desire like butter atop a biscuit and caused him to want to stop talking and make love to her.

"How come I'm not your real wife, Duncan?" Dossie asked him.

There was only one thing he did not like about Dossie. She could stop him with a look, a wholly trusting, wide-eyed, straightforward gaze that made it difficult to deceive her or even to give her less than all of the truth.

When Duncan came back home in the morning, Dossie gave him his coffee and a happy smile. He touched her hand when she set down his cup and said, "Good mornin', Little Bird."

"Mornin', Duncan," she replied. She noticed that he twitched a little in his shoulders. Well, Dossie had changed his call for good. As Jan said, it was lewd for her to call him Uncle. Dossie had made the house smell good and she knew that pleased him. The air was freshly stirred. There were aromas of all of the things Duncan liked most — coffee, frying pork, biscuits, and Dossie.

"You got a way with those chickens, girl," Duncan said in a loud, cheerful voice when she set a plate before him. "These're the prettiest eggs I have ever seen." He pulled her dress when she turned away, and she lost balance into his lap.

Later when he finished eating Duncan came toward her and put her face between both of his hands. He looked and looked at her as if putting together a puzzle. She kissed the palm of one of his hands and then kissed the other. She kissed him on his neck and his shoulders — standing up on her toes to reach him.

"All right then," Duncan said the following morning. She was working with her birds and was consciously putting on a show of great industry because there was a charged air between them. Duncan said the same thing a couple of times more and drove his feet into the hard-packed dirt. "I figure I will put up a better chicken house. I'll get a dog to keep the foxes out and give you company. Then I guess you ought to marry me on purpose, Little Bird—legal. What you think?"

Dossie thought she'd never seen Duncan Smoot act so flitty-fly—being silly like a boy.

"Dossie, you gonna marry me?" he asked.

What will Hat say? How will it be for Noelle? What will Jan and Pet think? It will not matter! Duncan is chief among them.

"Yes." First and foremost she was pulled to say yes, because she'd never said no to Duncan Smoot. Since Dossie had put her hand in his when they walked away from the Logans, she hadn't ever said no. A tickling came up from her vitals. She said, "Yes."

And then she thought some about the chickens. Duncan is gonna make a pretty new chicken house, and we will grow our own baby chicks and have a dog! "Yes," Dossie said.

"No one will stay home when the Smoots give a fest!" Hat cried out at the news. Determined to make a moment of Duncan and Dossie getting married, she took up planning the wedding party the very moment she heard it from her brother's lips. Her absolute delight was unmitigated by any consideration of the magnitude of the tasks involved with executing a wedding dinner party. She insisted that the entire town would come.

"No," Duncan protested weakly. "Your party is a lot of fluff and fun, Hattie, but..." He broke off when he saw Hat's face fall. When had he seen her look so joyful? Perhaps he could endure her excitement. Duncan laughed and gave Hat the cudgel.

Hat engaged Miz Mary Figgs Van Waganen, a noted seam-stress in Russell's Knob, to sew a bride's dress, various other essential clothing for a bride, as well as undergarments and a negligee. Miz Mary Figgs Van Waganen's fee for the trousseau was a case of good Scots whiskey. Miz Mary Figgs Van Waganen raised her glass for more of Hat's berry liqueur when she made a contract that Duncan would conduct her into the town of Paterson to purchase the cloth goods.

The hustle and bustle of wedding preparation made Dossie melancholy despite Hat's infectious good humor. Her escape had come when the Kenworthys and all of their people were making preparation for Helene Kenworthy's wedding. Dossie and the young mistress's dower furniture had left Kenworthy's island aboard Bil's punt in the midst of the excitement.

"He did not pluck you from the sky or from the river, did he?" Hat asked in a sweet, solicitous voice when they sat and sewed. She had a feeling about Dossie's sad face — that she might be sick for her home.

"I come off an island. We rowed from before sunrise, set sail, and reached the port of Havre de Grace before sunset," Dossie answered. "Mr. . . . Duncan knows the place Bil first brought me to. He showed me where on the map is the port of Havre de Grace. He knew I was put aboard the boat in Havre de Grace. He showed me where the island of the Kenworthy people must be, though there was no spot on the map for it. I started out there, Miz . . . Hat."

Dossie was a changed gal from that day. She remembered the storm of activity to complete Miss Helene's wedding clothes. Master Kenworthy had given his wife the choice of the two slaves who would be sold to raise the extra funds, and Mistress had decided to get rid of old bent-back Ca'line and Sister, the incessant young chatterer who attended Mistress Helene. Sister was expendable since Helene's husband wanted no slaves, just a hired woman, to attend his wife. Sister figured to bring a bright price for she was a skilled lady's maid. On the first news of her impending sale, Sister fell silent and her face collapsed in horror. She appealed to her young mistress, but Helene refused even to look when Sister was attached on Mr. Woolfolk's coffle.

Jan wanted to resist the wedding party altogether. But whatever they said and whatever they did, the Smoots were his people, and he had to be with them on Uncle's day. Dossie's day, too. Yes indeed, it was going to be Dossie's big day. And if he truly loved her, he'd want her to have a special, happy day, wouldn't he? What he really wanted was to talk Dossie out of marrying Uncle. He wanted to trap her in her hen yard when Uncle was not there to see, to grab her, to shake her shoulders. He wanted to tell her he dreamed about her and dreamed that she would slip out from under Uncle's grip.

The truly shameful feeling he harbored was that he loved Uncle, too, and missed him because of her. He and Pet had lost out to her. Uncle didn't belong to them so much anymore. Pet didn't care because he had his papa. Ah, it hurt that Uncle had shoved them off so easily, so thoughtlessly! What had Jan done to be pushed off so? How had he lost his place with Uncle?

And now it was awkward as well. Where was he to stay? With Noelle, of course. But she was in a boil about Uncle's new arrangement. Her feelings were raw.

Two days earlier, Jan had driven a wagon into the clearing laughing and calling out with high hilarity, "Auntie, Auntie, Auntie!" His boisterousness startled Dossie. Jan had begun calling her Auntie in a loud, teasing voice, and it annoyed her and Duncan. Alarmed, Dossie had run out to the clearing, and

Jan hollered again, "Auntie, Auntie, Auntie, come and look at your butter and cream!"

He showed her three tightly packed crates covered with straw and one large crock of cream. He was very animated. He danced about. Dossie gave herself to duties in the chicken house to escape him. She was frightened of Jan in this condition.

When Duncan came, Jan was snoring, sitting on the side of the porch with his pants undone where he'd gone to pee. Dossie tried very hard to pretend that she hadn't been hiding from him. Duncan did not upbraid him until the spirits had worn off in the morning. At sunrise Duncan slapped Jan to rouse him to his senses so that Jan's face was slightly bruised when he stood before his uncle. Duncan fumed and demanded that he drink coffee in large amounts.

It was never a contest of strength or skill at fighting or self-defense. Uncle beat him, and he accepted the punishment as he had always done. He was, as Uncle said, a drunken fool. He was not fit to live amongst decent people. Duncan's last, most cruel remark was that, though he had tried to pound away all parts of Charlie Tougle from him, Jan would never be anything more than wild and dangerous like his father.

It was planned that Duncan and Dossie would go before a justice of the peace and formalize legally in Paterson, as Wilhelm and Hattie had done. Ernst Wilhelm thought it mattered to be on the books amongst the whites and, for once, Duncan agreed when Ernst Wilhelm said colored people needed as much good legal paper on them as they could get. Only to himself did Duncan acknowledge that he was nervous of Dossie's free status. He wanted to be sure couldn't nobody drag her off.

At least twenty chickens were to be killed for the sake of the wedding feast. Swine were to be slaughtered, and rabbits, squirrels, and possums would give their lives to celebrate the day. Hat arranged a veritable army of hands to handle the food preparation, and the Smoot and Wilhelm homesteads were a hive of enterprise. Children sat chomping cakes on the steps of the Smoot house when Noelle strode up one week ahead of the day. She dropped off two large sacks of nuts and set some young children to cracking them out of their shells. She went to the kitchen to pay respects to the hostesses but announced she was looking for Duncan.

"I come empty-handed except for some nuts, girl. I mus' talk to your husban'," Noelle said to Dossie with a tone that was just short of being brusque. Though Dossie was immediately and unquestioningly deferential, she could feel Noelle's extreme pique, and it worried her. She knew she had the authority to question any woman wanting to speak to the man who was to be her husband, but she knew also that she could not upbraid Noelle, her own teacher in many things.

"What you want him for? What's the matter, Noelle?" Hat asked, affronted at Noelle's manner and already wearing a dusting of flour on her bodice. She didn't want to relinquish the day's fine humors on a fracas.

Dossie had been gauging Duncan's mood all morning from her own subtle, intimate indicators. He was excited and a bit nervous, and he had been fuming about Jan.

Wanting to get to the meat of the thing in the air, Hat demanded to know what was going on. Again she asked, "What you want him for, Noelle?"

"Him pounding on Jan," she answered simply, then turned to face Dossie. "You tell him that Jan was saucy and forward and takin' liberties with you?"

"No, ma'am," Dossie replied quickly, anxiously, but wondered if she ought not to have said she did. She wanted to be loyal above all to Duncan. Was it right to dispute him? But she did not want to lie. What did Noelle intend to do?

Hat got absolutely quiet at Noelle's words. Her first impulse was, as always, to defend her brother. She had a great fear of having to take a side between Duncan and Jan or between Duncan and Noelle, and she knew very well that her cowardice meant that Jan and Pet had suffered. Even when he was wrong, especially when he was wrong, Hat was Duncan's ally. She wanted to pummel Noelle and make her shut her mouth.

Jan had gone to Noelle, built a fire, hung the aromatics, rubbed himself with grease, and sweated in her lodge. She joined him after some hours of smoking and praying on his behalf. The sweat was cathartic. The hemp pipe she gave him made him light-headed. Noelle built upon the heat and prepared a switch of stinging branches. She slapped Jan's back with the switches to bring his blood rushing. She stung his chest, arms, and buttocks lightly.

"You are not at all like Charlie Tougle. If it matters to you. I knew the man and you are not like him. You are like your mother. We loved Cissy most of all. She was the head of our band. We were a band: Cissy and Duncan and Hat and me. Then Charlie Tougle came and took her away from us. The one good thing he did was make you. But you do not replace her." She paused and lowered her voice still further. "And you are not like Duncan either. You have not gone to the mines," Noelle said, tracing the outer rim of Jan's ear with her finger. "Forgive me, child, I ought to have stopped him. I didn't know, child. I didn't know what makes a man. Here is the child of the ancients!" Noelle cried out loudly — throwing her voice about the room. "Here is the child of the ancients!" she cried again as if challenging her gods to recognize him. She gave Jan a drink from a gourd, covered him, and let him sleep.

When Jan woke, Noelle made up a tea to purge his guts of the liquor he'd drunk. She prepared his mush. She buttered bread and poured honey on it.

At dusk on the night before the wedding, when the bloodiest work of animal slaughtering was done and the air was saturated with smells of singed hair and roasting meat, the neighbor women collected out back of the Wilhelms' kitchen. Many had brought elements for stews or cakes, breads, jams, and cheeses for the wedding fest. Hat and Dossie circulated with platters of sweet rolls and hot cider and roasted potatoes and roasted seeds and nuts and apples.

Noelle, the only woman in the gathering wearing the old-style beaded buckskin dress, seemed out of step with the other women. All of them wore calico, even the two young wives of Chief Aaron, a distant relative of Russell Sitton. Old Sarah DeGroot, born when few women wore anything but skin dresses, wore a fancy cotton gown and sat in a rocker covered in shawls and warmed quilts. She was prune dark and frosted with white hair, and she began the storytelling in the old language that few still understood. She still spoke the former masters' prattle, the slatternly pidgin Dutch of decades before. The younger grown women stood, leaning against a porch rail or against the house, and spun on their drop spindles or used their needles for making stockings. The little gals combed and plaited each other's hair and listened to words they hardly understood.

Dossie was too nervous to rest, but Hat settled at last and guided the women's talk to the market. "Is your girl wantin' to work, Honey?" she queried. "Dossie can stand the help with her eggs and her sellin' and I know my brother will pay your Sally to go 'long and 'sist her." It was Hat's clever way to remind the women that her brother was a very successful man, and they were here to celebrate him. Ah, and well they knew it! Hat then laid out a whole plan with a precision that suggested she had practiced her words.

Harriet "Honey" Vander smiled graciously. She was even more pleased and flattered than she chose to display. Most of the women who had daughters were eager to find some work for their older ones amongst the women who needed to hire helpmeets. Honey was excited to be asked if her daughter could work. In fact, she had dreamed of this for her girl. It would do her Sally no harm to be in Harriet Wilhelm's orbit. And it would do her no harm to be in the orbit of Mrs. Wilhelm's son and nephew. Sally was at the age that she must be seen. And she must be seen to be a modest, hardworking, healthy-looking girl. No man in Russell's Knob wanted a wife who would sit on her rump and preen. For that, they went in town.

"Ma'am, she's a good, obedient girl," Honey said to Hat, then turned to look at Dossie. "Miz Dossie, you won' hafta give her nar' a penny if she don' do just what you ast her. She's strong. I be proud if you take her on. She'll serve you well."

Sally's face lit up with circumspect excitement. She wanted to show all of the modest, obedient attributes that her mother was extolling, but she was excited to be going to the market. She wished it was considered proper for a girl of her size to jump up and cavort. She squeezed her younger sisters' hands until they squealed and pulled away.

"Thank you, ma'am," Dossie said to both Harriets for their plans for her. She felt built up, too. Hat had taken and given her a place and elevated her to a knob of respect. And Honey Vander must trust her fitness to let young Sally come into her orbit. Dossie felt content, accepted, and only once or twice for the remainder of the festive night did she think about her husband and worry about her marriage.

Dossie dozed off listening to the women's market palaver. Hat's eyelids fluttered, though she did not drift to slumber as most of the others eventually did. Had Nancy Siscoe slipped from the group when some of the young women sneaked away to meet their beaux?

Nancy Siscoe did leave the group, did go in search of Duncan, did find him, but left exhausted of her self-esteem. He hadn't done anything but finger her and kiss her and had acted more drunk than he'd actually been. Nancy fumed to herself that, at last, Duncan truly had a ring in his nose. For a long time she had been the easy trouble, the dalliance. But now the new little cow had it all.

The wedding foursome left Russell's Knob for Paterson before sunrise on the day. Dossie was resplendent in the dress Mary Figgs Van Waganen had made. Her eyebrows had been shaved to half-moons, and purple agates hung on gold wires from her ears. The dress's collar was high and white and laced magnificently. The cloth was a plaid design that was perfectly agreeable to Dossie's shape, for it emphasized her enviable bosom and, with its folds and flounces, celebrated her delicious butt. Hat, too, was beautifully dressed in a new gown. Duncan caught his breath when he mounted to sit beside Wilhelm at the front of the four-wheeled trap. Ah, beauty is a complex play of familiarity and surprise! Duncan said nothing, only turned to Ernst Wilhelm and smiled. Because Hat suggested it, Ernst Wilhelm had dressed the horse with a fresh-polished holiday bridle, and the group set off for town with a merry sound.

In the office of the justice, the marriage ceremony went smoothly except that Duncan and Ernst Wilhelm had lied that Dossie's papa was a freeman called Jim Bird whom they'd known for many years. Dossie started when she heard her name called as Dossie Bird, and Duncan winked at her. She wanted to laugh. Her most important day, and she wanted to do nothing so much as laugh aloud! She smiled while repeating her vows and lit the room.

If the morning's ceremony was Dossie's high and festive pinnacle, then the evening's party was Hat's. All of the town did come to celebrate with the Wilhelms and the Smoots, and Hat felt a thrill to see them assembling in the clearing and filling the barns.

Because there was far less shame in being a woman put aside than in being the sole inhabitant of Russell's Knob who did not attend the wedding fest of Duncan Smoot, Noelle Beaulieu attended. She observed to herself that, though Duncan Smoot is a pirate, he can't put aside something he don't own — that he ain't ever owned. When Jan came to escort her, Noelle's chin was thrust forward, and her cheeks were held tight, and she'd prettied up for the occasion.

Not a soul missed Duncan Smoot's wedding celebration. As dusk descended, torches were lit and hung at intervals. Some people were, at first, shocked that Jan had gone and got the very best fiddler in Russell's Knob, a well-traveled girl called Charity Toynton, to accompany his dancing. Charity, an abandoned bastard child that no one had the bitter heart to smother, lived with and worked for the Van Waganens. She was called Toynton because she was discovered, in infancy, some months after the disappearance of Prosper Toynton.

The bride and bridegroom were seated on a dais to observe the dance, and Jan began the show by nodding to Charity, who brought her fiddle to life. Jan let her play and only tapped his heels intermittently. He brushed against the floorboards with his thick leather clog shoes as he looked at Charity's fingers on the fiddle. All eyes bore into Charity until the spectators realized that Jan's feet had become active. Then they turned to gaze on him. Jan Smoot, nephew of the bridegroom, danced for the bride — for Dossie, the beautiful queen of the day. Jan and Charity meshed and were kept to a beat by a drummer who drummed in the old ways. They furnished a wildly beautiful duet of fiddling and dancing. The jigs and turns were entrancing and complex.

The duet continued with mounting fury for several songs, then Jim Scout added jug playing, and the cadence soared. A mouth organ was played, and a band formed as several young shavers worked at spoons.

As master of the dance, Jan took Dossie's hand and pulled her off her throne and pulled Uncle to his feet and gave one to the other. Jan drew them to the center of the floor and led them in the dance. Duncan grinned from ear to ear and grabbed Dossie's waist and spun her around the barn. His dancing was exuberant and graceful. No one had ever said the Smoots were inelegant dancers. Here again Dossie had worried. But it mattered little, because Duncan held her and swirled her and she fixed her eyes on him and was borne along. Finally he let her go to Jan for an extended turn about the floor. At this signal all of the party began to choose partners and form up for reels and breakdowns.

Dossie danced with most all of the men while Duncan rotated through the women — stepping gaily but keeping a corner of his eye on his wife. Except that when he danced with Hat he drunk in her beaming face. Hat was so rapturous that it made Duncan proud of himself to have given her a reason to swell with pleasure. They stepped sprightly and in perfect concert. Their family resemblance was obvious, and they made a handsome pair of dancers.

"You had better watch out for your husband, girl," Noelle said to Hat with tipsy laughter when Hat stopped and caught her breath from whirling about the floor. "He's got plans for you, I think."

Noelle was the one woman who did not dance a turn with the bridegroom. She had promised herself that she would not. "The European dances are useless," Noelle said out loud but to no one in particular. "They can't cause rain or ward off a danger!" It annoyed her to see Hattie swirling around so merrily. As always she was getting her way! She had Duncan tucked up tight, and now she could work on marrying off the boys. And Hat wanted to believe that Duncan and Dossie would fill up the porch with children. Noelle knew they would not. If Hattie believed differently she was fooling herself and dreaming still. Hat knew, and she ought to tell the Dossie Bird because a woman ought to know what she is getting in marriage.

"He's following you with his greedy eyes. You better have your safety," Noelle said to Hat, who was blissful in all of the revelry.

"Shut your mouth, Noelle."

"He's dancin' roun' like Pan with a flute. He's gonna catch up with you, girl."

"You jealous, Noelle? You can't let us have no fun 'cause you're sour."

"I'm as always jealous of Mr. Wilhelm," Noelle answered quietly and pinned Hat's eyes with her own.

"Hush up, Noelle," Hat snapped. "You're jealous of everyone." She rolled her eyes and walked away. She caught up with her husband and linked her arm in his. The gesture surprised Wilhelm, and he grasped at Hattie's waist.

Jan had barely managed to contain himself. The worst had happened. Dossie had married Uncle. He felt exhilaration in his dancing. His soul flew around the barn with the opportunity to show her his capering. He had kicked it up to delight only Dossie. He loved her so much, and his eyes loved her so much. He had looked at her all of the day. It was allowed. All eyes could drink in the bride on this one day. When Jan reflected on it, he wanted to cry. This one day had convinced him that he loved her completely and fatally and that she would disappear into Uncle's pocket and he would know she was there.

So many things had been there — in Duncan Smoot's right-hand trouser pocket: his tobacco, some smooth stones he fingered, some string, a leather strip, and once an unusual feather was there when Jan and Pet had sneaked into Duncan's pants to pilfer a coin or two. The feather hadn't come off any bird they'd ever seen. It had a large eye at the center of it. Neither boy knew what Uncle used the feather for, nor could they imagine. Then Jan had seen Uncle use it. Jan had crept out of his bed in Noelle's house and followed the happy voices. Uncle was using the feather on Noelle's body, stroking and titillating her all over and in every place upon her. Then she had turned the feather on Uncle. When Jan told Pet about it they talked for hours, and Jan said things about Noelle that made him ever after regret he'd watched. Though from that time, Jan became a confirmed watcher. Dossie was part and parcel of Uncle's pocket now. Did Jan love Dossie so much because she belonged to Uncle? Belonged? She was his wife now, and Uncle belonged to her as much as she belonged to him.

Dossie was so beautiful on this day from sunrise until the last torch had burnt in the clearing. When it was black dark Jan watched her walk into the house with her hand in Uncle's. She had sat for hours, then had danced and gone back and sat again. Once she had been given a small cake from Uncle's hand, and she bit into it and smiled directly at Jan. He knew it was meant as a small smile of happiness for all of the excitement around her. But Jan also imagined that Dossie taunted him with her eyes. She was a little vixen who was pleased with herself for succeeding with Uncle. Later when Jan fucked Charity Toynton in the horse stall, he thought about Dossie's studied innocence and the contents of Uncle's pocket.

PART THREE

"ONE OF PORTZL'S BITCHES had some pups. That's the prettiest," Pet said, smiled shyly, and deposited an animal at Dossie's feet. She cradled a pan of peas, pulling them out of their pods. At first she mistook the animal for a lamb. For days the wedding gifts had continued to arrive. Small sheep and goats were popular.

"Oh, he's pretty!" Dossie exclaimed.

"Oh no, ma'am," Pet responded in a peculiar, uncomfortable voice. "Is a bitch for a job. She'll make a good lookout around those chickens. She was my choice 'cause Hickory Short's bitch was wild for my Portzl. So Portzl did the job, and I got my pick. She's for you. Uncle says you need a dog." He gave her a fleeting, furtive smile.

"Oh," Dossie cried and raised her hands to her face. Her face broke apart in smiles and giggles at the sight of the fat, clumsy dog tumbling about the porch. "Oh, thank you, Pet!" She reached down to stroke the small dog. It had a dark black fur, a large head, and molasses-colored eyes.

"Better not spoil her. She'll be good at runnin' off a fox or any other thing worrying your chickens. Her bitch is from a line of foxhunters. She'll be keen for them." Pet stooped and ran his hand over the dog's back, then picked her up by her scruff and held her to his chest. "She'll be big and clever like Portzl. I guarantee you." He nuzzled the pup about the head and neck. He handed her into Dossie's arms.

"She'll cry a lot at firs' 'cause she misses her mama," Pet went on talking and walked into the kitchen. He fixed up a small pallet of buckwheat hulls in a sack and found a rag and knotted it and put the baby dog in a corner near the stove. He dangled the rag above her head, and the puppy grabbed it in her tiny teeth. Pet and Dossie giggled together, both sitting on the floor beside the dog's bed.

"Don't let Uncle put her out in the chicken house yet. She's a baby still. You've got to be her mama." Pet's voice was gentle. But he soon got nervous of the closeness as if afraid some feeling would come over him and he might touch his uncle's wife. When Dossie squatted near him he smelled her pleasantly yeasty privates and fought not to respond to the charm of the aroma. He took up the puppy again and nuzzled it. Dossie thought that Pet was very sweet with animals he liked. He stood up and still held on to the dog.

"She's got brown eyes like you got — pretty — fiery bright but sweet," Pet declared to the great surprise of them both. "Uncle said, 'Pick out the bes' dog for my Dossie. Don't take jus' the prettiest one. Get the bes' one.' I know about dogs. That's the bes' one."

He returned the dog to Dossie's outstretched arms and she hugged her little helpmeet.

"Duncan will love her and me, too."

"Yeah," Pet said and patted the puppy again. "Uncle is crazy 'bout you. He will walk over hot coals for you." He suddenly wanted her to know just how strong Duncan felt for her. He wanted to be sure she knew it. He wanted to warn her away from dallying with Jan.

The cat had got out of the bag as far as Pet was concerned on the afternoon that they'd tussled with her donkey. Now he was afraid of what might happen. Jan was very good at seduction.

"Jesus, Jan. You gonna get your jasper chopped off if you try anything with her," Pet had whispered. Jan was staring at Dossie's bodice, moist from sweat and her donkey's snorting breath. His longing was adolescent, urgent, and obvious.

She'd rushed up and caught sight of them slapping at the flanks of her she-donkey. "Eee-ah!" she'd cried in an odd, shrill voice. The animal, whose rump had collapsed in intractable donkey rage, stood up at Dossie's voice and rotated her ears back and forth. Her sudden movement tossed Pet, who had braced himself against her rump, into the mud and shit. "Ee-ah!" Dossie called again, and the donkey snorted amiably. The donkey's swishing tail put more dirt on him, and Pet jumped to his feet, cursed the animal, and slapped her sides again.

Dossie got even more exercised and sweat damp. "No, no! Hold off. She is my beast if she needs a slap! Fix the wagon so's the load is even, one side to the other. Uncle taught me. If the load ain' balanced, the donkey will balk. A donkey ain' as dumb as a horse," Dossie had lectured him, repeating Duncan's words. She'd taken hold of the bridle and talked into the jenny's ears and stroked her head and neck. She used soothing touches to calm the donkey. She lay her face on the animal's neck. She looked like a pretty butterfly resting on a fallen log.

"Ah, you saved us, Miz Dossie," Jan said pleasantly, teasingly. "That oaf, Pet, crossed your donkey, and she refuses to haul our goods."

"What!" Pet had exploded. He was so mad at Jan he could have slugged him. His clothes were covered in mud and donkey shit and sweat, and Jan was laughing? "That hardheaded old thing needs a whip on her back! We ought to have brought a whip, Jan! I told you we'd have to drive the old donkey to get her to haul a load."

Dossie hung on the donkey's bridle and looked about the ground for a thick stick to hit anybody who raised a whip to her donkey.

"Aw, Pet, if a donkey don't want to move, it won't. You can stand and give it stripes until your arms are worn out. It'd rather drop and die than pull a load it don't want to. Is't not so, Dossie?"

"Yes," she whispered. "Duncan says so."

"See, I tol' you. A whip ain't no good on a donkey. Ain't that what Uncle says, Dossie?" Jan's voice was ever more full of mirth and teasing.

"She's a good donkey. She'll haul if I tell her," Dossie had said, and she'd locked her eyes with Jan's.

Pet nearly lost his breath in fear of the look. He had seen his cousin's methods of seduction. He knew the danger of a woman looking long into the eyes of Jan Smoot. His face was startlingly handsome when he was smiling and sweat frosted him.

In frustration, Pet hollered at her, and Dossie jumped. "Tell her to pull the wagon dammit!" The donkey raised her ears in alarm.

"Shut it, Pet!" Jan had said. "You're spooking the animal. Please, Dossie, tell her to take these cigars uphill for us, won't you? They're for Uncle. Tell yer donkey she's doing a favor for Uncle, not for us," Jan had said sweetly and stroked the animal's head. "Don't mind Pet, Dossie. He's drunk on whiskey. It makes him irritable. What mus' we do to please your donkey?"

"Even the load. You got the crates goin' crosswise and sloppy. Donkeys don't like things in a mess. One way or the other — all of them crates. Then the donkey will pull that wagon to hell and back," Dossie said. She'd laughed then, delighted with herself for saying one of Uncle's bold and dangerous sayings and saying "hell."

Jan had laughed, too. It seemed like the three of them had stood for a long time just laughing at her saying "hell" and sounding like Uncle.

They reloaded the wagon with care for the feelings of the intractable animal. Pet remembered that he'd done twice as much of the hauling work because Jan capered, spoke to the donkey with humor, and paused to gaze at Dossie each time he stood straight with a crate.

6

THE WOMEN FROM RUSSELL'S Knob set themselves apart from other colored women and the white women who came to Paterson to sell at market. There was a proud manner in the way they brought their wagons into town. They arrived together. They sat high up in the seats. Their shawls were not tattered nor were their dresses. Though they went to the colored area, they set up together and kept to themselves. They had regular, staunch customers amongst the white matrons as well as the better-situated free blacks. They were singular in treating all of their customers with courtesy. They were typically not harassed by other market women of any color, for they were believed to be great knife fighters. And it was known that the men of Russell's Knob were protective of their women and vengeful in extreme ways.

Paterson's professional women frequented the market also. And, of course, those with allowances spent freely. Hat watched one dolly-mop with particular interest. Very pretty, very young. She had money for embroidered handkerchiefs and candies for her friends and hot corn. Arminty was what she was called, Hat learned from Mattie Ricks, the corn seller she'd paid to find out. Hat never lied when she told Ernst Wilhelm that she knew what went on in town. Though the girl was painted up like a fancy, she seemed a little shy, a little uncertain of herself. No doubt dropped into the circumstance. But the little whore was spending Ernst Wilhelm's money. And him pawing over his wife like he was a sweet old tomcat. All the while he was having cake. It was a bad example for his son. This is what Hat had told Noelle was the reason for accomplishing the thing they'd done. But most of it was her anger at Ernst Wilhelm and his audacity.

Hat had her mind on this thing when the boys arrived.

"Why should it be only a whore that has a frolic — that has fun?" Hat muttered. Dossie looked up with a startle. What had Hat said?

Hat smiled when she saw Jan and Pet. They were, for grown men, beautiful and unmarred. They had both their arms and legs and all of their eyes and teeth. They were handsome.

"An' Hat," Jan called out. "An' Hat, there's a contes'. You ought to come. There's a dancin' contes' and I'm takin' 'em up and gonna beat 'em!" Jan spoke loudly. Hat squelched his voice by frowning. She disliked tipsy behavior in town.

"Jan Smoot! Arrest yourself!" Hat cried out. She noticed Pet and wondered at his quiet, thoughtful demeanor. She followed the line of his gaze to where it settled on the little doxy, Arminty. Did he know about this girl and his father? Or was it that he was cut from the same bolt as his father?

"An' Hat, you got the chance to see me dance," Jan trilled. He gabbed Hat's hands and pecked them with his lips while peeping at Dossie. "Come see me dance." His voice became quieter and seductive.

"Jan, I ain' goin' in a tavern to watch you dance," Hat answered and pushed him away.

"Aw, why not?" He frowned mockingly at her.

"I got too much to do for frolickin', Jan. Hush," she said.

"Come, Dossie," Jan said suddenly. "You can come and sit and watch me beat 'em all," he bragged. Her teeth were so white when she smiled at him, and they shone brilliantly in contrast to her dark skin. Her lips no longer had a childish pink line caused by furious licking, and now they were wholly dark and smooth and set her teeth off beautifully. Jan thought she must be using a tonic. He thought he must, one day, put his lips on hers. "Please, Dossie, please come."

"No!" Hat answered. "We do not frolic in taverns in this town, Jan."

"Why can't Dossie come if she wanna?" he said suddenly like cracking a sharp leather strap. Pet, standing behind Jan, jerked at the words.

"She's workin', Jan," Hat said after a long silence. She wanted to fuss and send him off but was always less successful at chastising Jan than she wished.

"Aw, she won't be long. She can come for a little bit." Jan turned to good-natured wheedling. "It ain't really a frolic. It's a contes'. I could win a prize!"

Dossie stood still and listened. At first it seemed that Hat would keep answering for her. Hat would certainly be able to tell Jan the reasons that Dossie must not go into the tavern to see him dance. Though she was a matron, she was also under the guidance of her husband's sister.

"Gwan off, Jan, Dossie cannot go to no tavern."

"Jan, I ain' goin' in a tavern to see dancin'," Dossie said for herself.

"Why not?" Jan quickly challenged. "Pet'll take you on his arm the same as if it was Uncle took you. You can sit and watch me dance." He came very close and looked directly into her face impudently. Dossie smelled his naughty mischief, the degree of his drunk. He was not so sweet when he drank as he once was.

"I don' wanna go." Dossie looked back at Jan directly — eye to beautiful eye.

"Yes, you do. You wish you could see me go at it. You want to see me dance, Dossie Bird." He spoke back her name with his uncle's call — as if usurping Duncan's advantage with her.

"No," Dossie said quickly. Jan's familiarity rattled her. But truth to tell, she did long to see him dancing. His performance at the wedding had been a sheer wonder. And she imagined the atmosphere in the tavern would be exhilarating. Why, she'd been in Minnie Stewart's place with Duncan. There'd been no harm in the tavern badinage and the laughter and the capering. Duncan had enjoyed it.

"Yeah, you do. You want to see me turn. You say you don't wan' to go 'cause you scared of Uncle. You think An' Hat will tell on you. You won't tell, will you An' Hat?"

"Hush up, Jan." Hat tried to busy herself.

"No," Dossie said. She wanted to be firm without being angry. Jan was trying her, and he knew it.

"He ain' such a big old monster, is he, An' Hat? Uncle won't be mad, will he?" Jan taunted. "Why, Uncle spends a fair amount of time in taverns himself. He won't be mad if you come just to see me dance. He's let you come in town. He mus' think you're grown. Please." Jan chucked Dossie under her chin in a gesture that, even though they'd been raised as cousins and were allowed to be familiar, was immodest, indecent. "Come on, Dossie Blossom. No drinkin' — jus' dancin. I promise. No drinkin', Pet?"

"No drinkin'," Pet answered sullenly.

"Even if Uncle get mad, he won't stay mad at you. Why, a wife has got a certain freedom because she can't be put away so easy."

"Hush!" Hat's voice got a bristle.

Dossie realized that it might be disloyal to Duncan to behave as if she were afraid of him. It began to seem unfriendly to her sweet cousins not to go along. It was like a tempest had boiled up for no cause, and she could quell it by going. Jan might sober some if she agreed, and she wanted to keep him well behaved. When Pet offered his arm gallantly, Dossie strolled off between the two young men.

The place was not at all like Minnie Stewart's. The street they went to was not any street Dossie had ever been to. She knew immediately that she ought not to be on this street or in this establishment. She realized too late that Jan was flat drunk on ale and his own exuberance for dancing. Pet seemed only to be following along behind the piper. And they were doing the thing that Duncan had warned Dossie never to do. Never go into the white-only places.

The tavern had mostly men inside — sports and workingmen — with a smattering of tough-looking, hard-drinking women. At the back were several colored fellows. One of them was August Vander, Sally's big brother. In this place, Dossie was the fly in the milk.

Jan would not have that they would sit at the back. He wanted Dossie and Pet to be center and near the front so as to see him vanquish the other jiggers. They did so to please him, and Jan's dancing won the audience. He had no trouble beating the reigning Irish-jig dancer, for he'd added some haughty flourishes that caused wild enthusiasm in the crowd. But the room exploded suddenly just after Jan had finished performing. Something got let loose, and everybody in the place seemed in a roil. A crude man grabbed at Dossie's breast, and Pet smashed him in the mouth and called him a stinking Irish bastard. This set off a brawl, and the sound of thumps, screams, clattering bowls, and shattering glass filled the place.

Pet was on his back when several of the Irish boor's confederates leaped on him. He was encircled and kicked and pummeled on the floor. Jan came off the stage, grabbed Dossie, and pushed her out the back door into the alley. He returned to rescue Pet and saw that August Vander and some other colored men had waded in on Pet's behalf. Shortly the room began to fall into one-on-one contests.

In the alley a sheriff walked up soundlessly and took hold of Dossie's upper arm, hoisting her off the ground.

"You the cause of this trouble, gal?"

"Oh, no, sir," Dossie stammered without raising her eyes to his face. When the man let go of her arm, he tore the sleeve of her dress.

The sheriff entered the tavern from the rear and watched. He exerted no authority in the brawl, calculating that the bogtrotters could trounce the niggers and save him the trouble.

The colored fellows and Jan eventually pulled Pet out of the tavern and spirited him to a colored doctor on the other side of town. When Pet was patched up so that he could be taken home, Jan and Dossie returned to the market and found Hat and Sally Vander waiting. Hat exclaimed at the sight of Pet and put him into her wagon with his head in her lap. Jan drove Hat's wagon, and Dossie and Sally followed.

Dossie's torn sleeve was the first thing Duncan noticed when the bedraggled group reached the Wilhelm place. Hat called out directives and made the others rush and fetch. She sent Jan to bring Noelle on the run.

Dossie's relief at reaching Duncan's protective sphere was immediately replaced with cold fear. His face was not soft. He demanded to know where her shawl was and acted affronted that Dossie was confused and could not recall. He looked at her like he thought she'd done something wrong when surely he ought to have been comforting her. Where was her shawl? Duncan was called to help with lifting Pet into the house, and his attention was diverted to the crisis. But Dossie had felt herself nearly singed from the heat of his glance.

When Pet was put into his bed and Noelle had arrived, Duncan directed Jan to take Sally Vander home.

"See that she reaches her porch safely. I won't have her people say the Smoots harmed her or let her be harmed."

"Oh, no, Mr. Duncan...," Sally tried to speak, but Duncan turned away and faced Dossie.

"You better sit and collect yourself, woman. I wanna know what went on in town," he said to her.

"It was my fault," Jan said quickly. "Don't be mad at her, Uncle. She isn't the one who was wrong. I talked her into coming in. I wasn't thinkin'."

"You better take the little girl home like I told you and leave my wife to me, Jan," Duncan said with a twist of his lips.

Later when Jan returned, Duncan pinned him. "Yeah, you the one who's at fault for this. I know it. What make you bring my wife into a place like that? You tryin' to take advantage of her? You tryin' to get her hurt bringin' her in a place like that?"

"No—was to see me dance in the contes'. She wa'n't drinkin'. She was sittin' with Pet," Jan stammered.

"Poor Pet got the shit kicked out o' him to see you dancin'! His life is hangin' by a thread, boy. You brought my wife in there to see you dancin' and cavortin'? Dossie ain't no cheap gal

like the ones you like. She ain't no Charity Toynton! You tryin'
to throw dirt on her by bringin' her in that tavern? You wan'
her to see you jumpin' an' preenin' an' let them bogtrottin' bastards look at her and grab on her?"

Jan had meant no harm—no disrespect. It had seemed like
a harmless thing for Dossie and Pet to sit at the back and watch
him vanquish the Irish braggarts. Then Jan recalled that, in
his drunk state, he'd cajoled Pet to sit up front where they had
a good seat and he could see Dossie's face from the stage and
note her delight. He didn't figure they'd toss the place if he
won. He had only wanted to see that look of wonder and wor-
ship of his dancing that had played on Dossie's face at the wedding fest. It was a small thing he wanted, a small smile. Why
should all of her smiles belong to Uncle only now?

"I could beat you down, and no man would criticize me for
what you done to my wife, boy! The women would cry, though.
Hat and Noelle would harangue me if I killed you. It's only
this that keeps me from it."

"Don't punish her, Uncle, please. It's my fault," Jan cut in
and put his hand on Duncan's arm. It was a restraining gesture,
as if he thought the man meant to beat his wife right then and
he could stop him. His uncle chuckled at his desperation.

Ernst Wilhelm debated going for another doctor, but absent
any knife wound or bullet hole, he deferred to the women's
decision that Pet had had enough questionable doctoring.
Noelle swung in beside Hat, and the two began addressing
Pet's wounds.

Duncan took Dossie home so that he could yell at her the
more and more loudly.

"You know better than go in a Irishman's drinkin' place,
don't you?" he cried out as if he'd been stuck with a poker.

How could she not know how foolhardy it was? How could she be so careless and foolish? Had she become so willful that she wanted to preen before a room full of bogtrotters? Had he spoiled her so? His face was thunderous — so twisted in fury that she could not recognize the man who had coddled her and protected her. She tried to answer him.

"No. No," she stammered. Then, in a simple, complete, violent repudiation of her words, Duncan struck her face. She cried out and leaned away. His open hand slammed her temple, her eye, her cheek, her jaw, and she fell to the floor.

The bilious contents of Duncan's stomach rose up and sickened him to realize he had done this. Duncan had seen Dossie's torn dress and imagined a ravishment. He got beside himself that his jewel had let herself be carried into this place. It was Jan's fault. He was the culprit above all. Yet Duncan had wanted to slap her. All of the wagon ride from poor Pet's bedside he'd wanted to punish her for having been there and wanting something that he was not there to give her, for being out of his light and needing help and him not there to help her. Didn't she know it? Didn't she know that now she was a wife in his pocket she shouldn't be gallivanting with the boys into taverns? Ah, with Dossie Bird it is innocence above all. It is ignorance of what all goes on in places like that. He had to slap her so that she would not ever go in such a place again. It was the only way to discharge the intense longing to go out and gut the white sonofabitch who had touched her.

That a lout had grabbed at her in the tavern, that Pet had taken him down with a punch, and that a brawl had then started was what August Vander had told him. August had reached Russell's Knob ahead of the others, carrying the story directly, first to Duncan. And so it was known about that Dossie had been grossly insulted by a drunk in an Irishman's tavern in Paterson. Duncan knew all this by the time the wagon approached and Hat was shouting out orders and Duncan saw Dossie's ripped dress. It was a flag, a bait, a poke in the eye.

Dossie was onto her knees like a dropped sack after he hit her. All because another man had touched her? Duncan demanded that she take off the torn dress. It offended him so deeply that her clothes were disheveled. She removed the dress and looked up at him. He'd seen the look before in women who had been slaves or girls who'd grown up in bondage. Submission. Fear of punishment and resignation that it is inevitable. Dossie seemed very small in her chemise. Grandmother showed him a picture of himself then, and he stopped.

You cannot do it. You must not. Dossie Bird cannot be punished like a child and she must not be slapped and flogged like a slave.

Later Duncan whispered in her ear, sobbing onto her face, "Pardon, pardon, pardon me."

Her jaw became hot. Her face swelled and was painful. She had expected him to embrace her and be only slightly put out that she'd disobeyed. Her ears had not rung this way since she'd come with him. He had slapped her. He, who had taken pains to convince her that the days of ill treatment were over, had struck her. She had not, in truth, considered the implications of her ripped dress. She had heard the sound of the cloth tearing when the sheriff grabbed her arm, but all the fighting and yelling had drowned out any further thought of it. There had been a frightening amount of blood on Pet's clothes, and Jan's nose had run blood. But Duncan's eyes locked on her torn dress even before he looked at her face, her frightened, tearstained face that itched with dried tears already spent for Pet.

He could not see past it. Duncan had been gripped in a fit of anger so fierce that Dossie saw the gesture — the strike — as it seeded and germinated in the few seconds before he raised his hand. The slap burst from him. He was so suddenly aflame with indignation. She was at fault, though she could not figure out how. Why was Duncan so angry with her?

Dossie wanted to touch him and sway him from his rage. Her fingers could be persuasive. She could insinuate them in his clothes and make him smile as she'd done before. Maybe she ought to have run at him, circled his neck with her arms, and pressed herself against him so that he could feel her heart and her circumstance and forget the dress. Surely the crisis was that Pet was injured, cracked up very badly. Yet Duncan had fixed his eye on the ripped dress and been completely focused on that bit of it. And the shawl. He said such rude things about her lost shawl as if it were a virgin girl dragged through the mud. Now was the time to be a little swallow that could fly the distance, slip in, search the tavern, and retrieve the shawl and bring it home.

Because Dossie had turned her face into her pillow and cried throughout the night, had let him also cry onto her swelling skin, and had finally slept with her nose caked and mouth open, she woke up more swollen, feeling her face chafed raw. Her knees ached also because she'd slammed onto them when Duncan had hit her, which was what he had done no matter what she woke wanting to believe.

Though Duncan was contrite, he continued fuming into the next days. He shouted that Pet and Jan were fools to think the Irish would accept them as equals in the tavern. He reviewed all of his previous lectures to them on the subject. He shouted at Dossie that it was little wonder there'd been a brawl. Pet had sat in an Irish bar at a table in the middle of the room with dark Dossie on his arm, and Jan had the audacity to dance their best jiggers into the ground.

"And what must they thought of you, woman? There you was sittin' in a white man's tavern with a white man!"

Duncan's shouting was so loud and furious that Dossie wished he would slap her again and leave off haranguing. No. She would not ever wish to be slapped again. She felt the bones in her ears still rattling. She wished only that the slap could have been the last of it.

Dossie hadn't thought about Pet being a white-looking man. He was as he'd always been — her cousin. They were all of them cousins — her and Jan and Pet. She hadn't thought about the temper of the room around them. She'd been caught up in the jig competition, oblivious to all but Jan's flying feet and his saucy smile. They had all three forgotten themselves in the place. They'd danced at the wedding. They had been the beautiful cousins then. But in that Irishman's tavern, they were somebody else.

Hat considered how tenderly her husband lifted his son and brought him into the house. Pet fainted once when he was shifted, and his head lolled on his father's chest. His father held it and kissed it there for the long moment that they worked to rouse him. She had never seen Mr. Wilhelm so tender. Hat herself cried out to see Pet's scars and bruises. She sat at his bedside and dozed only when he neither moaned nor trembled, when his breathing was neither shallow and quiet nor rattling loudly.

Hat and Noelle kept Pet still in the bed. They laid plasters across his chest to draw the pain from him. At first Pet writhed and moaned, but then Hat brought her chair to the bedside and fed him whiskey by the spoonful to ease his pain. She held his hand and bathed his head.

When several days had passed, Pet's vigor began returning. He felt the warm things that lay across his body. He felt the touches of his nurse mother. He fought against coming wide awake because her bending over him—her bedside vigil—was so pleasurable. He tried to remain still so that she would continue to peck at his face with her lips while she tightened his bed and drew the blankets under his chin. When he could control himself no longer, he opened his eyes to hail her.

"Mama."

Hat smiled broadly, and Pet lost his pallor at once in response.

"Oh, you are back!" Hat began wiping Pet's moist forehead with her apron. She called his father, who rushed in to the bedside, and for a moment Pet thought he had died and gone to heaven. His parents were together, both smiling at him.

"He has scars as well as bruises, Ernst. Why does he fight so much?" Hat asked her husband later, sounding like a child asking for an explication of a Bible verse.

"Ask your brother, Hattie," Ernst Wilhelm replied.

Hat was leery of Duncan, nervous still at what she imagined he would do to Dossie. She had confronted Duncan that first night. "Brother, you should not be harsh with her."

"Hattie, I ought to box your ears for lettin' her go off with them boys," Duncan had shouted.

"Is she a child or a grown woman?" Hat had answered back and further riled him.

"Hattie, you were wrong not to stop her." Duncan glared, and Hattie did feel culpable. "She ain't a slut to be hangin' about in a public house. You know that even if she don't. Your husband would chastise you if he'd caught you in a public house full of drunk Irish and your dress was torn and some bogtrotting bastard had your shawl wrapped up round his jasper!"

"Punkin, please...," she had gasped.

"It's finished, Hattie."

So Hat had dedicated herself to nursing Pet and forgot about Dossie, Jan, or anybody else. She satisfied her nascent curiosity about her son and examined all of the things from his pants pockets and his chests while he slept. She ran her hand along the bottom of his drawers and found billets-doux and all else. An embroidered handkerchief buried deep below some shirts gave her pause, and Hat tried very hard to note the design, then put it back as if it had not been touched. She looked and looked at his face as she bathed his head and swabbed his ears, nose, and eyes.

Hat confiscated several flasks, cigar cutters, pipes, and pipe-cleaning implements. She was concerned at the number of knives that Pet seemed to own. She had a boot maker in to measure after she and Noelle scraped and bathed Pet's feet and trimmed his toenails. She gave away his old boots.

Pet was powerless to resist his mother's ministrations and intrusions, since he was weak and in pain. He was made to wear one of his father's sleeping gowns and be covered in shawls when he was propped up for feeding. His head was shaved to ensure his fever did not return.

Hat enticed Pet's appetite by filling the house with cooking aromas, though after consultations with Noelle and her medicinal texts she placed Pet on a strict regime that allowed only broth and tea and mush and benne wafers. Hat was frightened of the damage the men's kicks may have done to her son's innards. Thus she gave him teas and flushed him and held the chamber pot before him herself so that she might note the color of his water as it flowed.

Jan's wounds, such as they were, healed up with Noelle's aid. He'd come out worse in tussles with Pet. The damage was done to his feelings. Guilt. He was guilty for all of it. He took it on himself that what had happened to Pet and what had happened to Dossie were his fault. He wanted to slip in and see Pet, but Hat wouldn't let him. "Gwan off, Jan," she'd said. Jan knew he better stay away from Dossie, and he did so. They all blamed him.

"I'm sorry, An' Hat," he said weeks later. "Pet's better?" Jan came up behind Hat with soft shoes as she fussed about in the kitchen.

"He's come back to himself. But no drinkin'," Hat admonished. She let Jan come close and brush her cheek with his lips, though she did not peck back at his. "He's not strong yet."

"I'm sorry he was hurt. It's my fault." For once he didn't raise his eyes and try to win her favor with handsomeness. His contrition was abject, but still she wanted to fuss and fume.

"Yes," Hat answered. "You made the trouble. You made trouble for her, too. You made trouble for her with her husband. Are you a wolf that can't come inside and sleep near the fire, Jan? Don't make no more trouble for Dossie. Leave her alone, Jan," Hat implored.

Jan had always wanted to call An' Hat Mama like Pet did. Hat never encouraged it. She mothered him, but he felt that she always wanted to remain his aunt. Like Noelle, she wanted to leave a slot for Cissy, her beloved sister, a ghost haunting their dinner table.

"Colored people have got to be careful. I think you forgot that. Dossie should have known better herself than be pulled in there. I should have stopped her. It's somewhat my fault, too. I should have slapped your face for asking her, before I let you pull her to go in there. I'm sorry I didn't. Your uncle is right to say I been too soft on you — so easy persuaded by your smilin'. I think your uncle has taught her not to be swayed by a honey-tongue fancy boy who would take her into a rowdy house. You're becoming a caution, Jan. You're becoming a dangerous kinda man for a decent colored woman to know!"

"I'm sorry. I'm sorry a thousan' times. But An' Hat, he's got no right. He's got no right to —"

"Maybe she was too young to marry him. Duncan is grown. He ain't no boy to trifle with. But she's accepted him. Dossie wants him — not you, Jan. She's living in his light because she loves him. She's his wife. She takes what he gives her. She's got her guile and her meekness and her special secrets to influence him, you know that." Hat touched Jan's hot cheek. Her gesture was a mock flirtation, and it stung him. She made it clear that she did not believe his love was sincere — chaste even. She thought he only wanted to fuck Dossie.

"I would not prick her finger if it would make her cry out. I love her," Jan pronounced very solemnly.

Hat was surprised.

"Her husband chastised her," Hat said to Honey Vander, though not knowing actually whether he had. Honey Vander heard the words in silence. It was a rash, punishable act to go into a white men's drinking place. Honey Vander had mulled it. She figured Dossie Smoot would think twice about her behavior in town now. Colored women had to win and keep their reputations at some cost. Honey considered that a lesson had been taken. Her Sally would now never consider doing such a thing.

Everyone in Russell's Knob knew what had happened in Paterson. Everyone knew how badly Petrus Wilhelm had been beaten. All of them knew that Dossie Smoot was at the middle of a brawl in an Irish tavern full of raucous dancers and drinking men. She was with her husband's wild, capering nephews without her husband. That her dress had been ripped was the subject of whispers. As it stood in the town's view, Dossie's reputation had a blemish that was expiated by her contrition and the willingness of her husband to forgive her.

7

AUGUST VANDER'S PAPA WORKED for Ernst Wilhelm in the brewery. As little shavers, Jan and August and Pet had ripped about together taking messages and eating corn cakes outside of Hat's kitchen. Though there was some envy among them now, Jan needed company and attention, and August Vander needed drinks. Pet needed a small band about to truss him.

"No colored men 'lowed in?" Jan asked.

"Not a one," August answered.

August Vander's currency for a lark — a long afternoon of ale drinking leading up to a night of whiskey — was his willingness to spark up things with randy conversation. "Not in the Alta Club. In this house are the prettiest dark gals you can picture. No white ones. And they're reserved for white men only — no Africans, no jumble boys, no 'Talians, no Indians, no Greeks. Just for your pale, white men. You know, your rebels and your redcoats, your Scots, your Frenchies, your Dutch," August Vander spat at saying "Dutch" as many did in Russell's Knob. "And your Germans," he added.

"Oh, I don't believe it," Jan piped. "Whorehouses in Paterson are wide open. They let in Europes of all kinds and jumble boys and blacks and whites and Indians."

"Them are bawdy houses. This here is a better house," August insisted.

Pet wouldn't admit it, but he was leery of going to Paterson. And especially he didn't want Uncle to know this and think he was a coward. He had heard Papa tell Mama that he and Duncan and some other men had gone down to town and cracked open the head of a blind-drunk bastard that stumbled out of the back of the same Irish tavern that had given him the beating. Then they went back and did it a second time so that the bastards would know they were hard and unpredictable. Mama purred with satisfaction at the news, and Pet marveled at the vengeful hearts of the Smoots. But he wanted less trouble from now on.

Pet breathed deeply and rubbed his sensitive ribs. He had promised his mother he wouldn't drink whiskey at all and would not fight (he meant to keep this promise!) and would "stay away from loose lollies." His mother had giggled at her own words and pinched his nose.

"Maybe you could get in, Pet," Jan said.

"What? Oh, shut up, Jan! You probably could, too," Pet said. "You got the price."

"But not in the Alta Club. That's a place for pale white-skinned men like you and your father," August said to Pet, "only." August looked straight into Pet's face. He had the eyes all the Vanders have that people called molasses bullets because they're the color that molasses becomes in the deep wintertime and they are hard like ice.

"What does it matter?" Pet asked. He felt the one glass of whiskey he'd drunk sear his stomach and roar to his head. He chose to be dumb to August's provocation. But a realization crept up on him that his pale face had kept him from knowing some deep tenets that Jan knew — that August knew — because their faces said something different from his face in the town. And he didn't know what they knew, or did he? He knew full well that he and Jan had no business challenging them Irish dancers in that tavern and bringing Dossie in there. Uncle was right about that.

"It don't make any matter unless you want to see what kinda pussy they got in the Alta Club," August Vander continued slyly.

"I don't believe they got such a house. We never been. I never heard of it. Uncle's never been there," Pet said, now feeling ensnared in some trap.

"Don't be stupid, Pet, we're colored men. How can we know about it? You the only white one," Jan put in. The liquor was affecting him, too. It made him careless and disloyal to his cousin.

"I ain't white," Pet said.

"Well, you look white," Jan came back at him.

"You and your papa." Again August spoke in a sly voice of instigation. "You the only ones look white enough to pass through those doors."

"I ain't no white man," Pet said as he'd said so many times before.

"Pet, don't be dumb about it. You know what you look like. You know what people take you for."

They all drank one more shot of whiskey, rode into Paterson, and Pet agreed to go in the Alta Club. It was a show for Jan and August — a lark. When had he been immune to a lark?

"Go on up there and go in and look around, Pet," Jan said. "You can bring us back the word of the beauties. You can get you a taste and tell us all about it. We'll never get to New Orleans." Jan and August guffawed and hiccuped.

Pet loosened up with the raucous laughing on the ride into town and put aside his vows to his mother. What did it matter? What was the big tick in being white skinned? For one brief moment of ale insight, though, Pet felt that August was envious of his white looks and was getting back at him. Maybe Jan was, too? Pet chuckled to himself because he had always been jealous of Jan's place among the golden gorgeous and the pretty browns and the lovely blacks of Russell's Knob. Jan was the beautiful one with his tawny skin and dark, curly hair and Uncle's majestic, formidable face. Jan's eyes were bright and always dancing. He was the one called handsome. Suddenly now, it occurred to Pet that Papa might be keeping something sweet from him by not letting him be a white — not sharing these privileges with his white-looking son.

The thought that carried Pet into the place was that it might actually be fun to go in just to see what there was and to tell Jan and August about it. It would be a unique pleasure to have something to brag to Jan about.

"Gwan, Pet. We'll sit in back with the wagon. Take your time, boy. You got money? You got to have dough." They laughed more, Jan stuffed his own money in Pet's pockets, plucked a bit of straw from Pet's hair, and brushed at his clothes.

"Go on, white boy," August cajoled. He wondered to himself why they didn't take their pooled resources and go to a house that welcomed all comers. Of course, he was the fool that had started this idea up.

They drove the wagon into a grove at back, and Pet had to walk past the barn to enter at the front door. Well, he knew it all then — or most of it — when he saw Freyda, his papa's horse, in the barn. His father's mount would not be in such comfort in a place that had not made his papa comfortable. She had been brushed. Her mane looked dry and fluffy. She wore a feed bag and looked at Pet with surprise. Whiskey told him to snatch the feed bag off Freyda's face and punish her treachery in some way, but when he put his hands on her a voice called out, "Can I he'p you, suh?" A small stable urchin ran up.

"Whose horse is this here?" Pet demanded.

The stable boy looked up frightened and stammered, "This Mr. Ernst Wilhelm's mount." Pet started at the boy's tone. "What's your name, boy?" Pet asked harshly.

"I'm Careful Jackson, suh," the boy answered.

"Humph," Pet muttered, in a complete fluster.

The madam admitted Pet to the Alta Club, after he showed her a persuasive amount of cash and recognized that he was not innocent. Pet entered the parlor and sat looking about for five or ten minutes. He stood up again, returned to the anteroom, and found the madam at her post near the door. Pet pulled another fold of bills and asked to be taken to Ernst Wilhelm. The madam took the money and said, putting her palm in the center of Pet's chest, "Don't take it out on that girl and don't tear my place up."

When the lovely girl opened the door Pet had banged on, she was wearing a shimmering blue robe. She was young, about his own age, and brown skinned. The girl he'd ogled at the market! In the room behind her, Pet saw his father also wearing a robe. His father lurched up from an incline, completely breathless with shock at seeing Pet in the room. He could not stand.

"A gentleman don't do that, Petrus," he stammered and struggled with the chaise. "Petrus, a gentleman don't bribe a whore to tell him what another man is doing. What you doing here, Petrus?" he demanded. Pet was brought up short momentarily by his father's chastising tone, but his equanimity, such as it was, returned when he saw Papa's discomfort.

"What you doing here, Papa?" Pet answered.

Ernst Wilhelm got to his feet finally, though the chaise was deep and plush and tried to hold him. "Don't trade words with me, boy!" he yelled. "I ask you what you're doing in here!"

"I'm grown, Papa. I come in here to get some pussy. I saw this pretty girl at the market the other day and I thought, since I ain't got a wife at home, I can use a regular whore," Pet said, though he ought to have been afraid to taunt his father. But Pet felt fearless now and inured to any pain his father might inflict.

"Go on home and snitch to your mama then. See if she cares," Ernst Wilhelm said. He was shocked at his own words. It was a show for the girl. He hadn't wanted to hurt Petrus's feelings — to attack his manliness. But he didn't have the courage to take an affront before the girl.

And it was unfair because Pet was not a tattler. "Keep your mouth shut, boy!" Ernst Wilhelm had often said, and Pet had always done that. Pet had never told his mother anything.

The young fawn-colored girl was called Arminty, Pet knew. He'd heard her fellow doxies call her in the market. She was as desirable as a cup of sunshine, and she watched the contretemps with some interest, tightening the belt of her robe and waiting.

The ride home was quiet. All three had got sober. Did August Vander seem to be smirking? Pet's head swelled and throbbed with wondering about this day. Jan and Pet headed to the

Wilhelms' house to sleep in Pet's bed because Hat and Dossie were at Noelle's house making jams and pies. Pet knew his breath and his complexion would give him away to his mother. She would know he was as untrustworthy as his father. It was as if a band had been put around his head and tightened.

"You know my papa had a girl in there?" Pet demanded in a fierce whisper and jabbed Jan in his side. "Did you know my papa had a cozy and a whore in that place?"

"No. How I'm going to know your papa's business if you don't? August knew it for sure. He knew what you'd be walking into. He's a kind of mean little bastard," Jan said lowering his voice. "But you been shunnin' me. I got to have a buddy for drinkin'."

"You're both swine," Pet said resignedly. "And Papa and Duncan and me, too. Jan, boy, I wanted to fuck her. Papa was sitting down on the divan with a robe round him. He was so comfortable. She looked at me with her little eyes, and I figured she'd go for it. It was the pretty little minx we saw at the market, Jan. How's a fat bastard like Papa attract a pretty girl like that, Jan?"

"He's got money and she's a whore. She may not look so good in the light of day," Jan said.

"I told you I saw her in the market, and you did, too. She's pretty. She ain't much older than us. And then I was standing there, and I wondered. This being the kind of place it was. I wonder did this girl have the right to leave if she wanted? Papa was fussing at me and I was thinking about taking this girl for a drink so I could pull on her and kiss her. Then I came awake to wonder was she a slave—this girl? You think she's a slave of my papa's like Mama was? That was when I left. 'Cause I got to thinkin' that if she was his slave girl I could fuck her if Papa said so. That made me kinda' sick and sober. I didn't want to think about that part of it. What you think, Jan? Is she a slave?"

"Damn, Pet. It ain't no slavery up here anymore. I don't know."

"Yeah, but some are still owned and folk get drug off south and sol' and some runaways are followed and drug back south. And gals get rounded up and forced, Jan" — Pet's voice began to sound plaintive — "like my mama."

"That gal is your papa's arrangement, boy. It ain't got nothin' to do with you . . . or An' Hat."

"I just don't want him keepin' no slave gal. He ain't got a right to do that."

"Ah, we live in a white man's world." Jan laughed. "Go on back down there and take your papa's girl if that's what you want. Set her free."

"Up here in Russell's Knob everybody is free. I'm gonna stay here and not go nowhere else," Pet said sleepily. He rubbed up and down on his right side with his left hand in a gesture that had recently become a habit.

"Not me. I'm going down to the city. With Uncle married, I ain't even got no place to live. I'm a vagabond already."

"In Paterson town? You got a new girl there?"

"Naw. I'm going down to New York City."

"Naw, naw, stay here. But you better watch yourself round Dossie or he'll know you got a burn for her," Pet said with self-satisfaction.

"He knows already. It's why he taunts me. It ain't right for her to be with Uncle, Pet. I'm goin', boy. I ain't gonna stay here all my life. An' she ain't neither."

"You gonna kidnap her — drag her off? Goddamn fool, I say."

*   *   *

It was far easier to capture women for bounty than men, for they offered less resistance, were more easily frightened by guns, and could be flushed out of hiding by grabbing up their young'uns. Conveniently, they were often found in whorehouses.

Two men rode into Paterson and looked up the local lawmen for a palaver. They had a warrant with a description of a young escaped slave gal said to be working in the area at the Alta Club. Their papers stated the young woman was a runaway with a reward for her capture. She was said to have run from the South. The sheriffs had a description of a pretty brown girl with a sassy, intelligent demeanor. They had word she'd been seen working in a high-toned bordello in Paterson. They said they'd traveled from Maryland and claimed to have received a warrant from a man from Tennessee who said that a part of his inheritance was the value of this one slave girl who'd run off.

Sheriff Emil Branch suspected the story was a lie but considered that one less whore in the town was a good thing. Many times these "escape" stories covered a blatant plan to kidnap a likely looking colored gal and have a bounty. But if there is slavery farther south, what does it matter to him?

"Don't try to snatch off no extras," Branch growled at the men. "This is a free town."

The stable boy from the Alta Club came up to Dossie's wagon at the market. He winked and waggled his fingers in agitation. Dossie was some bit frightened, though she recognized him. She'd seen him with Philomena Johnson, the boss of the Alta Club. The Alta Club's cook was always happy to get large, fresh mountain eggs, and Philomena Johnson herself enjoyed an outing to market. Dossie knew the woman's business because Duncan had explained it to her. In fact, he had cited the Alta Club as her warning. Be good, be careful, or you might end up like one of these women.

Careful Jackson spoke as plainly as his snaggleteeth allowed. "Ma'am. Ma'am. Tell Mr. Ernst they tooked her," he said. "Tell Mr. Ernst that they takin' his gal back to slavery. They got her in the jail." Dossie looked at the youngster with her eyebrows disappearing into the top of her head. He was smaller than her, but upon close observation he appeared to be an old man. Dossie heard his words. But why was he talking to her? Why tell her Mr. Ernst's business?

"Please, ma'am, take word to Mr. Ernst Wilhelm that a sheriff come and give money to Miz Philomena and tooked Arminty. She gone down in the jail. Tell him 'cause she his tuck-up," the boy insisted. "She his girl." Careful Jackson squeezed Dossie's hand to press her to action and released it when she nodded.

"I give him this word soon's I can," she promised.

Philomena Johnson had no compunction about taking money from the bounty hunters. In her view the girl was neglected. During Pet's convalescence Ernst Wilhelm was inattentive, and Arminty had had to make do with her little savings and was teased by the other girls who said her fat old bastard had dumped her. After the ruckus with Pet, he'd stopped coming with regularity. And then her stomach began.

Sheriff Emil Branch was too lazy to pursue thwarting the bounty hunters, but he offered them no real help either.

"Now, Mr. Wilhelm," he said when confronted by Ernst

Wilhelm at the jail. "Just because you want your comfort here don't mean you can take some other man's legal rights away." Branch's own feelings about white men who consorted with the colored were complex.

"That paper don't mean anything!" Wilhelm growled back at the men. "That gal don't belong to no man in Tennessee!" he shouted.

"Now you don't know that, Mr. Wilhelm. This paper says she's the property of Mr. Sanford Crawford of Tennessee," Branch answered.

"Legally the coming child's his, too," one of the men said with a cracker sneer. "By the look of her we'uns'll be back home just before it come — back to Mr. Crawford. He'll thank you for the boon, sir."

The nasty, unnecessary words made Ernst Wilhelm grunt. He was stunned. He hadn't laid eyes on the girl in a month. Surely it was only one month. Had it been longer? Perhaps it had been longer and he'd forgotten. He had neglected her. How long had she been in the jail?

When he was allowed to see her, Arminty begged him to kill her himself so that she would not be taken back south. She pleaded for him to use his hands to strangle her. Ernst Wilhelm's complete panic caused bile to rise into his mouth. He left the jail with one hand over his mouth and one on his gut.

Ernst Wilhelm put it together in his own mind while he chucked up his last meal that he would shoot the man who had spoken in the sheriff's office — if he did not gut him with a knife. His own guts calmed when he thought of buttermilk and fixing a plan with Duncan and the boys.

"Counter them. Use the paper, man. Now is the time. Show them that paper and say she is your slave," Hat said, entering her kitchen, seeing Wilhelm and Pet hunched over, whispering. She knew about the scene in the sheriff's office because Mattie Ricks had hired a dogcart and a boy and had come quickly and stealthily to bring her the news for a bonus fee.

"Hattie," Ernst Wilhelm sputtered. "How . . . ? Is Pet been tellin' on me?"

"Hush, man. Pet don't tattle. I know what you do. You the kind of man a wife has to keep her eye on. Take the paper and make the case. You may get her away without having to shoot anybody."

"No, Hattie."

"Take the paper, Wilhelm. I give you your freedom and you give me mine. It's a bargain." Hat handed him the bill of sale.

"Mama . . . what?" Pet began.

Hat raised her hand and stopped him from speaking. It was only since she'd nursed Pet back from the brink that she felt like she was in the right place with him. Before they seemed to her to be children both together — Mr. Wilhelm's children. She'd always felt like Mr. Wilhelm's child wife instead of a grown-up woman because he'd always had the power to make her small and tearful. She felt a break and realized she wanted him to go and had a way to be rid of him.

"Listen, boy, but don't interfere. This is between your father and me," Hat said.

I know about it all, Pet wanted to say to keep her from confessing more. Hat looked at him and quieted him with her placid demeanor.

"Ernst, I've honored you as my husband because you kept me from a worse situation. I thank you for helping me and bringing me back to my home. And I thank you for my son. We are both free of our bond."

The paper Hat handed Ernst Wilhelm was more a receipt

than a bill. It was a very small piece of paper to have had such moment. All those years ago he had laid it on the table carelessly. She looked at it. He'd not known then that she could read. Naturally he had assumed that she could not. Anna Beth could not. But Harriet Smoot could read. She read the state of herself as represented on the paper. It said that he, Mr. Ernst Wilhelm of Bergen County, New Jersey, had the authority to take her up and keep her unfree. Whether the market had been legal or not, Hat had been bought.

"Hattie. What are you saying?" The shock of it all was just hitting him. To rescue Arminty would mean that he'd lose his home and Hattie and Petrus and Russell's Knob whether he used the paper or not. He would have to take Arminty away. He'd have to see her to safety. A wave of indignation washed over him. Hattie was forcing him out! In all his gallant plans for the girl's rescue he hadn't thought about what would come after. Now he stood to lose all.

"Did you think you'd be able to have your cake and eat it?" In the circumstance, there was little satisfaction in seeing Ernst squirm. Hat felt a real sympathy for the girl caught up in jail. "I s'pose it's why I kept it. It is proof that I had no choice. It always pissed me and besmirched my feelings for you. It is at least an insult to be sold and bought. It leaves a bad taste. Gwan an' take the paper. It may free her."

"Hattie," Ernst Wilhelm managed to say. He reached for her hand, but she retreated from him.

Ernst Wilhelm might have let the man ride off. But when he saw the way Arminty was shackled and the state of her nakedness, he shot the man in the back of his head, kicked his body over, and took the keys from his belt. When he imagined what humiliation the bastard had served up to Arminty in the jail, he wished he'd beaten him to death.

The others were surprised and dropped open their mouths. Pet gasped, "Papa!"

"I had to do it. Look at her!"

"You've lef' us some trouble, Wilhelm," Duncan declared.

"Shut up!" Ernst Wilhelm exploded. He took off the shackles that bound the insensible woman. Arminty did not speak, did not scream or cry. She did not make any sound. Lost in a laudanum faint, she lay nakedly exposed to the air on a bed of feed sacks in the hunter's rig.

Wilhelm covered her, and Duncan tied his own horse to the wagon, got in it, and drove to Noelle's home as smoothly as possible.

Noelle felt Arminty's stomach and said her baby was safe for the time being. Noelle said the girl needed a good, long rest in the bed to build her up. She said they'd given her laudanum to keep her quiet and to keep her from crying herself into ill health. Noelle rubbed Arminty all over with her fingers and bathed her head.

"Hat, Hattie, Hat, Hattie," Ernst Wilhelm said again and again—calling her and hoping that some words would follow. Was there even a way to explain himself? He had great difficulty actually saying anything to Hat. How to say in words what he felt—what he felt he was obliged to do? Finally Hat herself restated the case and drew out a plan. Ernst Wilhelm would take the girl who was bearing his child to safety in Canada. There was nothing else to do. He ought stay with them and care for them because he was, all would acknowledge, completely responsible for them. He was an outlaw himself now. He must sign over his business interests in this country to Petrus. This she said coolly, and Ernst paused to consider it. All of his property in this country would come to his first son. He would take the cash money that was on hand with him, and Petrus would send more when he could safely do so.

Hat's lack of passion alarmed Ernst somewhat. She was a Smoot. She was cunning.

"I worry that I am leaving so much responsibility on Petrus's shoulders," Ernst said with some attempt to soften the parting.

"Ah, he can do anything you can and he is younger and stronger, and he will have me to help him," Hat said with a harsh self-assertion that stung Ernst Wilhelm.

"Yes, you are right. He can take the reins," Ernst conceded. "I will worry about him though . . . and about you."

"Save your worry for yourself," Hat said sincerely. "We will cover it for you. We won't put a lawman on your tail."

Harriet Smoot was certain that hers was the only heart that had never been softened to love and entanglement as women's hearts were expected to be. Her first and only love had been her brother. He'd been a merry, playful boy once. She hadn't known the man who took her off in marriage. Some contract had been made with her papa. And though Ernst Wilhelm rescued her from a horrible circumstance farther south, she had never known a choice in the matter. It was Wilhelm and his money that had chosen her. And none of the subsequent days spent as husband and wife and as parents had changed the ugliness of their beginning. He had been voracious in wanting her, and she never had wanted him. And everyone—including Duncan—had colluded in her acceptance of this as marriage. He had her blessing to go.

Hat assembled belongings for Wilhelm as if he were going on a trip and would return in a day or so. She collected his shaving cup, razor, stockings, and chemise for sleeping. She added a box of bayberry candles for the sake of sentiment and lay down, closed her eyes, and let sunrise come on as it would.

Petrus and his father sat together talking throughout the night after Ernst Wilhelm had signed papers and passed them to his son. Several times Petrus had wanted to lay his head on Papa's knee and have his hair tousled. But they were no longer in this relation—father and child. The son was grown now and taking the reins from his papa.

They struck a bargain that made the young man fortunate. The last thought Pet had before he let himself slumber—head on the table—was that his papa was such an enviable adventurer. He would never have Papa's boldness of character. He'd never have the gumption to leave a world across the ocean in Dresden and come here and live so long in these mountains and then go off again into a new country. Damn! Pet knew for certain that he'd never have that kind of spunk or wanderlust. He was his mother's child.

When the sun came up, Ernst Wilhelm went to speak to Hat once more. She awoke, startled. Her hair was disheveled. He looked at her and thought that she was as pretty as a biscuit still—even with dried matter about her eyes. Had she cried because he was leaving?

"We must go, Hattie."

"'We,' Ernst? You taking my son with you?"

"Petrus and Jan are riding with us to the border. They will

not cross. They'll come back. It's best if you go up to stay with Duncan and Dossie. Some lawmen may come looking for me and the boys."

"Better change your name. Gwan. Send them boys back. Don't let them cross the border. He's my boy. He's mine."

"I won't."

"Good luck to you then." She put her head on her pillow and turned her back to Ernst Wilhelm.

Pet and his father drove up to Duncan's house in one of the larger beer wagons with two of Wilhelm's sturdiest horses pulling it. Noelle and Dossie made a straw pallet in the back of this wagon. Noelle spoke to Jan and Pet in a husky voice. "Lash these goods up tight. She's still weak. Don't toss her roun' too much, or the baby liable to come early. She's not strong enough to bring it."

Noelle reached and took Pet's face between her hands and spoke to him. "You come back here in one good piece, boy. You b'long to us. Your papa has made his bed and can lie in it with his own conscience. You're our baby. You're our ol' shoe. We want you. You come back here." Noelle spoke to Pet as if she were calling down spirits to influence him. She grabbed his shoulders and squeezed.

"Yes, Imi," he replied with the old childhood name him and Jan had used for Noelle. She placed her palm on Pet's chest, then on Jan's, and closed her eyes to murmur prayers that Grandmother would look after them on the road. She gave Grandmother no exhortation on behalf of Ernst Wilhelm or Arminty Brown, for these two were to be left to their own fates or someone else's prayers. Noelle firmly believed that prayers, like butter, must not be spread too thinly. Her gods, she knew, were miserly in parceling out blessings.

Duncan could have cut the route to Canada without his eyes. He had traversed it many times leading others along routes through New York to the border crossing. But his role in this plan was to stay back and muddy the water.

Few but Noelle knew Duncan had been a conductor for years. Ever else he was or had been, he was a smuggler of people and goods.

Dossie packed up cooked eggs and some fatback and dried meat and many, many hoecakes. She added potatoes and apples as an afterthought. She envisioned them eating potatoes roasted over a fire that Jan had raised, Arminty's strength building up because of the hot vittles.

At the dock on the border, the boys were falsely jocular so no one would weep.

"When he's grown up, send your son back to learn the business, Papa," Pet said shyly and slapped his father's shoulder. Ernst Wilhelm pulled him and held him and kissed his lips and ruffled his hair as if he were a very small boy. Ernst had been far younger than Petrus when he had left Dresden so many years ago. How could he have known he'd have so beautiful a son as Petrus and leave him to take another child to another country?

"Yes, Uncle Ernst, send your son back to us when he is big," Jan said and clapped Pet's back. His uncle pulled him close and kissed him and bade him take care of Petrus and Hat and himself and all.

The cousins were raucous on the trip home. They were drunk when they left Rochester riding southward. They became drunker still, stopping at taverns in New York. When they got to Schoharie and smelled the fragrance of the hops barns, they sobered some and got to longing for their home. Jan knew Pet was grieved at parting from his papa. He, too, was sorry to see the old bear depart for Canada.

As the boat docked in Canada, Arminty rose and stood beside her man. Yes, indeed, now he was hers. She trembled. She became nervous of her appearance. Allowing that she had been ill and jailed, she wanted to be pretty now that she was drawing up and assuming a new role. She was soon to be a mother. Her man had shot a man to keep her from going south when he could simply have tossed her aside. The facts were deeply sobering. What would happen next? The equation was simple. For what Ernst had done thus far, Arminty would belong to him for as long as he wanted. She was standing next to him in broad daylight! She brushed her clothes and patted her hair, then moved closer to him and picked at his coat to remove lint and flecks. She lost balance with the movements of the boat, and Ernst grasped her gently to brace her.

"Are you ready, Mrs. Brown?" he asked with true kindness, for he was sympathetic to her nerves and delicate situation. They had decided to take the name Brown—the name Arminty had used since leaving Tennessee—so that they would become Mr. and Mrs. Ernest Brown when they entered their new country.

"Yes, Mr. Brown, I am ready," Arminty answered in a familiar, cheerful voice that sounded like a small dinner bell. It was the lighthearted, delicate, and musical voice she'd acquired and practiced to please her man. The return of this sound was reassuring to Ernest Brown. He took Arminty's elbow and led her from the boat. He stepped on the dock first, sighed deeply, and reached both hands to assist his new wife. He felt guilty about Hat and Petrus. Why couldn't he be some Oriental potentate with as many wives as he wanted? Why couldn't he have them all? Often it is the hard choices that are very simply and unequivocally made.

8

DUNCAN RODE UP TO the Wilhelm house to find Hat. She was seated on the top step of the porch with her skirt drawn over her legs, tucked up under her like a child, like a woman rarely does after her body gets out in front of her.

"Gwan in an' get your bonnet, Pippy. I'll show you a patch of berries that has sprung up new," Duncan said with exuberance. He sat on his horse and called to her. "Stir yourself, girl. Hurry up!"

Hat got her bonnet and let Duncan pull her up onto the saddle in front of him.

"He ain't keeping my boy, is he?" Hat asked with a quavering voice so unlike herself. Sitting sidesaddle, she nestled against Duncan.

"No, Hattie. Your boy is coming back." Duncan rode uphill and around bends at top speed until she laughed and held to the horse's mane and begged him to stop. They came upon a crag set in a hillock that had been a childhood hideaway and in it was an abundance of blueberry bushes. They dismounted, filled their buckets, and filled their mouths.

"Hattie, if Wilhelm hadn't brought you back I would've spent my life looking for you. I woulda gone south to get you," Duncan said solemnly.

"I know that, Punkin," Hat answered, indulging herself in berries. "I've lost my husband, Duncan."

"Yes, Hattie, but you're still as pretty as a button," Duncan said and smiled.

She kissed Duncan with her arms encircling his neck. "We better get back, though, 'less your wife puts you out," Hat joked. "I've got work to do. I've got to keep an eye on things until my son comes back." Duncan heard determination and was pleased. They mounted the horse as before, spilling many berries and giggling like youngsters.

Dossie looked out at their approach. As Duncan and Hat came up, she contained her enthusiasm at some effort. Duncan and Hat were so happily engaged that Dossie did not want to disturb them — to break them apart. She was still cautious to presume with her husband and his sister. Hat needed Duncan, especially now. Dossie waited and let them ride up and tie the horse. She stood when Hat came onto the porch, and Hat nodded to her with formal courtesy as the woman of the house. Hat held out the buckets of blueberries and grinned.

"We want some cream, Dossie Bird," Duncan called.

"No cream!" Hat shouted. "Duncan wants to eat them berries right out of the bowl. Nay, Duncan, we will wait for a pie."

"It look like we could have many a pie. Look like y'all got a secret place for berries. These're the bes' ever seen." Dossie caught their merriment.

"Shall I turn you a crust, Miz Smoot? When we was children we had to pick double what was needed 'cause Punkin always ate half of what we pick," Hat teased as she tied an apron around her waist. "Dossie, when I was small as a top, I loved my brother so much I followed him all over the house, the yard, the bushes. When he go pee, I go behind him. Cissy used to

switch my butt for always trying to trail after Duncan. Me and
Cissy were kept nearer the house, and we had to work the
chickens and cook. We did sewing and mending, too. Most
everything we did was in the house and in the yard and the
nearby vegetable patch and the animal pens. We didn't get to
run off fishing and go hunting. We didn't go tracking and riding horses. We wasn't allowed to ride with Papa and the uncles
up to the Indian camp."

"Aw, Pippy," Duncan cut in.

"I told Duncan once that I would marry him when I grew
up. He say, 'No, Pippy. You my sister. I can't fuck you. I got to
have a wife to make babies with. You got to get a man of your
own.' He laughed at me. He told Cissy what I said, and she
boxed my ears. Then she demanded that I only sleep in her bed
and I must work next to her. I had to stay well within her distance for shouting or I would get my ears slapped. It was really
Cissy that loved Duncan so much that she wanted him for her
own and wanted to trail off after him — hunting, fishing, doing
all of the boy things. She was the better fisherman. She was
good at trappin' squirrels and possums, too. She wasn't 'lowed
to, of course.

"When I got bigger Cissy wouldn't let Duncan and me put
our heads together on a thing without her. One day Punkin
was letting it go next to the barn door and I was standing there
talking to him. I must've been looking at his jasper 'cause when
Cissy came up, she grabbed me at the shoulders and pulled me
around and slapped me until my head rang with pounding
bells. 'Don't you never do that, Hat!' she hollered. 'You ain't
s'posed to look at or touch a man's member 'less you be a dirty
girl!' I said back when I could catch my breath to do so, 'Cissy,
Punkin ain't no man!'" Hat rolled out her crust with an

explosion of laughter and loose flour rose in white bursts about her, landing on her apron.

"Hush, Pippy. Gwan now," Duncan hollered in from the porch, and the women guffawed.

"You might ast why my papa sent me off with a slickster. It was 'cause I started to show womanliness and I was a pretty girl. My father's youngest brother started to notice me. Papa was concerned. He looked around for a husband for me. He didn't much care as long as he wouldn't have a problem with his brother. See, he worked his own little brother like a mule, and he needed him. He didn't need me. He had Cissy for keepin' the house. So he married me off. Duncan was 'way in the mines, or he would have saved me. Cissy cried and begged Papa, but he didn't care about her either. My mama might have saved me, but she was dead."

"Aw, Pippy, it's done and finish now," Duncan called out. He knew the hurts that Hat had suffered for being a pretty little girl coveted indecently. He was the one to have rescued her, but he hadn't been able to.

Was it 'cause he was scared or in Charlie Tougle's thrall that he hadn't stepped in to save Cissy? And Pippy paid so dearly. And Cissy paid.

Duncan stood just inside the door and spoke quietly, "I'm sorry, Hattie."

"Which part of our lands is Cissy's share, Duncan?" Hat asked, sloughing off weepiness. "Shouldn't Jan build a house and think of tomorrow? You better tell him, push him to build a house and settle down. Jan needs to get a good girl and make some babies. We need some babies around here to keep us company." Hat spoke in a loose fashion as though she'd suddenly become tipsy. "You, too, Duncan. You and Dossie can make some babies." Hat went to Dossie and grasped her arms. "Dossie, you got a job to do, girl. We need a baby."

"Aw hush, Pippy," Duncan said, finally becoming truly annoyed. Hat's voice was beginning to ruffle his nerves. He lit a cigar because he was no longer in a conciliatory mood and smirked to think that Dossie would have to suffer his stinking breath. He intended to drink and smoke cigars and fuck her because she must give up her bed to Hat and sleep with him.

When Duncan was done drinking and smoking, he went to the patch alongside the house and chewed some mint. Then he returned to the house and found that Dossie and Hat had retired into Dossie's bed and were soundly asleep.

Red, one of Mensah Paul's youngsters, came up in the first light of day. "Mr. Duncan Smoot, sir," he called in a well-modulated voice as he came onto the porch at the back of the house. Dossie shook water from her hands and wiped moisture from her face. She had heard Red's approach and cleaned her face to meet him.

"What all is the matter, boy?" Dossie asked.

"Papa says a lawman from the town is heading up to see Miz Hat. He headin' here if he don't fin' her home at her place."

"Duncan," Dossie called back into the house in a quiet, direct voice. "Come, boy, and sit." Before she'd spoken his name a second time, Duncan had risen, called to Hat, and taken up his shotgun.

"Red, gwan back and tell your papa to come up quiet and stay hid," Duncan said. Dossie put a corn cake in the boy's hand.

"Mr. Smoot, I ain't come with no force of arms, so I'll ask you to lower your shotgun," the lawman called out as he rode up and saw Duncan standing on the porch. Duncan lowered the gun very slowly. "I'm here to ask you if Miz Wilhelm is here. I'd like to have a speak with her. If you don' min' I'd like to see is she here, sir?" The sheriff spoke deferentially, respectfully.

The shotgun, the defiant stance, the suspicious stare, were all a show. Duncan knew the man had come alone. Everyone living up and down the mountain knew that. And he came confidently, fearlessly, with no bluster, so they also knew that he was — or had been — one of them.

The man dismounted, and Duncan said, "Come up, sir. Mrs. Wilhelm is visiting. She's not feelin' so well, though." Dossie would have laughed at the sound of Duncan's voice if the air was not so thick with danger. "Dossie, give the sheriff a cup of coffee, won't you? Hattie, come on out and talk with the sheriff," Duncan called out so amiably, so falsely friendly-like.

Dossie was happy Duncan gave her a job to do so that she was not standing and staring at the sheriff. Her heart felt like it would stop when she recognized the man who had grabbed her arm in the alley while the fight was raging in the tavern. She was so shocked she might have turned to a block of salt.

"You got a familiar face, Sheriff. Your mother is Bessie Stringley?" Duncan asked, eager to exploit his knowledge of the man's background.

"Yes, sir," the sheriff answered. "Now she is Branch, sir. My papa is Emil Branch, as am I."

"Emil Branch. I'm pleased to know you," Duncan said. He reached to shake the sheriff's hand and led him to sit in a porch chair. "This is my wife, Dossie, sir," Duncan pronounced grandly when Dossie offered up the sheriff's coffee.

"How do, ma'am." The sheriff nodded his head respectfully. His eyes lingered on her face for a split second longer than they might otherwise. Yes, he had seen her face before. Yes, he remembered her. She had a quiet, demure, butter-wouldn't-melt-in-her-mouth manner now, but he had seen her in the alley behind the Irish drinking hole when her husband's nephews were getting shellacked. Instinct told him that the fight had started on account of her. Ah, these jumble niggers and African Indians and subversive white men don't accept that there are some places they are not welcome!

Dossie was struck to think that the sheriff must be a man from Russell's Knob. His manner told on him. He was not a lowlander, though he was their sheriff. Her thoughts became consumed with hoping that the subject of the tavern and those doings would not come up.

Emil Branch decided that Duncan Smoot was a lucky man. His wife was pretty. And he had had his hands on her! He was not truly surprised to find her here. These people are mixers, amalgamators. Everybody who knows of them knows they take in runaways. And yes, his mama had come from up this way. Her people were among the whiter-colored ones, and she'd left and married a lowlander and lived like an ordinary white.

His gaze returned to Dossie surreptitiously. Miz Smoot's figure was full and well presented. Though her mien was quiet, composed, he imagined that if she smiled her face would spring to life. Her eyes were inquisitive despite her good manners.

"I know your people, sir. Your mama was a very pretty young woman, son," Duncan bantered, and his words startled the young sheriff. Branch's cheeks became red; he looked again at Miz Smoot, then lowered his eyes.

"She still is, sir," Branch replied. "Very pretty, sir." His voice remained courteous, though it had a slight bristle that a stranger had mentioned his mother so familiarly. The show of pique—the possessiveness—was a tell that Duncan noted. The sheriff was not duplicitous then. He was letting his honest feelings show. Duncan thought that he could read Emil Branch and perhaps trust him.

"I'll warrant she is. We ain't seen her around here in a long time, though. Tell her to come home and see her people. We want to see her," Duncan said. He took up the role of sweet patriarch with the young sheriff.

"I will give her your regard, sir," Branch said, then turned his attention to Hat. "Ma'am, Miz Wilhelm, may I ask you where is your husband?"

At the question Harriet Wilhelm did something wholly unexpected by the others. She burst forth with a loud fit of crying. "I don' know! I don' know!" she wailed. It was a shocking departure from the dignified reticence that Harriet Smoot Wilhelm was known for. She shrieked, "He's gone off from me! I 'on't know to where!"

"Fix her some tea, Dossie. Won't you fix Hattie some tea? It may make her calm," Duncan said as though they had been nursing Hat's hysteria throughout the night. Dossie wondered when the two had agreed on this subterfuge. "I b'lieve I tol' you, Emil—Sheriff Branch—Miz Wilhelm ain't feelin' so good now," Duncan continued with a deadly solemn face.

"Mr. Smoot, does she have any idea where her husband, Mr. Ernst Wilhelm, is at?" the sheriff asked Duncan as if Hat had gone insensible.

"Sheriff Branch, my sister don't know a thing about where her husband has gone."

"There is a story," the sheriff began and was quickly stopped by Duncan's raised hand.

"Sheriff, my sister has heard the story. You see what it done to her to hear these things. We don' know what Mr. Wilhelm did or where he gone since he lef' here some days ago."

Dossie brought the hot tea to Hat, who jerked and whimpered but held the steaming cup competently and no drop was spilled.

"Mr. Smoot, whereabouts are the boys? Miz Wilhelm's son, Petrus, and your nephew, Jan. Where they gone, sir?"

"Now, Emil, them boys is grown. They ain't gon' tell Miz Wilhelm and me whereabouts they going for a fine time," Duncan said smoothly. He smiled and elicited a smile from the sheriff.

"Where you think they went, Mr. Smoot?" Emil Branch came back at Duncan with a smile still on his lips.

"Oh, they went to New York, of course. They crossed the line to see what pussy's like up there," Duncan pronounced coolly, and the young sheriff's ears became crimson. "They're likely to be gone awhile."

Ha! The old man had done it. The sheriff couldn't continue now with his examination of the wily old codger without pursuing this unsavory conversation in front of the women. The old man had seen his embarrassment — seen his color. Is reason enough to paint your face when going for battle! These old Indian niggers know what makes a white man blush, and they know how to push him. Emil Branch fought to regain his composure.

He should never have let the old man talk up his mama. Had Duncan seen the hungry way he'd looked at his missus? Emil Branch fumed internally. He would have to drop his inquiry for the time because he was flustered. He couldn't escape the mountain child's reverence for elders. Ah, old Duncan Smoot had pinned back Emil Branch's ears! His defenses were down.

"I hope don't nobody else come up here lookin' for Mr. Wilhelm, a somebody whose mama ain't from roun' here," the sheriff said resignedly as he stood.

"They wouldn'a got so far as this, Emil," Duncan replied.

"You ain't meanin' to kill lawmen, are you Mr. Smoot?"

"You have some pie?" Duncan answered. "Dossie, bring the sheriff some pie," he commanded. "Wrap up some eggs and a pie for the sheriff's mama, Dossie! I'll freshen your coffee, Sheriff Emil. You eat blueberry pie while my wife makes up the basket." Duncan put the lawman back into his chair with a fatherly slap on his shoulder.

Dossie exited to the henhouse. She hitched up her skirt when she got out of the sight of the men and ran about collecting eggs. She was anxious to have the sheriff gone. Here was the man who had torn her dress! Maybe he had the shawl? Though there was no direct connection between them, there was the fact that he had touched her. She was frightened of him and frightened to consider what may happen if Duncan discovered this. She put the eggs in a basket and wrapped up a blueberry pie from the safe for the sheriff's mama.

Despite Branch's great annoyance and his eagerness to leave, he enjoyed the bracing cup of coffee and the pie. Here in the highlands there was a crispness to the air that embellished coffee. Of course "thiefing" the Jamaican beans when they came off canal boats guaranteed a good cup. Highland water is good, too, and good water makes good coffee. And women in the highlands could turn a handful of berries into ambrosia! The sheriff wiped his mouth and bid the women farewell with cordiality and some reluctance. He nodded to Hat, though she never lifted her eyes to his. He inclined his head at Dossie with an impressive show of courtesy.

"Mr. Smoot, thank ye and good day, sir," Branch said and took the basket for his mama and hitched it to his pommel.

These mountain people — these hideouts — these residents of Russell's Knob are a jumbled-up people, Emil Branch thought. They're made up of whatever is thrown together in a pile. They're the children of amalgamators. They're the children of whites who won't stay white and reds who won't stay red and blacks who won't stay black. Call them jumbles or hodgepodge people or whatever harsh moniker you can stick onto them. His own mama had come from here amongst them. Thank God his father had whitened him and raised him amongst decent, white folk. Emil Branch realized that he despised the bit of himself that connected him to Russell's Knob, though he loved his mother. But these mountain people are audacious. They are proud. They are straight-backed fuckers.

The sheriff rode away from Duncan Smoot's house scratching at himself gently like a man thinking about something pretty. Emil mused lasciviously on Miz Dossie Smoot's dark black breasts that were likely capped with delightfully darker, puckered nipples. They were sweet on the lips, he was sure. He felt his annoyance rising. She was too young to be married to that old man. "That old nigger acts like a king up in these parts — these old backward hollows where no sane white man would come," Emil fussed to his horse.

Emil Branch had always lived as a white, though he knew his mama was not a white woman. She was pale skinned and had come down out of the mountains to marry a lowlander white man she loved. But Duncan Smoot had pissed him. Calling up his mama's name and saying her maiden name with a kind of possessiveness that suggested the man had known his mother very well. How dare he! But Duncan Smoot had dared—he had dared to impugn her whiteness. How dare he suggest that his mama was other than she'd been living! His mama had not denied her home. She had simply left.

Emil Branch rode back to Paterson musing on his mama. She was never completely at a remove from her mountain beginnings, and she had sneaked and taught her son some of the ways. Running in her shadow most of the day in his earliest years, he'd learned his mountain manners. Over the years he'd become merely dutiful to the thickset, ivory-colored woman whose straight, black, ropey hair now had wisps of gray flecked throughout. Yes, she was still a very lovely woman to gaze on, though he did not see her often. Emil knew that she would raise her apron to wipe something moist from her hands at first sight of him. Her hands were always in something damp, and she always liked to dry them before touching him.

She was glad to see him and had moist hands that she dried as he approached. She took Miz Dossie Smoot's basket happily. She was surprised and a little thrilled to know he'd gone a mountain to speak with her People.

"Miz Smoot. Ma'am," Emil Branch called out when he came up behind Dossie on the next market day. Hat thought she ought to appear busy so as to seem neither concerned for her son's whereabouts nor cognizant of her husband's. So Hat and Dossie had set up as usual in their accustomed place. Dossie had her back to the pathway that wound behind the market area. She started at the sheriff's voice and turned quickly and had a momentary look of alarm. She lowered her eyes as soon as she saw Emil Branch's face. She replied in a friendly voice, "How do, Sheriff."

"Miz Smoot, I know you'll never call me ought but sheriff. But just know that my name is Emil to my friends," he said in a self-assured manner that was like Jan's. It was because of this similar tone that Dossie felt compelled to answer, "How you do, Sheriff Emil?" Oh, she caught up her own breath and held it. She hadn't meant to use his name. No matter that he'd asked her to. She had not meant to cross over the line and call him by his call. She halted and stepped back and looked again at her shoe tops. It was wrong for her to have said his call name and have it tossing around in her head. She wanted to shrink and go back to her duties.

Emil Branch advanced on Dossie and lifted the market basket. He'd seen the cringing look before. In fact, it was the look he got from all the colored except the tough old birds like Duncan Smoot or the arrogant cocks like Jan Smoot and Petrus Wilhelm. Emil Branch suddenly wanted to stand up close enough to smell Miz Dossie Smoot's body and think of touching it and then be able to recollect the smell and the touching picture for later on. He'd felt her in his grip once! It was delicious to think of it. He hadn't meant to tear her sleeve. It was accidental, but it was a beautiful, erotic serendipity! The sound of the cloth ripping and the shocked, frightened look on her face had given him a bone. Hadn't been for the brawl he'd have taken her in the alley right then. And, he realized, he wanted her to know it.

"Mama was truly thankful for your eggs, Miz Smoot." The sheriff caught sight of Mrs. Wilhelm, who looked up when she heard his voice. Her eyes did not fall to her shoes. She looked straight at him, then looked away toward the middle distance. She did not confront him, but she did not cower. Her placid stare was like her brother's and it acted as a caution.

"My mama wondered if you might 'low her to buy from you. If you would be kind and put aside a basket of your eggs, I will come on market day and fetch them for her." He again used his pleasant, reassuring voice.

"Sir, I be happy to." Dossie then took the basket, lined it with straw, and asked, "How many, sir?"

"She says ten — one for each day and three for a cake on Sunday." He laughed and again called Hat's attention.

"She would best take a dozen, sir, to be sure," Dossie said, a bit overproud of her counting and reading skills and her cleverness in commerce.

She placed twelve eggs in the basket and handed it to the sheriff. He touched his hat brim and lay ten cents onto the crate that she stood near. "Good day, Miz Smoot. Good day, Miz Wilhelm," he said and took leave.

At the following market day, Emil Branch did appear again with a basket to buy eggs for his mama. He was friendly. He was deferential to Hat and excessively polite toward Sally. His true attention was, without doubt, focused on Dossie.

"How is Mr. Smoot, ma'am?" he asked, to draw her into a converse.

But it was Hat who broke in on his plan by answering. "He is very well, sir," she said.

Emil Branch touched his hat brim with politeness. He put his dime on the crate when given his eggs, but he did allow his finger to brush one of Dossie's when the basket passed between them. Did she flinch at his touch? He couldn't be sure if it was not just simple surprise that he had breached etiquette.

The sheriff noticed a change on the next market day. Miz Smoot and Miz Wilhelm and the young girl, Sally Vander, were accompanied by Jan Smoot. Though the young man appeared to be lounging idly at the wagon, he was watching his uncle's wife like a guard dog. Emil Branch got tense with resentment and thought that Jan Smoot was a haughty, jumbled-up cur with tawny skin and curly hair in need of bear grease to press it down.

He was cordial to the women and pretended to ignore that Jan was looking at him. But Jan was not deferring to him. It was that mountain pride that gave Jan Smoot the stuffing to act like a white man in the town. *He figures he's a different kind a nigger and the rules don't apply to him!* Branch mused to himself.

In Jan's presence, Emil Branch did not even smile at Dossie, and she did not smile at him. She only accepted the basket, counted out the eggs, nestled them safely, and handed the basket back to him. Her fingers slipped away from the basket quickly so that he could not touch them. The sheriff walked off with only a slight inclination of his head, then caught the sideways glance of Jan Smoot. He turned back to Dossie and spoke loudly. "Ma'am, my mama credits your good eggs for building her vigor. She misses the clean air of the highlands, she says. I'll come again if you don't mind. I will take your eggs to her." He spoke ceremoniously, with an excess of courtliness that startled Dossie and pissed Jan.

"Oh, yes, sir," Dossie replied as if she were afraid of his displeasure, and he was encouraged by a spontaneous courtesy.

"Until next week then, ma'am," he said and tipped his hat again.

Dossie allowed a small expression on her lips — a small jot of courtesy. Did she want his attention, he wondered. It would be much easier to seduce her if she actually did, but not requisite. He was as easily aroused by reluctance and fear in women as by willingness.

PART FOUR

"The Grandmothers say that when you get your sweet soul's delight—your one special jot of luck—it is a dossie." Hat spoke and used her hands in a movement that seemed like throwing a powder into the air. "A dossie," she said while flinging her fingers apart. "A dossie is an ember in the hearth that snaps and pops in among the flames and, though small, keeps the fire roaring. It's a small, brown bird that answers your hunger. A dossie is a precious thing—a small found luck. When a man in Russell's Knob considers himself lucky, he says he has a dossie in his pocket." Hat smiled girlishly.

"True?" Dossie asked in genuine wonderment. "How you think my Ooma knows this? She's been nowhere near to here."

Hat stood and cupped each elbow in the palm of her hands crosswise her chest in her stance for the serious consideration of facts.

"Well, the Grandmothers know it all. Maybe Grandmother came to her in a dream and gave her the name. We are pleased to have you. You are a found luck for the Smoots," Hat said and smiled with satisfaction.

Dossie. She recalled that she'd been stopped in her tracks—mired in her thoughts. She puzzled. Had Grandmother called on her Ooma in a dream? Bil and Ooma had never said a thing about Grandmother that she could recall. Can Grandmother know about them and guide them and them not know it? She'd wanted to ask Hat, *Who is Grandmother? Is there a way to know her when you see her?*

Instead she asked, "Ma'am, what is a gal's good luck called?"

"Ah," Hat answered. "It can also be a dossie, of course. But a good woman wants a nest, a comfort. She wants to have her children and make a nice home and build up her people. So she dresses her hair and plumps up her tits and swishes and sways about and smiles and waits patiently and, if she makes a good, sturdy weir, a pretty skimmer fish will get caught in it." Hat chuckled and squeezed Dossie's jaws. "A woman's luck then is called a jimmer. You hear Honey Vander call her husband Jimmer? His given name is William." Again Hat used her pretty hands to illustrate. She held them one atop the other and moved them over her lower self like a fat, old man coming to the dinner table.

9

DOSSIE RECOLLECTED THE PRETTY story that Hat had told on that day so long back. Hat had used her hands to point up a tale of luck and the Grandmothers and all such other fanciful nonsense. A dossie! Was she the lucky one or the one who brought luck for someone else? Why hadn't she got a jimmer then? Why couldn't she get a fulfillment? Were the gods of all the other people so dead set against the Smoots that they worked against them thriving? Was she making herself worried unnecessarily?

Jan drew in his breath and spoke into Dossie's breasts as if he were unable to raise his eyes to her face. "Please don't make me do this 'cause I won't be able to stop it if you ask. An' I won't be able to stop even if I hear you ask and know you mean it. I'll keep on anyway," he said. "You better be sure. No squealing about force later on. You better stop me now!"

Dossie did not, of course. She had taken off her bodice and shown him what he'd come to see. She made his life complete with her hardheaded plans.

The puzzling thing that made Jan dizzy, made him aroused, made him ashamed, was that all of the shuffling and sorting and pulling together amongst the Smoots was pushing him out of their circle, and Dossie was the root cause of all the shuffling. And now she wanted a fulfillment. She wanted him to complete her dream. All he wanted was Dossie, wanted to fill her like a Christmas stocking, wanted to eat her like a cake!

He confronted her in the chicken yard. He came to stand before her and block her path. He moved in front of her and seemed to be pulling her into a dance. He stood the ground and would not be avoided. She was surprised at how wide Jan was. She thought of him as tall and slender like Duncan. But here he was taking up the width of the yard. When she turned away and walked into the chicken house, Jan followed.

"What the matter, girl? You sick? You sorrowful for what?" he asked.

"Watch yourself, Brother. I'm not your young sister no more. I'm a married woman, and I got a woman's troubles," Dossie answered.

"I s'pose if you wasn't married you'd be pleased to have your troubles," Jan said knowingly. He brought back a feeling of camaraderie and reminded Dossie with his tone that they were friends and cousins.

"I want it so bad!" she said with a frustrated belch that filled the chicken house with a sour scent. "Is a child. I want to give him my baby. Is the only gift I can give him. He's got everything else. I am tryin', Jan." Dossie turned to face him and spoke as if they were continuing a previous confabulation.

"I do everything he want me to do to please him. I do everything that Miz Sienna says. She has a yard full of children. She ought to know." Dossie's unhappiness spilled out suddenly like milk overturned and running off the edge of a table.

"I done all," she continued. "I feed myself secret teas and I rest myself like she said. She say that soon as the first one comes

I won't be able to stop them." Dossie chuckled and swiped her face. "I touched her bed for luck, Jan," she said as she turned her face up to his.

"I want to fix myself to be like other women. If a man whispers in their ear, they are all filled up with a child! How come not for me, Jan? I am wishin' and prayin' for a fulfillment. I want my baby so bad. It's like a hive of bees in my head. I am always thinkin' and hopin'." Dossie moved among the chickens and seemed ready to kick at them.

"Noelle would say you must fool the ancestors. You must act like you don't care if you're fulfilled. She says they want to surprise you with your dreams, to take you unawares. So don't beg 'em," Jan said in the damnably contrary and mysterious way he shared with Noelle. He pinched Dossie's cheek. It was the same advice that Duncan gave.

"Aye, but she don't have a baby herself," Dossie came back, then regretted her snappish words when she saw Jan's smile fade a bit.

"That ought to tell you something."

"Aye?"

"She don't want a child. She's got all the child she wanted with me," Jan answered good-naturedly.

"Miz Sienna said to hold my knees up after and let his seeds take they time to find a comfortable place. Hat says that, too. But Duncan..." Dossie stopped talking when she saw Jan's eyes get very large with discomfort.

"Why won't Noelle take me to see the old women healers? Hat says they could be a help with a woman's concerns, but it takes an anointed woman to carry you there. Noelle act like she don't want me to go. She still dislike me because Duncan married me? Is not my fault," Dossie said. She looked at Jan with the disingenuous, self-satisfied look of a successfully seductive girl. "Is nothing you can do to make my case with Noelle?" she appealed.

Jan was ashamed to know what he knew, and so he thought he ought to do whatever was wanted to help Dossie. An' Hat ought to know it and tell her. But she believed only what she cared to about her brother. Jan knew it for a fact. Jan fought inside himself to know whether it was his naked want or his feeling for fairness that agitated him. Didn't Dossie deserve to know? Would Duncan give Dossie the truth and risk making her disappointed with him? Had Duncan got the balls to tell her about himself? Not likely. Jan wished he could be happy that Uncle had failed at some big thing at last. But he couldn't be pleased to see Dossie torn up. He loved her so much. He wanted her to be completely happy.

And then he decided to tell her.

"He can't do it? What you mean, Jan?" Dossie asked.

"He ain't got what it takes," Jan said.

"He does, too!" she retorted.

Jan got pissed then that Dossie didn't understand. "I mean I think you can fuck him until you turn green with wear and you'll never make a baby with him. It is hopeless, girl."

"What you sayin'? You know this is true?"

"His seeds are bad. He is without the proper pepper," Jan said with a fiendish chuckle. Dossie raised her hand and slapped him on his impudent jaw for the insult to her husband.

"He didn't tell you?" Jan accepted her slap, held on to her hand, and kissed it. "Of course, he wouldn't tell his pretty prize a thing like that." Jan's unruly feelings took a meaner turn. "I mean, of course a man knows things like this even if his gal don't. Uncle'll do anything not to seem less a man in your eyes. He knows his sauces are no good for making babies. But you'll get a baby eventually if you're naughty or if you take some-body's baby from under a bush. Or you can raise a baby whose mama got killed like Noelle did."

Dossie sucked in her wind in absolute bewilderment at Jan's words. She hadn't considered this. That there was this flaw, a failing? Duncan Smoot was without flaw in her mind so that her reaction was to disbelieve. But it confirmed a suspicion of her own and it explained what Hat and Noelle had whispered about. There were also whispers that Nancy Siscoe had uttered at the nuptials. When you come to understand and acknowl-edge a thing that changes the course of your life in your mind's eye, you are left standing stiff with an open mouth.

"They coulda told me. They raised me," she bleated.

"Noelle don't give up Uncle's secrets, and An' Hat's his sister. She tries to act like she don't believe it. It was for him to tell you, little girl. You know that. It's on account of a fever Uncle had when he came back from the mines. It left his seeds flat, though he is still much a man. He has even been to a doctor in town." Jan's voice began to soften. All trace of taunting was gone. "I used to dream Noelle would bring up a baby with Uncle and settle down and we all could be one little family together. I think Noelle dreamed it, too."

"All of you know it, but you don't tell me." Dossie sounded folded in and greatly peeved. Sulking about it made her feel small and sadder still, for she knew she was a lucky woman. She had some ease from drudgery, and her husband was atten-tive. But now that she knew he couldn't do it, she felt a crushing sense of ruined hope and a crushing responsibility to keep it secret. She couldn't give up her husband's secret. She must, at least, do as well as Noelle had done. She wanted to give Duncan a gift of legacy, to build a line and fill her porch with her loving accomplishments. Now she knew she would be a childless, pitiful, secretive creature!

And they all knew it! Did they laugh? Perhaps Noelle did . . . and Nancy Siscoe.

Jan's peeved tone and acid words cut in on her reverie. "He has spoiled you. What makes you think loving him and marrying him would mean you was supposed to have it all the way you wanted? You still think he is a god and you're going to be God's wife? You want to be the mother of all God's children?"

"Once even Noelle said it was my destiny," Dossie said. She fingered the ties on her bodice.

"Well, she was drunk and so are you." Jan laughed loud enough to flush birds from the trees.

Indeed Dossie was drunk with it now, her plan, her strategy. She wanted to be Duncan's child's mother — the one wonderful thing he couldn't do for himself. She sat with Jan on the porch until it was no longer possible to see.

"You give me a gift, Jan," Dossie said bluntly from out of the dark.

"Must I buy it or steal it or kill it for you? What gift you want?"

"You the only one who can do it." The words were so completely the ones Jan would have chosen for Dossie to say that he became frightened his senses were gone off. "He will think he did it," Dossie said.

"Why you don't ask Pet to do you this favor?" he replied. "He's proven." Dossie said nothing. "Ah, but you're thinkin' I look like him. I'm a sure thing. You pretty hardheaded about your big plan."

"Yes," Dossie said with deadly quiet vehemence.

"You willin' to lie baldly and keep up lying until you die?" Jan asked her.

"Yes," she declared.

"Fair is fair. He never told you about being sick and unable," Jan said, testing all of her sores. "So you got a right to lie to him." Jan finished in a perversely amiable way that worried Dossie. "He knows he can't do it, little girl," he said, calling her "little girl" now to keep her his baby sis for the moment. Oh, but she was a woman he wanted to fuck with every inch of himself—to know his jasper had disappeared all the way into her. She caused him a furious itch in his leathers, and he was sure he had a baby for her. But did he dare do this to her and himself? She was such a curious one. She pretended to have a wide-eyed innocence of everything, yet she was bold enough to think up a scheme to get him to make her a baby.

She don't give a fig for the damage it'll do to my soul, Jan mused. Her and Noelle were troublesome women. It was just Uncle's bad luck that he'd got them both. Too bad Uncle's little dossie had a will and a destiny of her own.

Jan decided he would do it. Even so he knew it was not the right thing to do. To love Dossie was to pull from Uncle. That couldn't be avoided. To choose Uncle over her was to betray her hopes and would be as if he loved her less. And he did not love her less.

And how did they know for certain that she was not Jan's true destiny instead of Uncle's? After all, if it was a Smoot augury, then it could be as easily his destiny. He was a Smoot, too.

And Dossie seemed unconcerned with sinning as long as she

got her prize. She was so damnably self-righteous in this thing. Women think fucking is easy for men, because men are always liking to do it and want to keep at it. It ain't so easy. And women think easy is casual anyway, but it ain't casual either all the time. Him fucking her to make a child for Uncle could be a grand plan, but it could be a mess. Jan knew that. Duncan fucking Gin Barlow's daughter had become a mess that had ended all chances that Noelle would take up housekeeping with Duncan. The old man had forced Jan to lie about it and keep on lying to Noelle. It was a cruelty done to a small boy who loved the woman he was betraying. So the old man was due for comeuppance — for a lie or two in the service of somebody else.

"You give me the baby, Jan, and I'll make him believe it is a miracle. You do your part and I will make him believe it. I'm younger than Noelle," Dossie said carefully, not wanting to rouse Jan's defenses again. "I'm more constant than any of his other gals. I was meant for him. He says I'm a wood witch or a conjurer because I make him love me. I'll make him believe I am a wood witch. Duncan says a wood witch is a pretty thing that comes out of a forest to snare a man." Dossie snorted a little, intimate laugh.

"Is he chucking your chin and kissing your neck when he says this?" Jan asked impishly, with some spite for her self-satisfaction. Dossie wondered that he knew his uncle's manner so well.

"A wood witch looks like a doe with plump sides or a rabbit the size of a dog. Sometimes she appears like a pretty, pretty woman and she will make a man think the sun rises and sets on her face," Dossie came back at him in a string of words that he knew to be Uncle's own.

"In that case Uncle is right," Jan answered seriously. "There is a wood witch operatin' hereabouts."

"I'll make him believe I succeed where other women fell down," Dossie said with a startling tone of confidence and manipulation. And there wouldn't be a sin if she was not taking pleasure. Certainly it would be like putting the bull with the cow. Dossie resolved to cultivate thoughts to drive out any others. She decided not to say so to Jan because he might be mad if he knew that.

"You got the stuffing?" Jan asked sharply.

"Yes."

"Is't all for Uncle then? No itch to be naughty? No care for anybody else? No small corner in your heart for this dog, Dossie Blossom? Girl, it will take a time or two," Jan said. "You got the stomach to keep doin' it and foolin' him all the while? We got to do it when he is aroun', not when he's gone off, you know. He is got to think it could be him."

"Yes. I can do it," Dossie said.

"All right. You don' have to love me any, little sis. I love you. I want you to be happy. One of us got to be in love, though, if you want your baby to be beautiful. I'll love enough for us both." They exchanged smiles, and Jan left Dossie on Uncle's porch where she belonged.

Ah, Dossie smelled so good—so desirable. Jan thought of her as a soup of flower smells. Uncle was coddling her. He was keeping her in comfort like a good wife should be kept. Even her common, everyday dress was clean and fragrant. She didn't smell like no stable whore like Charity. What would happen to her if he took her away from Uncle? He knew he ought to do this thing to make her happy, to simply give her his gift. But what all would be let loose if he did?

10

EMIL BRANCH SAID THE day would come—that he alone would decide it. There was no choice for her if she wanted to avoid trouble. There were people who wanted to know about Duncan Smoot. They would like to know what was his true enterprise. Emil Branch knew Duncan was one who thiefed the barges and transport wagons. He knew Duncan was up to other stuff as well, and some people could profit by knowing it. He would have his way. There was no escape—no avoidance. If she screamed out . . . if she told on him. Go ahead and tell her husband or her cousins. Let them try to defend her honor and end with ropes around their necks. He said he knew about Owen Needham. He knew the fool had come a mountain to try to grab her back for a bounty. He knew the fool hadn't survived his consequences.

Emil Branch had been pleasant, friendly the first time he took Dossie's arm and led her away from her market stall. He asked her to come with him to speak with his mama. It was only a few steps, he said. He said his mama could not come out amongst the crowds at market for she was not very well. She wanted to meet the wife of Duncan Smoot. He'd said it sweetly—that his mama said this to him.

Then Emil Branch had made a lascivious sound and pushed

her against the slats of a shed at back of his mama's house. He fingered her, drawing circles around the nipples on her breasts and sticking his hands between her legs. He rubbed his hands all over her dress as if he meant to measure it for someone else or memorize the body beneath it. He smooch-kissed her neck and ears. He covered her face with his lips.

"You think because I don' haul him in for his thieving that I don't know he's a thief. I know what he is. I know all about him. And I know about you and where you come from and how he got you here. I want some. I'm gonna have it. And you ain' gon' tell him a thing. You do, I'll kill him. I'll kill 'em all."

Emil Branch sat on a barrel, smoked a cheroot, and watched the tears and gatherings from Dossie's nose drip off her face. She saw the sappy accumulation staining his pants and was shocked that his exhausted sausage had not penetrated.

"I wonder is Duncan Smoot really your husban'—a legal husban'? Did the old nigger take you in front of a preacher or a justice of the peace? Or did he just take you behind the barn and tell you you was his wife an' mus' do like he say? Look like the old nigger grab up a little girl and say she is his wife 'cause he wan' her. He ain' got no more legal right to keep you tied to him than I do if I wan' to. You sign any papers? Aw, a gal like you can' do no signin'. You don't know what man ain't got a paper on you—sayin' you b'long to him. You come outta slavery. I know it. You wearin' a fine dress now, but you was once upon a time somebody's miserable slave before he snatched you. I'ma grab you up an' take you away with me. I'ma go west an' take you with me for my appetite," Emil Branch taunted her.

The next time he took Dossie away from her stall and pushed

her into the shed, he accomplished a quick, sharp, painful penetration.

After this Dossie considered a pigsticker. She found a knife among the many and various ones that Duncan had. It was a more formal weapon than the cleavers and gutting knives she was familiar with. She drew it out of its sheath and familiarized herself with the way it felt. She cut herself to test it. Throughout a day of duties she stroked and handled the weapon. She ran through her mind should she or shouldn't she and when she would do it — at what point would she chance it — thinking to be forced no further. What was the mark?

Dossie had become enmeshed so quickly. Emil Branch had grabbed her in the alley and torn her dress, but he'd seemed almost apologetic when he came to Russell's Knob, when he came to the market stall. He'd fooled her. She'd thought she had no reason to fear him.

Take a stand with the knife. Threaten him enough that he would kill her. If he dropped her, then she could crawl and die somewheres that Duncan and 'em could find her body. Pray they make her sacred to themselves and speak of her again and again — like they do with Cissy and Lucy Smoot. And if he defiled her body pray God the skin would die away and rot quick and the bruises would disappear. Dossie promised herself that she would beg Emil Branch to leave her body in the highlands where the vultures could finish off her flesh when he has done. Then Duncan could see the unblemished bones if the merciful vultures picked her clean, and he would put them bones out next to the honored ancestors. It was a dreadful measure of Dossie's despair that she began to think that this death and only this could bring her out of the trouble. Further and further she descended under a cascade of bad thoughts on account of Emil Branch.

This was, of course, her retribution. She hadn't done it yet. But she had planned. She and Jan had discussed it. They had agreed that her desperate desire merited a desperate strategy. The Grandmothers were making her pay for the sin she was contemplating. Was that it?

"He got hidey-holes all aroun' town where he kin do his dirty business in," the pretty, plump-faced girl said when Jan paid her. Mattie Ricks, a hot-corn seller by occupation, was a member of a cadre of colored who watched goings-on on the streets of Paterson. People walked by her. Some bought her corn and butter. She noted them and could be hired to tail them.

"He likely got her in a alley behin' Caretaker Street an' the Market Street. His mama got a shed there. He worryin' her? He hurtin' her? Maybe, maybe not," she said. Jan scowled and Mattie Ricks laughed. Ah, she was young to be so coldly convinced! But Mattie Ricks knew what she was talking about. Few colored women who made a living on the streets of the town had not had some experience of Emil Branch. He was known to use his lawman's prerogatives for personal matters.

Dossie knew Emil Branch was dead because she was certain she would not be breathing and moving if he were alive. She took as evidence of her survival that her arm trembled, that the arm belonging to the hand that reached out and took up the knife and ran it into the man's back trembled. The courage that powered the knife's plunge into Emil Branch's back was forged from the conviction that she was willing to die to stop him. She was willing to die to save Jan's life.

When Emil Branch recovered from Jan's surprise attack, he took a low knife fighter's stance. His nakedness hung in defiance of all decency, and he moved at Jan.

Dossie grabbed up her knife that Emil Branch had thrown atop her clothes. He believed it was a sham when he stripped her and threw it aside. He considered her protests a game. A black gal will always want a white man, and every one of them wanted to be roughed up some.

Dossie closed her hand over the handle. And because she had been touching and stroking and practicing with it, it came into her hand smoothly, effortlessly.

She plunged it to the handle in Emil Branch's kidney and, like a practiced fighter, she followed the blade's plunge with thrusting her body behind it to sink it. She turned it in his flesh to quiet his nascent scream. But still there was screaming. She hollered out and sat back on her haunches.

Her thrust nearly finished Jan as well, though, for Emil Branch tightened his fingers as he was stabbed. For an excruciatingly long moment the three were tangled. Finally Jan was able to dislodge dead Emil Branch. He squatted.

"Cover yourself up, Dossie Bird," Jan said very quietly. It was a startle. She flinched at his words and reached to gather her clothes.

"Steady yourself," he commanded and gave her a pull from his flask. "Bear up," he managed despite his squeezed throat.

Then Jan proceeded in a string of actions that unfolded as they did for recognition that every action is one more advance toward death. What had they done and what will they do with dead Emil Branch? By the time her mind had spun out the sequence of events, Jan had a plan and had set something in motion and she was borne along.

Jan cleaned up some and went to Dossie's marketplace. He waited hidden until Hat's attention was turned away. When she set out to look around for Dossie, Jan caught the eye of Sally Vander, the only other person to have an inkling of what was in the air. Jan drew her to the side of the wagon.

"You know lyin' is wrong, little girl?" he asked in his boyishly sweet, friendly manner.

"Sir, I'ma youth, but I ain't no baby. I kin tell a lie for good purpose," Sally answered.

"Tell Miz Wilhelm that Miz Dossie had to go off to do a thing 'cause my uncle call her. Tell Miz Wilhelm you mus' ride wid her 'cause Miz Dossie have to take a wagonload for my uncle and me."

"Yes," Sally said.

"Stand up now, Sally, an' help us," Jan urged her. "Don't speak about nothing else. Whatever you seen down at the market — or heard — don't talk about it. If you love Miz Dossie, don't tell nobody, not even your mama!" Sally nodded assent. Yes, she loved Miz Dossie and she saw Sheriff Emil strong-arm her.

"Can you handle the donkey and the wagon?"

"Yes," Sally said emphatically.

"Take them into the alley behind the market. Drive slow and steady and casual. Then stop, get down, and go on back and get a ride with Miz Hat." Jan put two fingers across Sally Vander's lips, and she pursed her lips and kissed back at his fingers knowing that it was forward of her to do so. "Keep our secret."

"Yes," Sally answered.

On market day there is much movement in the hills—wagons on every road and thoroughfare. Like a swarm of bees the market women from Russell's Knob coalesce at market day's end. Their wagons are thick on the roads home. Sally was successful at her lies. Seated beside Miz Wilhelm, she was appropriately quiet. In a not-altogether-chaste dream, she cherished and built upon her pact with Jan in her imagination.

Jan wrung what help he could from Dossie. They put the sheriff's body in the wagon and concealed him under straw and burlap and unsold eggs. They waited for the factories' shift change and rode out of Paterson under cover of grim-faced exhaustion and drunken frivolity. They escaped town and took the body to the burial place.

At the grave site, Dossie was transfixed. "There's more to killin' a man than just killin' him," Jan said with little visible emotion other than weariness. It followed steps. Jan was systematic, and it was shocking to Dossie that he was so practiced at burying.

She watched Jan's movements and responded only when he called for her attention. It felt as if all of her had poured into the knife thrust. All of her yeast was gone. All that was in her vitals had been vomited or drained away. There was a painful radiation of muscle spasms in her thighs. Her legs were soupy. She had lunged onto Branch's back when he left off pounding her and turned to killing Jan. He had been pounding himself between her thighs. His jasper was rigid and voluminous when he taunted her, then shrunk, then bloomed again and discharged while he slammed it into her. He grabbed her neck, and she thought he'd wring it like a chicken's. He grabbed her breasts and mashed them and tore at them with ferocity that caused her such pain she was on the lip of unconsciousness when Jan hit him.

Dossie had imagined dying—being killed by Emil Branch. Her own death was the only outcome she'd figured on. She never thought she would kill Emil Branch. She'd only imagined that it would be herself dropping to the ground dead at Emil Branch's feet at the spot of greatest impact with his fists, his gun, his hammer, his own knife, or his belt or a rope in his throttling hands. She only saw pictured a murderous impact that would crush her like an insect. Ah, people make all sorts of plans and pacts in their head—plans to die and pacts to kill if this or that line is crossed! But juices overwhelm these schemes and dreams and ideas. The unavoidable, blood-boiling, stomach-churning physical reactions and uncontrollable sauces of emotion change everything.

Jan put Emil Branch in a hole on top of Gideon Smoot, one of Lucy's grandchildren. Buried years ago, Gideon had already been joined by a bounty agent. Jan performed the work on the sheriff's body with the determination Dossie was accustomed to seeing from him and Duncan when they were about the duties of hunting and fishing and keeping their hides and traps. Jan was quiet and keen, careful, slow moving, and precise. There was no reason to be superstitious about it. Rebellious, flinty, confrontational Gideon Smoot was likely laughing, pleased to accommodate a somebody that had needed killing. Gone was gone. What bones were left to mingle were mingling in the grave just like the souls attached to them were mingling in the great stewpot of the hereafter.

Jan drank some whiskey when he was done. He emptied his

flask over Gideon's grave. He sang and he traced steps with his toes and floated his arms out beside his body and whirled and turned. Dossie thought of that first night she had listened to him dancing and cavorting.

When they reached home at last, Jan lifted Dossie to the ground gingerly. She became warm and nauseated at the sight of Duncan sitting on the top step of the porch. Why was he here? Dossie slipped through Jan's hands onto the ground and her guts heaved up.

Duncan let out a sound that was only partially formed as the word "what." He roared at the sight of her and rushed off the steps and covered the yard at a run.

"Duncan, you my god," she said in a wispy voice when he lifted her. He carried her into the house and laid her on her bed. He brought a cool, wet towel to her forehead and wiped her face without asking to know what had happened.

"Jan, gwan and get Noelle and get Hat to come," Duncan ordered without noticing his nephew's wounds.

Dossie roused at the words and cried out, "No! Don't call nobody to come. I take care of this myself. Bring me a tub of water."

"What happen? Y'all took a tumble on the road—a bad spill?" Duncan spoke to Dossie in a soft, solicitous voice, then turned and shouted at Jan, "Boy, do like I say and get Hat and Noelle!"

"No! No!" Dossie cried again. "I 'on't wan' nobody to see me."

"We mus' get somebody. I fear you need some fixin', girl. You fell down in the yard. You got knocks and bruises on you, girl. Gwan an' fetch a doctor, Jan," Duncan said. "Go in town and get a doctor!"

"No!" both Jan and Dossie shouted. "There is more to this

thing here, Uncle," Jan continued. "Let's us leave her to fix herself. Let's us talk about it."

"What happen here, boy?" Duncan shouted. "You bring my wife back here bleedin' and broke up. What happen?"

"Was Emil Branch. We kilt him. She's in one piece, but we got trouble, Uncle. Emil Branch was attackin' Dossie and she kilt him," Jan squeezed out the words with great effort. Only then did Duncan see the thick red bands around Jan's neck, his bruised eyes, and the gash at his hairline.

Jan propped himself unsteadily against the doorjamb.

"Son, what you talkin'...?" Duncan's words trailed off as Jan slid toward the floor.

Duncan took his nephew under the arms and supported him. He'd heard his own voice call the young man by his baby name. It was a visceral response to the sight of his welts and his faint, and Duncan brought him to a chair and sat him in it. He poured a mug of ale to revive Jan and get the story.

"Son, what happen to y'all?" Duncan asked in a coaxing, paternal voice.

Jan gave forth the story painfully, haltingly. When it all had come out, neither could speak.

Duncan sat in the rocking chair and sawed back and forth on the floor, emitting deep grunts. Then he leaped up suddenly and stood with his fists poised.

"I ain't help her. I open the door for that bastard. I knew his mama and I bragged on it. I didn't think what I was sayin'. I made a enemy of him and he made my Dossie pay. I'm gonna dig him up and take off his balls and burn 'em, Jan. Then I'ma go down to Paterson and spoil his wife some."

"No, Uncle. Stop that talk! Dossie already paid him full. We better be smart, or she'll swing."

"He ain't been paid full for what he done!" Duncan's voice sounded like the wavering cry of a sheep and it unsettled Jan. "A woman got a right to kill a beast attacking her!"

"Colored woman ain't got that right, Uncle—not 'mongst the whites. Colored woman ain't got the right to kill a white man no matter what he do to her. You know that. Emil Branch was a lawman besides. They'll show you a colored woman swingin' from a tree as easily as any man!" Jan said bitterly. "Her an' me and you, too. She'll hang and so will all of us if they catch us!"

"Now Dossie got a killin' on her soul, what she gonna do? What she gonna do, Jan? She mus' been so scared. My min' ain't clear. Help me, son. Help me, Jan. Help me to take care of my Dossie!"

Jan looked at his uncle and was surprised. Duncan Smoot was unhinged. All throughout the proceedings since Emil Branch had died Jan had been musing that what he must do was bring Dossie to Uncle, and Uncle would grab them both up and know how to turn away the rest of the world. Duncan was the heart of their refuge. Jan had spurred Dossie and kept her from fainting by saying that they would soon get home and that Duncan would be at home and all would be well. But she'd got sick at the sight of him.

In the past Jan had wanted to set the old man back on his heels. But he studied him now in silence. A man so accustomed to venting anger and meting out punishments is now shaking with indecision?

"The harm was done to her, old man," Jan said sharply. "Dossie's not no lamp on the mantel that the sheriff knocked to the floor and broke." His voice was sober and angry.

Duncan looked up at his nephew like an inquisitive child. "You think God is punishin' me for what I done?"

"I hope there ain't no God that cares so much for you, old man, that he'd let this happen to her."

"I wanna talk to Noelle and find out what the Afric gods got to say 'bout this."

"Uncle, it's late in the day for bringin' up religion and spells and such," Jan chided.

"Get Noelle! Get Hattie! We got to get her some help!" Duncan cried.

"You got to be quiet some, Uncle," Jan said in a cool voice. "We got to think about what's been done and who ought to know about it — for they own protection. Your wife killed a white man, an' we don' wan' her to hang."

Suddenly Duncan honed his attention on his nephew as if only then questioning some facts of the events. "How come you ain't stop him, Jan? Why you let it fall to her? You been followin' her, been watching her. How come you didn't kill Emil Branch when he was rapin' my wife?"

Jan had expected the onslaught. He'd raked himself over coals to explain why he hadn't he come up quicker. Why hadn't he knifed Emil Branch?

But he'd lapsed in his watching and, when Sally Vander said the sheriff had come by, he went to find the shed that Mattie Ricks had told him about. When he reached it and heard Dossie's screams, there was one long moment when he couldn't see where she was. He heard her cries. She was beneath the man and obscured by him. Branch might have been holding her with a gun or a noose about her neck. Jan had hesitated only so much as that moment. Then he'd picked up a post with a nail in it and slammed it into Branch's back. Branch roared and turned to face him and was upon him quickly. They mostly grappled and tried to subdue each other. Jan couldn't catch hold of his naked opponent as his skin was slick with sweat. Branch had hold of him tightly, though, and began closing his hands around Jan's neck, putting him in a perfect lock and throttle and cutting off his air.

"I set out to kill him, but he bested me," Jan confessed to Duncan. "She killed him to save me, not herself. She put her soul in jeopardy for me. I won't let her swing for it."

"What you sayin', boy?" Duncan flared indignantly, and Jan stood toe to toe with him. He wanted to hit somebody. Jan saw that and understood it. But Jan knew he would not allow it. Duncan would have to rein himself this time. He would have to hold himself back because of Dossie. She had borne the harm! It was for her to raise her voice and scream and make vows. She had been raped, she had killed the man, and she was shaken.

Duncan quieted. He sat down and slumped in his chair. He held his head down, bent forward.

"Husban'," Dossie said when she rose the next day. At the sound of her voice both men's hearts came alive with hope. She stood in the doorway, and her woolly hair was every which way on her head from lying down and tossing. "I did not do it willin', husban'," she said. The words tumbled fast. Her eyes filled up with water when Duncan touched her cheek. There was a quality of ghostliness in her expression. "I was scared that man could hurt you."

Duncan placed his finger over her lips to seal them. "Hush, girl. Hush, Dossie, don' say nothin'. Nobody blame you! You must know it!"

Duncan and Dossie sat at their table and ate hoecakes. For all of their travail, they looked like childhood sweethearts. Duncan held a cake to Dossie's lips and she smiled and bit into it to please him.

Jan sat on the porch and considered what they'd tell the others — An' Hat, Pet, and Noelle. They would have to know what had happened and would have to be part of a solution.

Later in the morning, Jan went out to the chicken house to take care of Dossie's birds and her dog. There was agitation in the animals because they had not seen their mistress. They were noisy.

"Mr. Jan, Mr. Jan," Sally Vander called out. Hiding in the familiar territory of the chicken house, Sally said her piece in a forceful whisper. "Folks sayin' she run away wid him. Mattie Ricks from down in the town is tellin' folks there is a letter to the sheriff's mama sayin' he meant to take Miz Dossie out West They say he chuck his wife for Miz Dossie and she lef' willin' to go. My mama say it can' be. I 'on' say nothin'."

Sally had concealed herself for some hours waiting for Jan to come feed the birds. She was guessing that he'd be the one who did this errand for the woman he was so sweet on.

"You be a good wife someday, Sally," Jan said. He couldn't help flirting and flattering the young girl. "You smart and brave, eh?" His attention made Sally giggle widely and show her prominent, brown gums.

Jan circled her waist and made her staunch in the enterprise by kissing her. "Don't say nothin' different — not even to your mama." He knew she would not betray them. "No matter what they ask you. You don't know nothing. Anything could be true, you say. That letter can work in our favor," Jan said more to himself than to her. "Me an' Miz Dossie are goin'. You gonna wait for me to come back? I'm comin' back, you know," he vowed, teasing Sally, using her poor heart to his purpose. "Don't pass up any good beau if he should come along, though, you hear?" Jan pursed his lips in a kiss. Sally turned and ran away.

Pet stood around expectantly for much of the morning. He felt something was happening that he'd been left out of. Later Pet and his mother set out together for Duncan's place. Both of them could feel a draw—a something in the air.

"Brother!" Hat called out breathlessly. She was in a lather by the time she was in sight of Duncan's porch. "Brother!" she called out.

"Come in quiet, Hattie. Don't holler," Duncan replied.

"Where is Dossie, Brother? Sally said she was doin' an errand for you and now folks are sayin' she's run off." Hat confronted Duncan at the threshold.

"Hat, I'm here. I'm sorry to worry you." Dossie's voice from inside the house was small like a penny dropped.

"Dossie?" Hat's forehead wrinkled up and drew tight in with questioning.

"What's goin' on here, Uncle?" Pet asked Duncan, but looked into Jan's face. Jan's eyes shifted and Pet felt betrayed. Jan had kept him out of something important.

"Is Emil Branch, Pet. Dossie had to kill him."

"Kill?" Pet blurted.

Hat sucked her breath in loudly. "Kill? How come she kill the sheriff?"

"He was rapin' her, Hat. He was violatin' her," Duncan wailed.

"He had his hands on my neck and she knifed him to save me," Jan confessed to his cousin. He felt his admission exposed him as a worm and he watched his cousin's face experience a range of expressions.

"Then it's a case of self-defense," Pet answered, though he knew he sounded naïve and falsely hopeful.

"The law won't see it like that, Pet," Jan said. "We're in a stew."

Kill the sheriff with a knife! Little Dossie had done that? Hat took Dossie's hand and led her into the bedroom.

In the other room the men had stood around Dossie obscuring her from view. In the bedroom Hat saw that her face was pained, that she winced, that she was close to a faint.

"Let me see?" Hat was frightened, but she faced looking. "I can maybe help you," she whispered while they removed the wrapper that Dossie had kept tightly closed up to her throat.

"He dirtied me with what he did, Hat. He changed me. I killed him. I'm not the same as I was," Dossie squeezed out in an odd, uncertain voice.

"We'll heal you up. You will be yourself again," Hat replied. Her words were gentle and urgent and conspiratorial. Perhaps she could keep her brother from seeing the thick bands on Dossie's thighs and arms. Maybe Emil Branch's finger marks on Dossie's breasts would fade before Duncan saw them. Maybe they could keep Duncan from digging up Emil Branch and cutting off his leather.

There were things in Emil Branch's pockets and Jan had

removed them before wrapping his body and putting it in Gideon's lap. There were two tickets for a train passage to Phillipsburg. There was a receipt for a wagon and a receipt for a horse, both to be picked up in Phillipsburg. He'd had a gun and a knife. He'd carried tincture of opium in a leather pouch in his coat and he had a flask of whiskey.

Jan looked around at all of their faces. He knew he must say the thing that no one wanted to hear. "She's got to go. We can't hide what happened if she stays."

"My wife ain't going nowhere," Duncan shouted out. "I'ma take her place if I gotta. I'll face the law."

"Settle down, Duncan. We got to have a plan," Hat said. She uncorked the whiskey and poured some of it for all of them. Jan's hands shook and she pressed his hands around his glass and squeezed. She poured his drink tall.

"What good will it do her for you to swing? A colored woman whose husband is hanged is in desperation," Hat said to her brother.

"If they come here hunting her they will make a show of it. A woman who has killed a sheriff will suffer. They ain't gonna just string her up in her Sunday dress. They'll abuse her and anybody who gets in the way," Jan put in. "If they come here they liable to kill others of the People. They will burn out the town. We can't visit that on our neighbors. I'ma give myself in and say I kilt him," Jan said. "I ought to have anyway. I give myself up and clear her record."

"I woulda killed him, too," Hat said with a sudden, big passion.

"We ought to go east to New York." Dossie spoke and the others turned their heads. They hadn't noticed that she got up to replenish her coffee, that she gazed out over her swept-up yard, that she thought of her first moments upon this porch in Duncan Smoot's heaven. She was contemplative. She was quiet — reticent as she'd once been in their presence. When she had first come to this heaven home, she never considered leaving it. Leaving her heaven now looked like it was going to be the only way to keep it a heaven for the others. When Emil Branch was destroying her, all she thought of was praying for Duncan to recover her bones and keep them here in Russell's Knob. But now she must consider the People. She must go now because what she'd done could get them all burned out. She ought to go because of Emil Branch's plan. If his plan would work, his people would think he went off alive and left them. "I'm goin' to the city with Jan and let the trouble here blow away some," Dossie said. "Leavin' is the best plan for coverin' up what happen. They likely won't look back east for him. He claim he left a letter for his wife and his mama. He said he was" — she put down her cup carefully as if her next words would cause her to drop it — "taking me out West into Pennsylvania, on to Ohio, and on to St. Louis. He said he would leave me off there. He'd have his chance to kill you if you thought it was worth it to track me." Dossie took up her coffee again, sipped some, then resumed speaking while all of them stared. "Maybe you wouldn't want to bother so much for a ruined woman. In that case I was free for him to take," Dossie's voice trembled and sputtered out as her hand shook.

Hat poured a dollop of the whiskey in Dossie's coffee and pushed it toward her. She made an encouraging expression of her eyebrows.

There was also in Emil Branch's pocket an advert extolling

the opportunities of the frontier that had been torn from a catalog of accoutrement for westward travel. Clearly Emil Branch had been planning to go west.

It was nearly impossible to convince Duncan that he must play his assigned part and only that — that he must sit on the porch and wait. And it pained Dossie that the People would think she was so dirty a gal that she would run off from her husband. But they must think it.

Duncan lay his head on his knees.

"I make up my own min' 'bout where I'll go," Dossie asserted. "I mus' go to New York for the story to hol'. I got to go for me and Jan to be safe and escape the rope. We goin' 'cuz we got to, Duncan," she said. "I'm the cause of this trouble!"

"No! No! I ain't lettin' you go," Duncan roared like a bear. His anger was newly roused.

"I killed a man, Duncan. I can't be too careful wid myself. I'm bol' enough to knife a man, I am bol' enough to go down to New York," Dossie declared and then added a short, sharp, ironic snort of laughter though she did not feel amused.

"No!" he said again. "You stay here and I won' give you up!"

"No, Duncan, you can't hol' out against the lawmen who will come to get me. They'll take me and Jan and they will kill you and all the rest of the People. They liable to burn out the town. I murdered their sheriff — or Jan did it."

"What you do when you got no choice is not hel' against you in judgment. I am sure of that," Hat insisted, trying to defuse Duncan's panic.

"No. I can' pay back the People like this. If me being here brings a wrath on my home, I got to run."

It was a stubborn barn dance. They each walked across the floor and scuffed their feet and breathed hard and each shook their head and wrung their hands. Jan and Pet banged their fists into their own palms. There was no other thing to do but follow up with Emil Branch's plans. There was nothing else for Dossie but to hide or hang.

Hat became the captain — the conductor. Sally Vander was sworn to care for the chickens. Hat sent Jan east to New Barbados on horseback with salable goods. He was to leave his horse there with the colored blacksmith until he came back upriver. Jan would then board the same canal boat for New York City that Dossie already had got aboard in Paterson. She, too, would have market goods, and neither would be much noticed onboard toward New York City.

At the riverside in Paterson, Hat pinched at and chucked Dossie's chin at parting. "I count you a lucky woman, because you have the choice of them. Both of them love you very much. I ought to be green jealous of you."

Dossie bent and hoisted her crate of goods. She wasn't no bundle of sticks anymore like when she'd first come. Even then she hadn't been weak — was surprisingly strong for a little gal. Hat considered ruefully that perhaps Dossie was thought small only for being up next to big and tall Duncan. She was a stand-alone woman now, though.

"Hat, I love Duncan alone. I don' love Jan. That's not why I'm goin'. It is for the plan to hol'," Dossie asserted.

"Look out for Jan, girl. You be careful of him. I'm scared the people down there will treat you bad an' he will die taking up for you. Duncan had a bad time in New York town."

Hat and Pet boarded a train going west from Paterson to Phillipsburg. Wearing a hard-felt hat like Emil Branch's, Petrus

Wilhelm and his hooded companion seemed to fit a certain description. Hat clasped Pet's hand and held close to him and thought that Pet was handsome — very big and imposing — in his traveling clothes. At Phillipsburg they took possession of the wagon and horse that Emil Branch had already purchased and then left Phillipsburg heading westward.

Duncan waited for the others to get gone. Then he, too, left surreptitiously. He knew he must seem to be gone off tracking his wife and her kidnapper.

11

THE LAST CUP OF COFFEE Dossie had in her homestead — the first cup of coffee of her new life — had been drunk in the dark before dawn and was a potent tonic. Later when she'd stepped onto the packet in Paterson, her going away seemed like a horrible dream.

When the boat came into New Barbados, Jan was there with his bundles. They mixed with other folk bringing farm goods to New York town for commerce as Hat told them to do.

As they boarded for New York, the captain of the packet boat raised his arm to keep Dossie from getting on. He declared he transported no females into New York unless they were high ladies, which he'd never had the privilege to transport, or if they had a stout man to protect them, a gentleman or a ruffian capable of keeping them safe. His only exception, he sneered, was for a workingwoman who was willing to give him a fee. Jan then stepped to Dossie's side, fingered his pigsticker, and showed his most dreadful, implacable face. The man accepted their fare and waved them toward a comfortable spot.

Dossie glanced out of the corner of her eye at Jan and wondered how well she knew him. The flinty scowl was chilling. It was a visage to accompany a lunging, gut-cutting knife wielder. Ah, the mountain people are haughty about their knife skills.

Even she—even Dossie—had shown proof with a knife. She got a curious feeling in her gut as the boat pitched and plunged toward New York. Dossie was convinced of them both. She and Jan had an answer for all comers. Between them two, they would be safe.

It gave Jan no pleasure that they'd had to leave like this, running from their hearth, her not able to sit in her comfort. Now that they had gone, he realized he didn't want it this way. He was already missing home, and he was frightened that she was left with only him to look after her. He missed Uncle. Dossie held her face still and lowered her head when anyone came near, but she did not weep as he feared she might. It surprised him some that she didn't crumble like a cake because her god was gone.

Jan flicked his pigsticker and scraped dirt out of his fingernails. Any and all onboard saw that the mountain boy had a pigsticker against trouble. Jan got annoyed when Dossie removed her hat and replaced it with a rude rag head scarf. Why'd she want to look like an old servant? Duncan would not like to see her like this. But did that matter now? They were no longer in Duncan's orbit.

Dossie felt a chill around the shoulders as they traveled away from their home. She encircled herself with herself, lay her cheek on her knee, and rocked back and forth. She sucked the fingers of her right hand into her mouth and closed her eyes like a baby child. The comfort was great! Cheek to knees she felt her own body warmth and recollected cold evenings around a fire watching Duncan. His face swaddled in his bushy mustache, sewing on his fishnets. Oh, to touch the hair on his face now! Dossie hungered to have her face muffled in rabbit tails from the pillow at the back of her chair.

Conversation onboard the vessel was high pitched and mostly regarding men and supplies going into the big conflict.

"You goin' down to join up?" a colored fellow traveler asked Jan. The friendly, dark-colored man was ebullient, sat down next to Jan, and took up a conversation as if the two were companions. "It's the colored man's fight!" he whispered to Jan.

He then raised his voice to say, "Ezra Oliver I'm called. They raisin' a army to free the slaves. I'ma join up. Can you'uns read and figure?"

"O' course," Jan snapped, not wanting to talk, then regretting his unfriendliness. There was a familiarity about the fellow that made him homesick at once, and at once comforted.

"You'll pardon?" Ezra added quickly. "I don't have no letters. Those that got a bit of the cream in 'em like you and some schooling is going' to rise in the army of the colored!"

"Jan Smoot is my name." Jan cringed a bit but was not offended by the man. He and Pet had been coddled. He knew it. He and Pet and Dossie had advantages, though they'd been up in the mountains and didn't know city ways. They could read. Why, they had even read Mr. Fenimore Cooper's book *The Last of the Mohicans,* because Uncle brought it home one year at springtime and had made them accomplish the book, though it was spring and they would rather have been fishing. Pet's papa, as profligate as he was, believed firmly in Bible studies and reading from the Good Book on idle evenings.

"We'uns better leave the boat here," Ezra Oliver said in a whisper, but with great punch when they came into a canal lock outside of Pavonia. Jan, wholly convinced of Ezra Oliver by this time, did not hesitate to respond. "Gather up your things and let's us hop off, Dossie," Jan said to her with quiet solemnity to match Ezra's. Dossie took up her goods unquestioningly and slipped off the boat with Jan and Ezra despite a sharp pain in her intimacies and a sick dizziness.

Ezra Oliver smiled broadly when they were safely on land. He explained that it was a common occurrence that colored travelers were set upon and robbed by brigands before the boat came into Pavonia. Folk who knew this knew to get off the boat.

Jan and Dossie followed Ezra Oliver into Pavonia on foot, and he led them to the folk who helped colored to cross to New York unmolested. They boarded the ferry, and both felt a frightening lurch in the gut at putting another river between them and their home.

"The smaller I stay, the less fighting you have to do, Jan. You can't change what is. Maybe your insides is too white to be a colored boy in this town." Dossie said and Jan spat on the ground.

It was not meekness. Dossie took low because, in many ways, New York City was like Philadelphia. She remembered the terror and confusion of the streets of that city and the fear, then comfort, followed by a complete puzzlement. Jan had never been in so big and busy a place as this no matter how he chose to behave. He himself was frightened, Dossie knew, and felt small and was liable to be incautious. Her legs shook and she was so frightened for them both that she feared she might wet herself and further the discomfort between her legs.

The dark skin ended at Dossie's lips so that when she parted them a pinker skin emerged visible. She licked at her lips and tasted them again and again, taking the salt she found there into herself. She needed fortitude now. She needed the salt. She needed to put down the discomfort and the fear. The wind had been in their faces for the whole of the cross to New York. Here was the place that Jan had painted up—that Duncan had described!

On the lane in front of a lot between two tall and top-heavy buildings, Dossie stood behind Jan with her eyes down. Jan became fidgety and uncertain. Duncan had warned him and threatened him about Dossie. "Don't leave her alone. Take care of her. Bring her back safe." He'd said that if any harm befell Dossie, and Jan survived it, he should run off to sea and never return to Russell's Knob. Jan had clasped Duncan's hand and sworn to that.

Jan and Dossie headed to the Five Points to find a flop and to find Worm, the man Duncan had told them about. Jasp Wardman was called Worm respectfully because his face and neck and even his hands were covered with ropey, swollen lumps from his many knife fights. Behind each ear hung a fleshy mass that appeared, at first, to be decoration. Duncan said the fellow had been a professional knife fighter in his earliest days on the waterfront and had been slashed many times. He survived all these confrontations and had the lumpy skin as proof. He was dark black skinned and covered his head with a bright red cloth tied at an angle. He wore a leather strap around his waist on which hung awls, hammers, and rusted metal stakes. This belt was worn over grimy, wide-legged pantaloons, as Worm eschewed trousers for a different costume.

"Ach! Is't the old boy too scared to come back to New York town hisself? He sent you, eh?" Worm hollered and clapped Jan enthusiastically when he learned that he was the nephew of Duncan Smoot. "That jumble boy went back to the mountains when 'em put they foot in his ass in this city! He knowed I ain't

228 • BREENA CLARKE

gone nowhere. I sent too many white men down to the devil's front door for to be scared of 'em. You is home, boy!" Worm guffawed, all while punching and slapping Jan familiarly. "Set your woman to picking rags. One of the gals'll show her how. You come for a mug of beer, boy," he roared.

"Dossie don't pick rags," Jan piped up indignantly before she could accept the work.

"Aye, she's the queen then. I know. Only on y'all mountain is the coal-black gal a queen," Worm said good-naturedly. His manner was very loud, but unexpectedly circumspect when he turned to look at Dossie. He glanced her up and down quickly though not leering. "Gal, sit here and watch dem other gals while I take yer boy for a beer." He smiled at the top of her head.

Dossie looked to the ground beneath her feet, not raising her eyes as she nodded.

Jan was so irked by Dossie's new demeanor and his mouth was dry from so much excitement that he left for a drink with Worm.

"It's cold up yonder in them mountains then? For it takes a dark piece of coal to warm the cock of a mountain man, eh," Jasp Wardman hooted. "A pretty coal! A real pretty coal!" He cuffed Jan collegially about the back of his head as they left the yard. Jan fingered his pigsticker and did not laugh with Worm. The man noticed Jan's pique and added, "No mud on your madam's shoes, young boy. No matter the color. Matter the cunt only, sure!" Worm laughed and spit and elbowed Jan companionably as they continued toward the tavern. Soon enough Jan became relaxed and reciprocated with brotherly jostling.

It was a short walk to the first grog hole they stopped in. Below the level of the thoroughfare, the room was packed with drinkers. Worm kept his big arm collared around Jan and led him through several rounds of drinks as they leaned against a wooden trough.

"Boy, you'll be a popular one in this town — like your uncle. You jumble boys can be a big success with the women here — and some of the men. You're a pretty one. I'd fancy you myself, but your hind parts ain't big enough for my taste." Worm guffawed and grabbed Jan's ass and squeezed. It was a move so quick and firm and surprising that Jan had no time to reach his knife. "If your girl is on the game she can earn a decent wage in town until she run out. You lay about and take in the town till you fin' you a rich game an' she can make enough for to feed you both." The porter in Jan's mug told him to relax, but his guts made him wary of the man. To whom had Duncan sent him? Only Worm's deep association with Duncan saved him from a fight. What would Duncan have done to Worm if he'd heard this remark about Dossie? The man would have lost an ear for certain or one of his sausage lips.

"Dossie ain't a whore. She's my unc — she's my woman. I'ma take care o' her. She gon' sit on her duff and lap up milk if she want," Jan said, his head suddenly clearing in the way of a practiced drinker.

Worm continued to smile as he spoke. "I hope she don't end up clawin' your eyes out 'cause you caused her to starve."

At dawn, Jan returned to the rag yard stinking to high heaven and coddling an achy, remorseful head. He smiled broadly when he saw Dossie. She wanted to show her annoyance at him, but thought better of it. She'd thought about it all of that night. She was not his wife or his woman. He had no obligation to her and she had no right to scold him.

Dossie sloughed off her pique because of Jan's jaunty walk

and his flushed face. He showed her the money in his pockets. He showed her the turns and capers he'd cut atop a table in Black Bob's Cellar, a good-time tavern. He spun and cavorted until his head caught up with him and tossed him back on his hind parts. Dossie smiled and sat at his feet to hear him tell about his adventures. She kept up her smiling despite the grinding throbs in her belly. Her night had been long and painful, such a bone-lonely time that her parts had ruptured and blood had run and the ragpickers had kept her dress unsoiled, had given her good rags to staunch the flow and a hot toddy. Perhaps it was best he hadn't been there.

"Oh," Jan hollered and leapt up. "We got us a flop. Come on." He grabbed Dossie's arms and tugged her to her feet. He started to run off down the thoroughfare without a thought for their grips, their satchels, and the provision they'd brought with them, which Dossie had guarded through the night.

"Jan," Dossie called quietly.

"It's for both of us together. It can' be no other way. I can' let you out of my sight no more. I promised Uncle." Jan had been so frightened when his head cleared from drink, and he realized that he'd left Dossie alone with the ragpickers.

The triumph of the evening before had come when Black Bob Simpson, owner of the saloon for colored and any who cared to join them at Lispenard Street, negotiated a deal for Jan to dance in his bar. Worm had touted his dancing and said that he was fresh from the highlands and knew the traditional turns and steps. When he took the raised platform that all comers showed their stuff on, he did the freshest, the most athletic, the most graceful turns in his repertoire. Bob hired him on the spot and offered the room on the second floor for him and his woman.

In the part of town that Jan now led Dossie to — whereabouts was their flop — there were lots of dark black gals on the arms of white boys or jumble boys as light as white. And there were, as well, white gals with their arms linked into colored men of all of the shades. Dossie started to countenance the palaver of the ragpickers and got scared of losing Jan to some other gal. His eyes were alight. Even though he did not truly belong to her, she knew they must stay together. Their hitch was beyond that a man and woman feel for each other.

To reach the room at the back of Black Bob's tavern, a big, dirty barn of a building, Jan and Dossie threaded through groups of women gathered in the hallway and in doorways. There were some smells of cooking and some sounds of small children crying.

Inside a large room on the first floor, women moved around a piano singly and paired up with men. Threading through was a fright, for the passages in the building were narrow and the walls and the floor wet feeling. When they reached their place at the very back of a passage, stepping over a foul lake of water in the corridor, struggling to keep their parcels dry, Dossie's heart was thumping like the tail of an excited dog.

They were safe — tucked up off to themselves — but it was wet and dark and stinking. They relaxed a notch behind the closed door, but the trapped atmosphere was stifling. They heard a great lot of caterwauling and crying and threatening voices beyond their own walls, and the thick air got thicker when Jan lit up a kerosene lamp so they could take stock.

The noise and the putrid smells assaulted Dossie. Her loins ached, but she was set on not letting Jan know it. She didn't want any curiosity or intimacy yet. No matter that they'd made a plan. Everything . . . everything had changed. Dossie and Jan sat on two small milking stools that were all of the unbroken furniture in the room except a stove. Dossie put her head on Jan's chest, reaching for a place of comfort and contentment. She clung to him like a plaster all through the first night. Things crawled about the room and splashed in pockets of foul water. Dossie hung on Jan and refused to acknowledge the pests in the dark. There were cries of women and loud laughter, factory whistles and squealing animals. At each blast of some unknown noise, Dossie pressed closer to Jan and squeezed her eyelids until only the sound of their two hearts and the scurrying of insects and rodents could be heard.

"Don't let any harm come to him because he loves you," Hat had said. My goodness! How would she manage to do that in New York? Some sliver of light shown through their window. Dossie batted away bugs that settled on Jan's clothes and thought about him while he slept. Hat had begged her to be careful with him.

Is this a woman's test then? Must she be careful and be the custodian of the future? It was the responsibility that she craved. Let the ancestors know it! Dossie fussed and fumed at the pests in their flop. They seemed much smaller in the light of day, and she wondered why she hadn't lit up some of her fragrant candles to drive them off. She girded herself and went to find a water spigot to clean up, to drive off the smell of blood and sick that clung to her.

After two more nights alone in the fearful place clinging to each other for fear of the crawling things and the boisterous people, he made love to her and she welcomed it. It was not at all like the plan for the baby. He did but knock on the door. He knocked gently. He seemed scared and she kissed his fingers to encourage him. He was not bold and swaggering. Dossie had counted on him being cavalier and joking and teasing the way through it all. The first time he'd talked of it for the plan, Jan had bragged on his endowment and made Dossie blush and giggle to cut the tension. Now he was solemn and methodical, touching her intimacies slowly, lightly. He put his lips to every lobe, every nipple, and every fold of skin on her.

The new entanglement with Jan burst like a sunup! The doings with him ought to be a shame. Dossie Smoot was a married woman whether her husband was here or not. But it was not a wrong that she felt in any part of her body but her head. Her intimacies were convinced! Dossie wanted to cry in the light of day knowing what she'd done to Duncan in the dark.

Still, how could they be blamed? They needed each other. Comfort and pleasure were vindicated because seeking them brought them and they were palliative. Dossie sang birdcalls and brought her lips to brush Jan's ear. How could they be blamed for succumbing to this passion?

"I crossed him, Dossie. I love him, but I love you more. I love him, but I love you more," Jan babbled when he was done, but still trembling and clinging and not entirely spent.

"Hush your mouth!" Dossie countered sternly, showing impatience with his surrender. Here he was saying out loud what she had whispered onto his shoulder!

Jan Smoot was the beautiful cock of the walk in Black Bob's cellar. Jan and his dancing quickly became part of the excitement the folk were there for. His exertions were the same as at home in the highlands, but the onlookers were hungrier. They took in Jan's spirited jigs with much enthusiasm, and he rose to their expectations every time he stepped on the threshold.

Women of all shades crowded into Black Bob's on days off from a charwoman's stint or factory work and they giggled at Jan's flourishes and called for more. The cellar was filled with jauntily attired men of all colors, too. Roving clutches of sharply dressed dandies and cocks created a sartorial contest on the streets of New York City. And the taverns were galleries and porches and proof against the cold and the stink, and they were well peopled in the thronging Five Points. And though much depended on the precinct, colored folk did promenade unmolested in many streets.

On her first night in Black Bob's, Dossie would have been a mouse in the corner peeping out of her hole if Jan hadn't pulled her into the center of the activity. Because of all that had happened in Paterson, Dossie was scared of the drinking gawkers and "hi-de-hos" that filled up the tavern, though they were friendly seeming and of a range of colors like that found in the Knob.

Jan sat Dossie at a table close by the raised area for dancing and put down a glass of ale for him and one for her. He gave himself a pull from a flask and told her to take one good swallow from it, too. He said, tapping the end of her nose with his finger like Duncan might have done, that a gal should only have a little whiskey lest she be sitting at a table with her legs spread wide and her skirts hitched up. Jan nodded toward some women in Bob's cellar who were sitting that way and slumped forward with their heads down on the table. Then he left Dossie's side to break into his combinations.

When a dark, thick man came and sat next to Dossie and said he'd give her as much whiskey as she could drink if she let him paw on her, Jan jumped off the stage and flicked his knife open near the man's ear.

"Git up, boy, before I cut you!" Jan said and Dossie felt the air get thick around them. She knew Jan Smoot was not as soft as this man and the others supposed. He could give back one jot better than he was given in any fight on any day. But the man wanted no fighting, and he got up and tipped his cap at Dossie and Jan with respect. Jan then looked around at the room, and one or two of the men looked back at him. They gave him a silent token of respect, and Jan touched Dossie under the chin in a way that said, *Here is mine.*

Dossie was relieved of the man's bother, but thought this was the same way she'd seen Jan touch his horse. It was a native gesture — pointing out what he claimed or wanted so others would know. Dossie shrunk a little bit in her seat. Had she passed from Duncan's pocket into Jan's then? It was a hazard to become the pocket floss of one man or another.

"Watch me, girl." Jan touched Dossie's face again to cause her to smile and he gave her another sip of whiskey before returning to dancing. Oh, she would use up the last of her eyesight watchin' Jan Smoot dance! It had always been like loosing a jar of fireflies and seeing their lights flash.

"A satin-black gal like you could earn a better living if you wanted." The woman surprised Dossie, and she nearly dropped the pail she carried. "You mightn't know it, but there's sports that would pay to touch your altogethers. Some men favor a black gal just as there's some that want a white one." Shulamith Cleary had never before spoken to Dossie, though they had several times passed each other in the narrow, serpentine hallway.

She now faced Dossie with her sparsely covered breasts held high, and the sight of them was compelling. Dossie fought to look at Cleary's feet.

Shulamith Cleary ran the bawdy house at the front of Black Bob's building and paid a premium to have the large room with the window on the front. Cleary's women, known to cater to all comers, lolled about displaying themselves in the window in the front parlor.

"Naw, ma'am, that is not for me," Dossie replied with caution and a tick of courtesy.

"Your jumble boy won't stay trussed up for long, lamp black. You'll have to eat when he moves on." Cleary guffawed and sprayed spittle in the close confines. Dossie turned away quickly and walked off. Better risk a cuffing for disrespect than encounter the pox breathing the air from this woman.

When President Lincoln's Emancipation Proclamation was rung in on the first day of the New Year, all of the colored folk in New York City were ecstatic in celebration, albeit some were solemn and tearful, too. They dressed and promenaded in their precincts. The colored swells and leaders and the white folk working for the cause of abolition held a great convocation on the day to read out and hail the edict. The Cooper Hall was full of them. The first day of the year—the first true day of freedom! Jan and Dossie, clutching each other's hands, circulated in the crowd. The proud, staunch men speaking up about joining the Union army and fighting Jeff Davis made them both think of Duncan and the folk at home in Russell's Knob. How were they faring? Were they going to be drawn into the fray? Sobering thoughts countered their giddy love and their silly excitement about the Proclamation.

It had all come at once. The freedom from bondage and the loving Jan.

On a stone-cold afternoon following three days of celebration of President Lincoln's edict, the police clamped down on public revelry. To quell emancipation festivity and quash it in the name of public safety in neighborhoods like the Five Points, the police swooped down in raids even on the paid-up establishments that considered themselves immune.

Dossie emerged from the front of the flop as a herd of constables rushed in and rousted the women in Shulamith Cleary's bordello. The entire building was put into a pother. Shrieks and curses went up. Dossie recognized it at once, the keening and howling she'd heard in other streets, the sound that had puzzled her until now. Now she knew why the women cried out in this way.

The cops pulled out all of the women sitting or working in the building. They charged up and down the hallways of Black Bob's tenement, and every grown woman who could walk out of the place was put in a wagon and taken to the jail. Mothers were forced to leave all their children but the infants they could carry in the care of an old grandmother and submit to the cops.

The noises in the police wagon when they were taken off was clangorous. Pushed in tightly, some of the women were loudly, drunkenly abusing the police and held their fists aloft. Some of the women moaned and called out for their children. Some comforted one another, clinging together so hard they appeared to be strangling each other.

"Calm down, boy!" Worm demanded. "Look to you face!

They'll have you down for panderin' and lock you up at de very leas'. They'll say she is workin' for you and both of y'all go down a hole," Worm roared, hoping to bring Jan to the sense of the situation. They must keep their heads, or Dossie could have a stay in jail.

Worm was influential in the Five Points on account of his longevity there. At the jail he arranged that Dossie be separated from the professional gals, and when she came before a judge, Worm stood and spoke on her behalf.

"She ain't no prostitutin' gal, suh. She ain't got the assets for it." Worm guffawed and leaned toward the judge as if speaking confidentially, though his voice was very loud. "Huh, don't nobody want no lamp black like her, suh. She ain't on no game." Worm roared and capered and elicited a round of laughter in the courtroom. He pointed to Dossie and hoped she had the sense to keep her glance oblique and her eyes wide. "She just a quiet kind of country gal that could get pulled into somethin' bad. The good Lord knows I knows somebody that'll take her in and give her a decent job, Your Honorable," Worm testified. "If we kin keep this pitiful one from goin' on the game, I pledge to try it, suh! I'm gonna keep this child of God off them damn—uh, beg your pardon, suh—dem turrible streets." Worm carried on his declaration to the judge, until the man banged down on his gavel. The judge declared he was reluctant to put a simple-minded colored gal in the slam when white women needed maids and scullery hands. So he released Dossie into the custody of Miss Abigail Cheltham to work as a maid, as Worm had arranged.

"Is the onliest way, boy," Worm told Jan. "If you all wants to keep her outta the jailhouse, you better let her work a decent job. Miss Cheltham'll treat her good and pay her a sum. And she kin come home an' visit ya from time to time. You won't lose your jewel." Worm, who knew the swell neighborhoods and knew where servants were needed, had, of course, already accepted a fee from Miss Cheltham for his facilitation and to cover the "costs" of his defense of Dossie.

Jan wanted to smash Worm's jaw, though he was so grateful to the man he could have kissed his pulpy, ugly face. He'd saved Dossie from going to jail. But what now? Outside of the courthouse Jan grasped Dossie's wrist and pulled her into his arms. He smooched her hard on the lips in defiance of all the lookers. "You're a brave girl, Dossie. You remember all what you've done? Don't lose your water now." Jan pressed his forehead against hers. Dossie smelled stale but amatory, and Jan wanted to use his tongue on her. He wanted to have something from her before letting her go — something like a taste in the mouth. Instead he pecked her lips again, pinched her nose, and said, "Tighten your leathers, girl!"

"Come and see me when you can," she said as if she doubted he would be allowed to.

They had come to town to escape trouble, and now she was in a swirl of it. And he was separated from her. What would Uncle think? Jan remembered that he'd told Dossie this when he swiped at her butt and kissed her neck. "Uncle can't see what we doin' and he can't punish us from so far," he had said, hoping to get Dossie to change the whole of how she felt in the world.

No, Duncan couldn't help them. They ought to cut and run and go on back a mountain now. There was a brief moment when Jan could have grabbed Dossie's hand and pulled her away, back to the ferries, back across the North River, and back to their home. But truth was Jan wanted to stay. He wanted to have this bawdy excitement even with the danger and the turmoil.

Jan's guts were in a roil because of the war, too. There was the plan for conscription of white men, and some white men were chafing at fighting for the slaves. Hell! It was more than chafing. They were kicking about it. New York City was a far more dangerous, tumultuous place than Paterson had been, even with all of the Europes there fighting over crusts of bread tossed from the elegant tables of their masters — the great masters of Paterson's turbines.

The idea of fighting did appeal to Jan, though. He liked a good fuss. Maybe there was an adventure to be had in marching off for a brief bit to fix what needed fixing. But was this his war to fight?

The People had a measure of freedom because they stayed on the outsides of things, keeping to themselves in their own small place. Jan knew that was how they thrived. That was the only way. Venturing forth from Russell's Knob had always been chancy.

New York City was full of enemy elements of its very own — uniquely its own. But the same cacophony of funny-talking foreigners that was loud and ubiquitous in Paterson was abroad in New York City — only more so. And just like in Paterson there were pockets for each group. And in each group a great many malingerers lay about drinking on the pittances their youngsters earned. They clung together in their knots from this place or that county and had regular fusses betwixt and between themselves and with the native-born whites. And though treated little better than the colored, they angled themselves up a notch or two with putting their feet on the neck of the colored. How you going to get them to want to fight for the colored? There were angry knots on nearly every corner in New York discussing the draft of white men that Lincoln had ordered to get his army. Swells with the money for it were paying poor slobs to go in their place because of the exemption. And the poor Irish figured they were getting the worst of it because they couldn't afford to pay off nobody else. And there were black men, enslaved and free, who were spoiling for the fight. And there were free colored waiting and hoping for guns and government uniforms and the right to fight and die. Ezra Oliver was eager and earnest and determined to go. Ezra Oliver had said a free colored man like Jan had something to fight for.

Well, Jan wanted to fight for Dossie. He wanted to do what Uncle had sent him to New York City to do — to keep her safe until it was safe to come home.

Hadn't Jan and Pet been running headlong in the streets of Paterson to escape a beating by some Irish and had to grab up a crippled Irish boy to use as a shield? Hadn't they been forced to twist his arms until he squealed to escape a band of his confederates bent on bashing them with stones? Hadn't Duncan sent them and some other boys from Russell's Knob back to Paterson with pigstickers and swagger to show the Irish boys that they would fight for a place on the streets of town? Ah, once a day Jan thought it: he could use Pet here. He sorely missed his cousin.

Dossie Smoot, a married woman, knew well how to serve a whim so that working as a maid was not particularly onerous. Not schooled in the terms and protocols of the position, however, she needed spur and reprimand from Miss Cheltham and all of the other servants. Dossie's employer, Miss Abigail Cheltham, was a well-read woman of middle years who lived on inherited income in an opulent town house on Lexington Avenue. A staunch supporter of temperance, women's uplift, and the abolition of slavery, she was also self-indulgent and fond of rich foods.

The requisite uniform for Miss Cheltham's service was one of two dresses—one for day and one for the evening. Both were pretty gowns and tight to the form, as Miss Cheltham wished. "If you gain an ounce by eating or by playing with your man, I will sack you!" she lectured Dossie when she arrived. She'd noticed the fancy boy her new maid had hung upon and wept for. "I will throw you out of my employ! Do not test me. There are a great many girls for service in this city," she declared at high volume. Her loud voice belied the delicacy of her visage and the essential quietness of her nature. She was no bully, only headstrong and full of opinion. She was tiny and shaped exactly like an hourglass herself. She believed it to be the height of style that her staff was as well turned as she. Here in the bon ton there was a stiff, rich style that included the ladies' maids.

"If she think you bringin' a baby, she'll throw you out to starve. Don't doubt it." Tilly, another maid, assured Dossie emphatically that Miss Cheltham was very serious in her warning. She reported that the girl before Dossie in the position of ladies' maid had got in trouble, her uniform swelled, and she lost her job with Miss Cheltham. The girl's lover then lost interest in her when her few dollars for his drinking fund were gone. "He dumped her though she was big with his baby," Tilly fumed.

Dossie smiled broadly, showing herself in her maid uniform to Jan when he came uptown for a visit. She whirled around in the alley behind the town house, and he saw that she liked her own appearance. Jan was taken aback and got in a pique. He said she was almost unrecognizable and that her clothes were too white. He tried to breach the clothing with his plundering fingers and got irritable at the challenge. Drunk enough to make Dossie fretful, he said that Duncan would be in a rage if he knew what she was doing.

"Oh," she answered, "it is rich to stop now to consider what Duncan would think, what Duncan would do!" Suddenly Jan's face was like Duncan's had been when he'd been angry enough to slap her.

But, yes, it was late in the day to consider Duncan's feelings. Duncan Smoot would feel betrayed by them both.

Jan could hardly stand being without her, though. He ran uptown whenever he could recover from drinking, and he hung about the alley until Dossie sneaked out to see him. It was more than an itch in the leathers. It was needing to know how she fared. Without her he drank more, ate less, and fretted a good deal. Dossie noticed he was becoming thin when she rubbed her hands over him.

"Come home. Quit from here and come home," Jan pleaded. "Come home."

"You know I can't," she whispered repeatedly.

And what was their home? Were they at home in their flop at Black Bob's? Perhaps it was too cruel to consider home. Were things too far gone to ever return to Russell's Knob — to Duncan? Duncan was their home. It was to Duncan they must return . . . or not.

12

DOSSIE WAS NO SMALL bit annoyed to find Jan well oiled when, given a leave from Miss Cheltham's, she had ditched her maid's uniform and run downtown to get to the flop.

Winter had left the city and had taken away the chill winds they stuffed up the chinks in their flop against. It left behind a sullen springtime of dense, stuffy air that gave over into a thick, noxious summer soup. They did not light candles to illumine their dinner. There was so little air from their small window that they did not even hang upon each other kissing.

"I've got a baby, Jan." Dossie told him the news in a sudden swoop and waited for his reaction. Jan sat straighter at the words and turned toward Dossie smiling, looking up with an uninhibited grin.

"Ah, girl! I'm as happy as a little monkey! How long have you known it?" He stood up and grabbed her at the waist and swirled her about the floor in a small dizzying circle. He would have broken into a full-out dance—a reel or a breakdown. But Dossie's body did not fly and dance with him.

"I learned from a doctor today," she said in a flat voice. Jan was puzzled. Dossie spoke as if she was announcing an old shoe caught in a fishing net. Now she had what she'd been wishing for.

"Are you not joyful?" Jan asked. "At last he's coming!"

"I am joyful. I am happy from my toes clear up to my ears, good boy. But what will we do? I want to go back home for my baby's sake. What will my husband say? What will your uncle say?"

Jan's stomach dropped. Now after all these turns and twists, here comes the child! The Grandmothers take their time. The sour truth in the midst of this joy—this excitement—is that they had sealed their fate. They could not now ever go home.

"We'll stay here. I can keep you and the child. I can bring in enough coin. You won't suffer."

"You promised Hat and Noelle to bring your babies back to the mountains, boy," Dossie said to him teasingly.

"We're a long way from home."

"Just so. We ought to go home. It's time to go."

"You want to go back to Duncan?" Jan growled angrily. "You got the baby you was looking for—your boon to Duncan. Now you want to go home to give it to him. You're a whore, Dossie Smoot," he spat out. "You're on the game as same as the others. You trade your cunt for what you want!" Jan grabbed up his hat and ran down the hall. He made the hidden turn in the corridor and suffered the momentary fear of the black dark hole. He came out the back of their warren to Prince Street, slapped at his own leg, and fumed and swore at the tangle. He wanted Dossie! He wanted the baby! He wanted to stay in the city! He wanted to dance! He wanted to go back to the mountains. He could not go back to the mountains.

"Well, let her go home!" Jan snorted furiously. Let her go and take her stomach back to Duncan without him! Could he survive in the city without Dossie? Dossie was his sticking post — his one tether. How would he be lighthearted enough to dance a jig if Dossie went back to the mountains?

And his uncle? Duncan would take her back in a flash. Did Duncan expect her to return to him chaste and unchanged? The ancestors were contrary to send a child now. There was no straight course in this life. There were only the twists and turns. In the midst of a fuss folk look for a straight, even path with a gentle slope toward the hereafter. But that is the chimera — the myth — the dream. The straight, gentle way does not ever come.

Duncan had kept the truth of himself from Dossie so it was not a fair marriage. But no one saw it that way, least of all her. And Jan knew his uncle would not accept losing his wife to his nephew in a love match. He might choose to be dignified about it, but he could as easily kill them in a rage and be seen by his neighbors as righteously vindicated.

"You are going back to Duncan then?" Jan said accusingly when he returned. His voice was dull and dark and his speech slurred. Dossie smelled his breath. He put his hands on her shoulders and pressed her down on the bed.

"You're taking my baby back to him? The old man couldn't do it so you're giving him my baby?" Jan yelled.

"Jan," Dossie said quietly — whisperingly because of the shock. "You promised. When a gal gets a baby, she must think of something besides her tuck-up. Me and this child cannot thrive in this town, boy, you know it. Me and this baby belong with Duncan."

Sobering quickly, Jan said, "It's three of us, Dossie. Me and you and the baby. We three will be together."

"Suppose we cannot stay together?"

"At the first trouble you run back to Duncan!" Jan shouted. "You think I'm not man enough to keep you in New York, is't? You want to return to 'Uncle' then?" Jan said with a blistering sneer. "You still love him, Dossie?"

"Yes, o' course I do. I've always got to love him 'cause I wouldn't have myself in freedom without him. Without Duncan you would have been raised by the man that killed your mama. We've both been saved by Duncan."

"Remember when you thought he was God?" Jan asked quietly.

"I remember when you did, too. I have thought it over and over. I'm not gonna fuck him no more. But I'm going home to Russell's Knob to face him and tell him we got to be together. Maybe we got to go away from home after that."

"Just remember you taking my baby to the mountains," Jan said.

"We mus' sen' word to Duncan," Dossie continued, framing a resolve. "We mus' tell him that things are changed and we're coming home to stand up to it."

"You mean to tell your husband you carrying another man's child? How you gonna say it?"

"We wait till we get there to tell it all," Dossie said. "I will just write that things are changed, that there is worry, that we must come home.

"What we going to tell him, Dossie, that he won't want to hurt you? I'll kill him if he raise a hand to you!"

"You gonna kill Duncan?"

"Yes, if he try to hit you. I ain't going let him do that especially with my son inside," Jan vowed.

"I will tell him that I love him, but I love you more. I'll beg him to love me enough to open his hand and let me and my baby out of it. I don't wan' to be a small, sweet thing in anybody's palm." Dossie spoke resolutely. "We go on home and see if he wan' us to stay. Then we leave an' come back here if . . . if it trouble him too much. Long as we can be together and our baby is safe."

Then they hugged and held each other.

"S'pose this is a gal in here?" Dossie asked him.

"I 'on't know. What you s'pose?" Jan asked her.

What had Jan done to Duncan though? He'd hit Duncan in his one only sore place and it was justifiable only by the measure that he loved Dossie and that it could not be helped. Dossie was right to want to go home. But Dossie was wrong to think it would be so simple as asking to be forgiven. A woman may do this easily enough. She may confess her sins and accept chastisement and wipe her soul clean. Jan couldn't do anything now but go off to the war and not come back to Uncle's hearth. Not all of his virtues, nor half of his sins, would change this one treachery. He had lost his home.

Since Minnie Stewart's establishment was a spot for colored folk to gather in Paterson, the telegraph man and the postman most often sent what they had for colored people to Minnie's place. She was careful, circumspect, and employed a network of helpers to find people and give them their news. Because of her close personal association with the bachelor postmaster, Minnie also received abolitionist newspapers and tracts, "French" periodicals, peacock ticklers, and other confidential postings without hindrance.

When a letter came at Minnie Stewart's hub for colored people's information, a reliable boy was dispatched to find Mr. Duncan Smoot.

June 3, 1863

To my dear husband,

My heart is filled with hope that you and all are well. We are coming home. Things have changed. Is it all clear there? We wait on your word.

Dossie Bird

She sent word they were coming home! Duncan's heart was silly with glee. He was exhilarated at seeing a paper Dossie had touched — feeling the writing and knowing her lovely fingers had made the letters. He wanted more news. But, of course, this more would come from her lips.

"Yes, come!" Duncan shouted and alarmed the dog and flushed some small birds roosting on a bush. Oh, yes! He wanted them where he could touch them no matter what had happened. There seemed to be no more danger of hangings and burnings. Duncan laughed to hear the birds chirping and rocked back and forth on the porch step hugging his knees like a small boy. "Come and bring Jan back and tell me about it all!" he cried out, hoping the small chickadees on the wing would take the answer to her right away. He got his mount and rode off into town to send back the word. "Come!"

This letter from Dossie was not the first news Duncan had of them. Dossie had written several bulletins of their doings in her sweet, careful script. Duncan became more regular at Minnie's after Dossie and Jan left so that he could receive them. He did not write back to them. He had others to spy and send him news. His first most reliable informant had been his friend Ezra Oliver.

Checking in at Minnie's — hoping and yearning — gave Duncan's days a shape and substance. Pet came to Minnie's, too, to wait and hope that news of Jan and Dossie would come. Pet looked for news from his papa and Arminty as well. That Papa's child had been a girl he knew. Pet wanted to know how Papa was faring in Canada even if his mother did not. He waited for a letter from Jan. He'd taken it upon himself to keep his eye on Uncle, to bring Jan and Dossie back, to put them all back together in their soup.

June 10, 1863

Dear Jan,

Please come home. Everything seems clear here. Nobody is looking for nobody. They all accept that Emil Branch is gone. I heard a lot of things said about Dossie. Most folk in Russell's Knob think she ran off with you after all. They think you used Emil Branch's disappearance to cover you running off from Uncle. Don't nobody give a damn about Emil Branch. Come back. He's desperate for her. After all, Uncle knows the truth of why you left. If Uncle says you were all this time hunting for her and trying to bring her back home and that he accepts it, then everybody else will go along. Mama loves you and Dossie and misses you. She is also in some pain on Uncle's behalf, to see him as he is. He is very melancholy. I leave it to you to say what you will to her about Uncle. Does she love him at all still? I know you've succeeded with her by now. Is she completely tied to you? Some folk say Dossie's a whore, but they say this of any woman who leaves town on an adventure. Come back. Uncle is sick for his wife. He wants her back, Jan. You got to bring her home to Uncle.

Your cousin,
Petrus Wilhelm

Several days after Duncan had posted his answer to Dossie's letter, he received Jan's.

June 12, 1863

Dear Sir,

Have no fear, your wife is well. She wants to come home. Is it safe to bring her?

Uncle, I am sorry to say that I love your wife, Dossie, very much. I was greedy for her. I could not help it. I have tricked her and seduced her. I am sorry. Dossie is too good and beautiful and I am so wild and dirty. She has a baby coming now. Please take her back and raise her baby and I will go away. I swear to go off to the war.

It is all my fault, Uncle. And it is your fault, too, Uncle. You never told her the truth about yourself.

Your loving nephew,
Jan Smoot

July 1, 1863

My Dear Nephew Jan Smoot,

Do you remember this truth? I could have let them old Munsees keep you and use you for a stinking saddle boy sleeping with their stock. They cared less for a motherless boy like you than a cow flop. I took you to raise, but I could not change you. You are just like your worthless father. Why should my wife suffer because of your nature? Bring her home and go away. To join the war is the very best thing that you can do.

Tell her that I love her as always and can hardly blame her for anything that has happened.

Your Uncle who raised you,
Duncan Smoot

By the time July was full upon them, the news from New York City was volatile. Newspapers in Paterson and the environs had, for weeks, been full of the discontent with the war conscription. Battle news and draft unrest elicited partisan excitement in the larger environs, and the patrons of Minnie's were alternately fearful or exultant. They talked about the war long and loud. Some even sympathized with the carping foreigners who thought it was not any of their affair to fight for Negroes. The bold and free black men in Minnie's thought it was fairer to give them the guns and the uniforms. They consecrated the floorboards with ale libation and pledged their passion and their grit to fight the rebels.

If he'd not been preoccupied with thinking about Dossie and Jan, Duncan might have thought about the pros and cons of the war. He might have chosen to take up arms. Hadn't he and the others he worked with long been the skirmishers in this conflict over freedom? He was not afraid to fight, but until Dossie was home, he could not think of anything else. He did fear for Pet, though. Could he keep Pet out of the fray for Hat's sake?

Back at the first of the year on the first day of Negro freedom when the document the president had signed took effect, Duncan had mused on the many folk he had helped along to their freedom. They could rest easily now, could relax vigilance. Their tormentors were on the run. Truthfully, it was only Dossie's freedom that Duncan cared about anymore. Was she now free to never be taken from him? He had long ago decided to feed himself to any lawman who came looking for the killer of Emil Branch. So it seemed that she was free of any threat.

The back and forth of haranguing viewpoints, circulating information, and the fear of uncertainty was a canker that grew daily in Paterson and was spreading to all of the outlying towns.

Then on a morning in July, word came that black folk were fleeing New York City on account of mobs of Irish and their burning.

"Go home and look after the homestead," Duncan barked at Pet. "Put your mama and Noelle in your pocket and keep them safe. Tell the People to fortify. I'ma stay in town until my precious comes," Duncan said.

The Irish and other groups in Paterson were working themselves up, too. There was liable to be fighting in town. These hard-pressed, poor whites were pissed at the swells that didn't have to bother with the war. And there were plenty of rich bastards in Paterson who paid a pittance to their workers and stood on the necks of the poor slobs. There was plenty of discontent around. And Duncan knew what any other colored in Paterson knew: when the pale poor get mad and fortified with liquid courage, they decide it's the "niggers' " fault.

"Come. Come back home right now and be safe!" Duncan prayed his letter's contents again and again. Dossie listened to birds, so Duncan confided to every little winged beast he saw in the hope it might take up his words and carry them to her.

13

THE NIGHT OF JULY 13, 1863, was a bad night to be a black in New York City. Homes and businesses and hangouts and flops and alleys and hovels and shacks of colored or the people who defended them were aflame. Even the Colored Orphans' Home got sacked and burnt up by a well-oiled, vicious mob. Ah, a price is paid for forgetting your place and circumstance when the white men and their women are in a roil and boil and are pledged to run colored out of New York City.

The draft was called and implementation begun, and these rioters were firmly committed to resist it. Some later said the sin attached to murder and thievery was waived these nights, for the mob had sworn itself to righteous rebellion on account of the draft — the call-up — the conscription. It was said their clerics took their side, and their women took up banner and truncheon and murderous cries.

The mobs set fires that ate up shanties and nice edifices alike if they were associated with colored. Wise folk abandoned their belongings and took themselves off over back fences to safety. Colored flooded onto ferries and sought shelter in police stations and the army barracks.

It was reckless of Jan and Dossie to ignore these soundings.

Their own lives had them pitching and reeling, and they hadn't paid the proper mind to the temper of the streets.

They came to their plan. Jan agreed to leave and go home with Dossie. They would face Duncan together, and now that Jan had made his pledge he was content — no, excited — to go back to Russell's Knob.

The bawdy joke of Black Bob's beginnings was that his father had made sons on all sides of the blanket. Bob's tenements were considered a safe refuge for colored on account that Bob was himself half an Irishman. Jan moved through the city to get to Dossie and bring her to safety at Black Bob's. He didn't want her to risk going through the streets by herself. Colored women were being dragged off into alleys. Neither young nor old were safe.

"Miss Cheltham took her carriage and went off to escape the crowd," Tilly cried and ran about like a chicken for the pot, gathering things she figured she'd not be stripped of on the street. Her agitation had her twisting on her hair and chewing at her lips. "She won't let herself be caught. And she ain't comin' back for nobody. Run! You must run. You cannot let 'em catch you an' kill your baby. You gotta think of the nipper and run off as fast as you can." Dossie laughed to see that Tilly had stuffed her pantaloons with so many of Miss Cheltham's clothes that she looked like a woman eight months along herself. But she quaked to see Tilly flying out of the back of the town house at top speed, hoisting her stomach and hightailing over Miss Cheltham's back fence.

Jan came up to Miss Cheltham's back door then and Dossie's heart took wing to see him. She wanted to latch on to him and not be loosed come what may. Her sense of safety returned despite the menacing, noisy crowds on the streets. Jan would have a plan.

Jan decided they would fly through the streets — would run — to get to their place. They had to get around the mob. They must not be overtaken uptown. They must get downtown. Their passage was arranged at the waterfront. All they must do is gather up and go home to Russell's Knob.

Dossie shrieked when Jan grabbed up a handful of soot and smeared her white uniform, tore at the collar, and ripped the sleeves to her elbows.

"Them bog whores, them bitches, will pull the clothes off you. You got on more undies than they've ever seen on their sorries. They'll rob 'em off you. Colored women are being attacked, Dossie!" Jan cried. "You got to get down to Bob's quick as you can. You got to be quick and brave and save yourself and your baby."

He heard himself saying the words. He was separating them both. She didn't fully understand that he meant they must go separately. They were to be pulled apart then. These two who had held to each other like a plaster to skin had to separate now. Jan convinced Dossie that their chances were best if they ran off down different streets. She was to skulk, to hide in doorways, to go aground if she saw a safe hole. Get back downtown to Black Bob's for refuge. The only way back to Russell's Knob was through Black Bob's. Go there! Get there!

A mob has got little brain and no heart, but numerous, countless, numberless hands and feet. The great flood of people that formed it was fed at every tributary and side street until all of the avenues were filled with enraged people. Events quickly assumed an alarming pitch in the western part of the city. Men assembled in groups as if according to arrangements. They moved along all the avenues northward. Men knocked off work in the various factories and workshops to join the crowd. The separate groups swelled and came together in lots near Central Park. All of the streets and avenues uptown became blackened with white people.

"I'll run off different," Jan said, his words sounding to himself as if coming from away far off. "I'll go down a different street. We can meet up at the flop. Nobody will dare come down in there — in Black Bob's place," Jan assured Dossie.

If he sent her off under cover, he could distract any followers for a bit to let her start off. There were knots of angry whites at nearly every corner. Dossie might be lucky and escape the marauders. God might protect her. She was good. She had been wronged and she was still good and had been brave and was bringing a baby. "Help her, Grandmother," Jan prayed.

Could he pull the threat from her? Could he distract her pursuers — giving them a tastier target? They were bent on causing mayhem. Colored women had been grabbed on the thoroughfares and fondled, and drunkards had wagged their jaspers at them or spit on them. Some colored women had been dragged into alleys and raped.

The sight of Dossie's back darting from side to side like a crab crawling was alarming. Her clothes were still too white, too crisp! Jan wished for once that she was a less visible treat. But what would that matter now? A mob has no thoughts, only eyes, and hands and feet and threats. Jan's last coherent thought was about Dossie and her safety and their baby's life. He danced. He slap tapped his booted feet. He pounded and whirled and cavorted on the pavement with bluster and mockery, and the mob of scowlers turned onto him and did not see Dossie, and when Jan started to run from them, they followed, and all his thoughts and plans outraced him.

Jan tried to keep his feet. His feet did, in fact, leave the ground as punches and kicks and gouges kept his body off the pavement. They threw him down and stomped him. They left Jan nearly lifeless and ran on when they saw another colored man, but Jan had no time to check his wounds or crawl away. More of the mob came up, and he took off his boots, thinking that he could run faster without them. Indeed he could. He threw the boots as bombs and hit one boy beside his head.

Jan Smoot ran as he had never before done in life. Duncan! Duncan had said not to run — he and Pet were not to run off from bullies! They must stand and fight. Hell! Now was time to run, though, to live another day if he could. Duncan would agree that now was the time to run. "Oh, God, just one more day to know that Dossie is safe and to kiss her — even if the next day must be my last. Please, God!"

The streets and alleys went by. The encroaching mob chased Jan westward until he was uncertain that he was heading to the beloved flop that he was trying to reach at Black Bob's. His heart nearly burst, but he held to the hope that Dossie had been luckier than him. Maybe she'd been able to reach the flop.

Dossie! She'd saved him from Emil Branch at some forfeit of her soul's innocence, no doubt. If he could save her and the child. If only she could take the baby back up to Duncan's heaven. It was the heaven she believed in.

Jan kept running. He surveyed the street before him. He thought he might reach some hideout near the riverside under the docks. When the crowd behind him swelled still more and trained on him and yelled to rouse their confederates and brandished bats and swore to take him and to hang him, Jan jumped into the river. He jumped in to chance being able to swim or to float to a safe place, or even to cross the river if possible.

He was pulled from the water and pounced upon. They trounced him and kicked him, and Jan latched on to the toe of one assailant. He bit it free. They beat him senseless and then hoisted his body to a street pole. A swaggerer came forth from the back of the mob and scalped a lock from Jan Smoot's head and tucked it into his belt.

The indomitable Worm came upon the end of the scene and was so shocked at the sight that he watered himself. Johnny Dancer? Jan Smoot hung on a lamppost? Worm lashed at the menacing whites with a scythe and nicked all that did not flee. The ugly crowd would have beat and burnt him, too, for inter-vening to pull Jan's body away, except that their interest was diverted to another victim, and they ran off at a call that another black was sighted.

Worm then saw an arrogant creature retreating who turned and stepped like he was doing a cakewalk. A prize hung from his belt. A stolen patch of scalp from Jan Smoot's head. Worm stood and looked good and long at the haughty, swaggering alley rat whose face was spread with dirt and red freckles. The one who'd taken the scalp turned and he trembled for one brief moment, when he registered that Worm was studying him. The hair swung at his belt and dripped blood.

"Mark that boy! Mark that one!" Worm roared.

Some while later, a few hours only, Worm sneaked up on the tough who'd taken Jan's hair and caught his neck in the crook of his elbow on Sullivan Street. He pulled his pigsticker and showed it to the boy, which caused him to freeze and drop his hands. Worm grabbed him by the belt at his waist and tore

Jan's scalp off it before sticking him in the gut, lest the boy's blood fall on his friend's nephew's hair. The boy's blood did gush and run unstaunched over the cobblestones from the hole Worm tore in him.

Because he must not leave Duncan Smoot's nephew hung and scalped on the streets of New York City, Worm brought Jan's body to Bessie Cronin, an unofficial undertaker in the Five Points. Though licensed only as a laundress, she dressed poor and colored people for burial, was in the employ of certain medical students who were in the market for cadavers, and had contacts for chemicals. She prepared Jan to travel home.

Worm made up his mind that night, in that alley where he gutted Jan's killer, to go and die somewhere other than New York. Now, after days of seeing colored folk's heads cracked and bodies burnt and women suffering more violation than can be redressed, he was considering the gate. Jan's mutilated body was the finish. This boy had done naught but dance, stepping high and smiling at the girls and shaking out his pretty curls for the delight of the drunkards. Worm's patience with New York had run out. And perhaps his courage, too, had gone. He'd likely used up all of what he'd been allotted for luck and guts in paying out the nasty little bastard that killed Jan Smoot. He had better go. Yes, Worm had better be good and gone before the bulldogs on the police force tied him to the eviscerated body in the alley on Catherine Street. When Worm left off Jan's body at Black Bob's, he boarded the ferry at Peck Slip and put his back to New York forever.

Dossie saw the place on Jan's head where the hair came away, and there was the horrific, naked plug out of his flesh. She did not faint. She did not fall. She was frozen still at the sight and her senses left her. There was a hole above his right eye! The eye was there—the blessed, precious, beloved eye was in his head though the animation, the light, and the changeable beauty of it and its partner were gone.

"Way back a ways they pummeled my son an' kilt him. They strung up his dead body and rained blows on me when I cut him down. I like to lost my ear. 'Twas a long while ago and the worse of it has wore off," said an unfamiliar woman who'd taken refuge behind the barricades of Black Bob's tenement.

If there is any one thing that will bring the body back to animation, it is the smell of coffee and the call of birds. When the thick-bodied, copper-colored woman that Dossie could not remember knowing brought her a cup of coffee, her body revived. Dossie was certain then that she heard the little King-fisher Woman calling but thought it must be geese following the river. It was a rally, a call to go home at once. And she gathered up.

When the ferry left the west bank of the North River, all of the colored aboard it were shaking quietly. The only sound from them was their rattling bones. Many other colored took themselves in the other direction. Their bones, too, rattled inside them like dried beans. They crossed town to escape to the outlying areas to the east into Brooklyn.

Dossie took up the arrangement that Jan had made for their departure and put his body aboard the ferryboat. The boatman was not happy to take a coffin box on his packet, but Dossie convinced him by showing him who it was in the box. It was Johnny Dancer, the boy he'd made the passage with! The boat-man became tearful. "Beat and strung up?" he exclaimed. "Ach! The toughs have gone mad to string up Johnny Dancer here." The boatman said that Johnny Dancer had spoken of his home, and he vowed to see Dossie and the coffin all the way to

Paterson. He installed her comfortably and kept a protective eye on her as she sat alongside the coffin. He brought her biscuits and coffee and told her about the time he'd had a mug of porter and watched Johnny dance.

When he was given the news, Duncan walked out of Minnie's in a daze and wound through the streets of Paterson, then went back to Minnie's and drank whiskey that he did not feel or taste. Colored folk were spreading news. Eyewitnesses were grilled. It was worse than '34 when he had run from New York. Jan had been killed! Her telegram had said "killed."

"Son!" Duncan cried out several times. Had Cissy called Jan to her on the other side? "Why you so selfish, Cissy? Cissy!" he cried angrily. It was always this way. The vindictive dead ancestors were ever after pulling loved ones to their side. He'd held on to Jan this side as long as he could, but the boy's mother had won him at last. Ach! Cissy might argue with Duncan's picture of things he knew. He had often been harsh with her boy.

"You take care of my Dossie now! Cissy, you bring her back good and safe," he whispered an entreaty to his sister. He put his head onto the table before him in complete surrender to the grief and the whiskey.

Folk fleeing the lynching and burning in New York City carried horrible tales to every crossroads and meeting place along the roads. Hat threatened to dash herself off a boulder at the back of the house when word of Jan's murder reached her. Duncan and Pet held her and allowed her to thrash at them in her grievous fury. Hat might not have cried so much if her own leg had been taken off. Noelle was stricken with pain radiating along her arms when she was told of Jan's death. She lay down on a pallet facing westward and refused to speak to Duncan, Hat, or Pet.

Duncan, Hat, and Pet went to the landing at Paterson to meet Dossie and to take Jan's coffin from the barge. Dossie revived at the sight of them, when she knew she had accomplished her duty. She had brought Jan home. Now she had leave to let go of herself and fall down in her grief.

Duncan saw her at the landing when she stood at the rail of the boat and thought she was changed though recognizable. Her body was different. He saw it instantly. He was swept with the wholly inappropriate idea to remove her clothes and remove his own and press their bodies together — their skins touching. It seemed the only right way to know what changes there had been. He felt ashamed of this feeling and ashamed of crediting these thoughts in the face of his grief. He knew the circumstances had changed somehow. She had written it. She was bringing Jan home dead. But skin to skin was how he longed to renew his acquaintance with Dossie Bird.

Duncan's house — Dossie's home — was familiar but shabby in some measure. Dossie saw that the curtains were dirty and hanging east and west. The house had not fared so well without her, she thought. On crossing the threshold she pushed back her cuffs and took up the broom. She collected dirt in circular swirls and brushed it out of the front door to thwart ill will. Duncan busied himself with bringing in water and warming up the stove. He moved slowly. Perhaps it was the drag of grief. Had he changed so much? Was it only sadness and shock? Did she seem to him to be changed? Did he notice a change in her? Had he noticed that she carried a baby?

Dossie stopped her sweeping and stood across the room from Duncan.

"I am three months along and it is Jan Smoot's child and I will not lie about it to you," Dossie said plainly, facing him. He better know right away in case he did not want her to stay in the house even for one night. She'd seen his eyes on her. She knew he had questions.

"Ah, the citified woman is bold!" Duncan said ruefully. "I thank you for being straight, Dossie girl," he continued. "You and your baby are at home."

Duncan wanted to rush up and entangle her in his arms with soft affection, to touch and hold her and assure her. But Dossie did not invite him.

"Not a girl anymore," she said kindly to keep Duncan from going back and getting honey names and thinking all was the same.

"Aw . . . no, no. I know it. I wan' to call you by a sweet name because you been in so much trouble. Dossie. I can call you that, missus?"

She smiled at him. "A cup of coffee, sir?" Dossie put the broom to rest in a corner and took a seat at the table.

"You want me here?" she challenged when both were seated. She reckoned she knew what Duncan was thinking. "You lookin' for Dossie girl to come back? She didn't come back. Emil Branch took her off. No, I dropped her myself. I lef' her right nex' to the body of the sheriff. I've been a real grown woman since. And now Jan is dead? I do what I want to do, Duncan. I drink whiskey, too, if I want.

Duncan looked at her and said nothing. Yes, he wanted her. And he wanted her to stay as he always had. And he was itchy about it as he'd always been.

Later they drank whiskey together. Dossie was modest. She had not become a sloppy, excessive drinker. She sipped, sat back in her chair, and listened to his talk of the doings about the place. She smiled. The sauces in his groin came to a pitch and he wanted so much to touch her and then he did. He reached across the table to stroke her face and then to touch her breast. Dossie didn't start. She pushed off his hand. She wore an unsurprised expression as though she'd waited to confront this moment and had designed a response. She'd never before pushed him with a gentle, firm reproof, in the way of this short sweep of the fingers. "Another time, Duncan," Dossie said so clearly and quietly and decisively that he wanted to bawl.

Pet's first recollection, the point his world began, was the delight in baby Jan's eyes when his mother bent over the bed in which they both lay. She sang to them. Both babies reached for her, both kicked their feet, both were taken up by Jan's mother. Both were satisfied at that first most alluring tit. When Pet tasted warm sugar and butter spun together in a toddy or in a pie, he thought of his aunt Cissy. He was sure this was how her skin had tasted in their mouths. She was a big woman, as he remembered, though he remembered also that they were very small then. She could lift and carry them both, and both of them would let their sleep heavy heads fall onto her. He and Jan had lost her so early! Cissy! Cissy! But didn't none of them—not even his own mama—credit that he'd suffered her loss, too. It was not just Jan who was crushed by his mother's death. And now he was expected to bear up under Jan's death? The fear that he might not be able to worried him.

August 15, 1863

Dear Petrus,

My dear Pet,

I received your letter and the cruel news of Jan's death. How can this have happened? I fear for your mother's state. Is she well? We loved him completely — your mother most of all.

Have you looked at the papers that I left for you? There is something that you should know. Why do you speak of the army? I am told you can arrange to pay for another man to go in your place. You can afford to do this I am certain. If it becomes necessary to do so. I recommend paying this bond so that you may remain safely at home to care for your mother. She will need you and the brewery will need you. Duncan and Dossie need you. It must be a troubling time for all of you. Pet, don't go to war. Find a way to stay and take care of them all.

Please come and visit me. We are so numerous here that I can't pull away from them and come to you. You have three siblings. Arminty thrives here.

Your Papa

Pet hadn't opened the document his father gave him on leaving the country. He thought it contained the pernicious receipt of his mother's purchase. He didn't want to lay eyes on that paper, though he knew its contents. When he opened the envelope that lay at the very bottom of a box of keepsakes, he saw it was a legally executed copy of his falsified birth certificate. He was named and listed as the son of a deceased white mother and his own white father and thus was himself completely white. A note accompanied the document.

My Dear Petrus,
You may need this one day.
                                 Your Papa

                                            August 28, 1863

My Dear Father,
You have been cruel to my mother. Though you began nobly by saving her, you have ever since hurt her. It was a deep wound to us that you warranted she was dead and I was white. Perhaps it seemed like the right thing at the time? What can one think of a man who has done the things you have done, Papa?

Shall I state it plainly? You falsified the record of my birth. You purchased my mother and made me and I intend to enlist with the United States Colored Troops in Philadelphia. My mother will attest to me. I am colored as she is and we intend to say so. Papa, you must see that those Irish bastards who killed Jan in New York were balking and rioting at having to fight for the colored. They didn't want to risk losing their lives on account of colored folks and slaves. I don't blame them for not wanting to fight somebody else's fight. But I hate them for killing Jan and I won't fight beside them. I want to fight for the slaves. I want to take up arms. All along me and Jan wanted to take up arms for the slaves. Even as boys we wanted to grab up Uncle's guns and right the wrongs.

I will speak for myself and I will fight for myself. I am a Colored Man. I will join up. I do it so that Dossie's baby that was made by Jan will be free and comfortable—a happy colored child. And I'll fight for Arminty, too. Perhaps if I fight and win, you and Arminty can cross back and bring your embarrassing brood.

Papa, I am going to fight for the slaves regardless of what you advise. Papa, you have followed your jasper halfway around the world. You are a fine one to say that I must stay on the porch and mind my mother.

Your Pet,
Petrus Wilhelm

Dossie's waters broke at dawn and she set off on a loud keening. Her body was wracked with her work, and her wailing was ear-splitting. At noontime, the baby seemed to go still, a small skiff in a calm. The struggling mother continued to wail and her throat became sore. When the midwife arrived, she was cross that the mother had been allowed to weaken herself with hours of crying. Martha Remsen massaged her patient with practiced hands, relaxed her, steadied her through the throes, and shortly after nightfall a little girl came forth.

"Your wife will need more than a root woman the next time, Mr. Smoot. A midwife or a doctor should be called sooner," she said to Duncan, when she had been given some supper, a glass of ale, and her fee.

Duncan leapt up in alarm, but was stopped by Martha Remsen. "She is at the end of her energy, sir. She is sleeping, but she will recover. She is young and the baby is robust."

Duncan sat back in his chair and thought about the long day when Pet was born. He glanced up at Hat's placid, pretty face and remembered that he and Wilhelm got stupid drunk that day and brought a white doctor in from town that they had threatened with a gun. The man was surly, and he scared Hat, and the boy only came when the doctor had gone onto the porch to smoke and Cissy alone was there to catch his slick body like grabbing up a trout.

Through the first hours Dossie's baby was fretful. Dossie slept, then roused before dawn light and saw Duncan by the window holding the baby and looking out. What did he look at in the dark? Who did he look at in the shadows? "Jan," she called in a hazy consciousness.

"No, Dossie Bird, it is Duncan," he answered very quietly, very softly. "I am sorry, Dossie. It is only me and your baby girl."

"Ah, Duncan, you so good," Dossie said as her confusion cleared. She had heard Jan's voice in her dream and she started to remember his words. He was not soft. He did not plead. He hectored. He'd invaded her deep dream state, and each time she had turned from one side of the bed to the other, it was to escape his voice and his implacable grimace. He was not coy. He did not smile. He demanded that she tell it all and make the terms she'd pledged. "Don't lie to him and don't soften to him unless he swears," Jan hollered at Dossie in her head, causing her ears to throb. When she was fully awakened, when Duncan had handed her a cup of water, when she sat upright in the bed, Dossie spoke out as though a hand pushed her at the center of her back and would not let her stall, turn back, or turn around.

"Duncan Smoot, you got a daughter now? Do you accept my daughter now? Jan made her for the Smoots. He said, 'Uncle will make my child fortunate and you will make him beautiful and, if she is a girl, she'll be a prize.'" Dossie smiled inside herself to recollect this talk, but her face was heavy with grief and could not express a smile just then. "Is it in you to know all of these things and call her daughter without hesitation?" Dossie watched Duncan's eyes and thought she would recognize if he tried to dissemble.

"Hush," he answered. For the first time since Dossie had returned with Jan's body, Duncan felt impatient, miffed at her. Is he so small a man as to be unable to accept what Grandmother has given him? "What will you call her? Will you name her for your Ooma?"

"No, no. Give her a name from your people? Is she your daughter then?"

"Sarah then," Duncan said quickly. "Sarah Smoot. It is my mama's name. She was Sarah Vanderhoven. She became Smoot just after the Vanderhovens split up. Some of the family went to Cincinnati calling themselves Hoven. The others stayed in Russell's Knob and called themselves Vander. So my mama became a Vander, then a Smoot. The People are curious acting sometimes, Dossie girl," Duncan babbled, letting his words trail off and smiling to himself.

There was a touch on her spine. She turned her head toward her left shoulder and saw his head very large. She knew his curls.

"Jan did not rape me. Emil Branch did that, and his baby left me when I reached New York. Jan Smoot, your nephew, did not do me any harm. He did not fool me or force me or wear me down with pleading or frighten me. I came to him with the plan. I wanted a favor and I begged him so that I could bring a baby for you. I wanted it for myself most of all. I was so jealous of the other women. I only wanted him to put her there. It is what he did finally as a gift to me...and to you. I was a silly and spoiled girl who wanted what every other woman had. Jan loved me and I knew it. I ought to have loved him at least by half of what he loved me, but I never did. He loved you very much and I knew it and I trifled with his love and his loyalty so I could have my prize and have you. I lost him. I know you threatened him not to harm me or lose me in New York. I harmed him. I lost him. It would be wrong for you to think that he took an advantage with me. He did not. I welcomed him. I coerced him. It was me who used him."

Duncan tried to take up talking as if he hadn't heard what she said. "Sarah Jane because of Jan. It's a good name: Sarah Jane Smoot. Sarah was Cissy's given name, too." He spoke almost as if he was completely surprised to remember his sister's name. "Papa coined her name Cissy to call her something different from my mama. Sweet, lovely Cissy. Her name was Sarah Jane." He paused in speaking, then breathed deeply, he sighed and held on to the child more firmly. "Dossie." He said the name in a way he'd never spoken it before. It was her name as it stood, not embellished with his endearments, fripperies, and decorations of speech. It was her as she stood before him with no desire, no lust attached.

"I take the weight for losing Jan. I have not been a wholly honest man. I didn't lie to you, but I kept the truth from you. And I was cruel to him because he knew all my secrets and I knew he'd one day love you more than me and want to tell you about all of my sores. And I taunted him for loving you and I shamed him into bringing you home and going to war. I know I'm the one to be the caretaker of the Smoots. But I ain't done so good all told."

Duncan handed the infant into Dossie's arms. It boggled his mind to think on what had happened to Jan. He knew now and was ready to admit that he had failed to save Cissy and Jan both and the weight of this great failure could only be mitigated by his complete embrace of the baby girl. Duncan Smoot is a man who has made big mistakes—eye gouging, burning and punishing, stopping or not stopping. Grandmother's very flawed instrument. Wherefore he is Sarah's papa? He is Sarah's papa because she is Dossie's daughter and he is pledged to Dossie, to Jan and to Cissy, to his mama and all of them back to Lucy Smoot, who turned her back on the barrel of a gun to free her children. He'd thought he was the pasha, the head of the clan. Perhaps his life is finally just this simple? He is the scarf on Dossie's arm and her standard bearer and her protector. He is here to make her daughter fortunate.

He has already given her girl a sweet name. He has coined it in his head in his own private baby parlance. She is Janny—she is Jan as he had always said it with the added fillip of delight.

Is Dossie some kind of a wood witch that she has enchanted him so? Duncan studied her face and allowed himself to renew his enchantment. The beautiful favorite!

"You must promise to be a gentler man if you want us to stay." Dossie's voice was steady with great effort. "I will not let you chastise my girl. You must leave the switch to me. You must increase your sweetness or we will go. Jan made me promise to make you sweeter or go away. I pledged it to him and I will not go back on this promise."

"Dossie Bird!" Duncan exclaimed. "Where could you go? This is your home."

"You must pledge it or we will leave Russell's Knob," Dossie declared and captured his eyes levelly. "Dossie is no rabbit now, Duncan Smoot. She is Mother Bear and she will be her cub's champion." She started to chuckle with herself. She remembered! Was it a fancy tale or a prophecy? At their winter work, Hat had poked fun at her brother's mysterious time away, saying that he slept with she-bears in wintertime all because long, long ago Duncan had gone into a bear den in dead of winter when it was so cold they could barely catch their breath in the biting wind. Duncan, against advice, had taken a torch into the bear den. They all knew Mother Bear was inside, had taken her children and gone to sleep. He came out a day later sayin' that he'd slept with the bear and her cubs and that they'd hardly noticed him and it was very, very warm and smelled very, very pleasant. "Everybody knows Duncan is the bear's fancy," Hat would finish and giggle uncontrollably. Noelle would snap her eyes and pinch Hat's arms.

"This is your home, girl! It always has been," Duncan declared rather than swear any specifics.

"Duncan, you are not God," Dossie countered.

"Dossie, I pledge to be a stalwart for you and your daughter, Sarah Jane Smoot," he pronounced pleasantly.

"Yes, Jimmer?" Dossie asked, testing him, pressing him, teasing him.

"Yes, Dossie, I swear it solemnly."

Why, he'd torched the devil's tail to bring her to the mountains, to the ancestors, to Jan. Even if the white men's God had put this mark on his register as a sin, still it will have been well done.

"Yes, Jimmer."

Even if the Afric gods curl their lips in displeasure at his deeds and his methods, it will have been well done still. Janny, beloved Janny! Sarah Jane Smoot comes to the world!

"Yes, Jimmer Fish, it is well done!"

Acknowledgments

A work may have one author, but it needs friends and supporters to become a novel. I would like to acknowledge the deft and delicate, intelligent and beautiful touch of Terry Adams, my editor at Little, Brown and Company.

I would like to recognize the invaluable counsel, conscientious representation, and friendship of my literary agent, Cynthia Cannell, and the Cynthia Cannell Literary Agency.

Getting here is only half the battle. The battle is being here and thriving, and it needs a sister-warrior. I acknowledge my great good fortune to have Cheryl L. Clarke, poet and essayist, as my sister, my colleague, and my mentor.

About the Author

BREENA CLARKE grew up in Washington, D.C., and was educated at Howard University. For *Angels Make Their Hope Here* she drew inspiration from the tales and legends of the settlers of the Ramapo Mountains, not far from her home in New Jersey. Her previous novels are *River, Cross My Heart,* which was a selection of Oprah's Book Club, and *Stand the Storm.*

Reading Group Guide

ANGELS MAKE
THEIR HOPE HERE

by

Breena Clarke

An online version of this reading group guide can be found at littlebrown.com.

A Conversation with Breena Clarke

What was your first inspiration for Angels Make Their Hope Here*? Did you have any inspirations later in your writing process that changed the way you had originally imagined the book?*

I first got interested in imagining *Angels Make Their Hope Here* when I happened upon a small book about a mixed-race settlement in New York's Ramapo Mountains. Inquiring about these people led me to discover a lot more about the African American presence throughout the Mid-Atlantic. I began reading first-person slave narratives published mostly in the nineteenth and early-twentieth centuries. I was and continue to be fascinated with the lives of people who self-emancipated from slavery.

Dossie, your protagonist, is one of the few characters not born in Russell's Knob. She is very young at the start of her northward journey — too young to fully understand where her parents are sending her but old enough to know that she must depend on strangers for survival as she is passed from conductor to conductor along the way. In what ways did you want to capture the impact of slavery on her life while also remaining true to the fact that she is still a child?

The most damaging aspect of the institution of slavery is the destruction of familial relationships through separation and the inability of enslaved parents to protect their children. It is in the interest of preserving families that the people of Russell's Knob built a community — preferring to live apart from the mainstream in order to stay together with loved ones. Parenting in the time of slavery was necessarily fraught with peril. Dossie's parents did the most difficult thing imaginable. They sent their child off to uncertainty rather than have her suffer as an enslaved person on the Kenworthy plantation. They embraced a hope that, with the help of others, she could become free and live a better life. For them, the "knowable horror" of the Kenworthy plantation was worth risking their child's life and separating from her forever. The life of an enslaved child held no guarantee that she would not be involuntarily separated from her mother and father. She might be sold, she might be put to work on another plantation, she might be beaten, she might be raped, she might be killed. The only certainty in her life was that the people who loved her could not protect her. They could only facilitate her escape.

Also, it was very important to me that the enslaved people not be passive actors in the emancipation of Dossie. I've read many autobiographical escape accounts and narratives and realized that the people who succeeded in escaping slavery — self-emancipating — were bold, cunning, clever, and lucky. The popular depiction of the slave mother is, forced onto the auction block, she reaches for her children with arms outstretched, pleading, crying, helpless, collapsed in the dust. Evidently there were those who made the preemptive decision.

There are a lot of different parents, and types of parenting, in Angels.

I think *Angels Make Their Hope Here* is a novel about parenthood. I'd like to think that my large-topic theme centers on this question: Who are the progenitors of our United States? The parents in *Angels Make Their Hope Here* make bold decisions. One of the boldest is Ernst Wilhelm's — to take his pregnant mistress to Canada rather than to see mother and child sold south. With this decision, he forfeits not only his privileges as a white man but most of his wealth and comfort in Russell's Knob as well. Once again, a parent is forced to decide between uncertainty and a knowable horror.

The people of Russell's Knob are, by and large, a skilled and literate group. While literacy is an accomplishment that many persons of color are punished for or are compelled to conceal during this time period, in Russell's Knob the tradition of the written word is a given. Can you talk about your choice to present a culture of literacy without making it a focus of the story?

For African Americans, especially those who experienced enslavement, the ticket to being free and remaining free was the acquisition of literacy. Because they are survivalists, the people of Russell's Knob consider education in the dominant European language, English, an important tool for survival. The African and Native American ancestors of these people were not blank slates before European contact, either in Africa or in the Americas. They were fluent in the languages of trade among themselves, and they would have considered it vital to teach their children the European languages. In Russell's Knob the people educate and train their children in systematic ways because it is the best way to ensure survival. Though it is largely a patriarchal society, there is respect for the courage and intelligence of women. I chose to structure the people of Russell's Knob in a matrilineal tradition so that I could imagine a society that drew upon the strength of women as well as men.

It isn't always clear to the reader what race some of the main characters are. Was that intentional? I'm wondering if Duncan Smoot, for instance, is a free black man.

I wanted to leave certain questions of identity open. Readers of fiction bring their own ideas about racial identity and national origin to the page. In certain genre fiction a kind of racial shorthand is used and readers are given clues. I like to thwart that a bit.

You would rather it be ambiguous?

Oh, no. I really don't want to make up your mind. I know you'll come to a decision. We Americans always do. I think the word *amalgamation,* which is employed most of the time as a derisive term in descriptions of people, can inform a more inclusive worldview of what a mixed-race identity is. I think what you'd find among the people of Russell's Knob is that they have managed to bring strength and survival skills from all of their ancestors and forge them to make a strong whole. To me, that's amalgamation. I think it's a positive concept for a multiracial, multinational, inclusive society.

Both Jan Smoot and Petrus Wilhelm have European-sounding names. What do their names say about them or their history? Are they nods toward their heritage, or something else?

Both of these young men are what might be described as mixed-race, if what we mean is an individual whose parents belong to two different races according to the widely accepted ideas about race in this country. Jan's skin color is described as appearing dark relative to the paler European skin colors. Pet has the same pale-white skin as his father, and outside the context of his home he appears to be of entirely European heritage. In Russell's Knob, the advantages that white skin can afford are mitigated by a deep tradition of inclusiveness, respect, and appreciation for African and Native American culture. I intended their surnames, first names, and "sweet" names to be sort of polyglot as, in fact, most of our American names are.

There are so many untold stories in American historical literature, and even pivotal moments like the New York City draft riots tend to get overlooked in favor of more simplified dichotomies of North vs. South, slavery vs. freedom. What sorts of historical details call out to you as a writer?

The most exciting part of researching and writing historical fiction is being immersed in a particular period or place. I find the nineteenth century breathtakingly exciting because of the crucial importance of the century in the history of African American people. I also simply admire a number of people who lived in the nineteenth century. This interest has everything to do with the significant number of autobiographies and biographies of formerly enslaved people that cover the horrific events of the enslavement institutions. I think it is important to make an important distinction: the women, men, children, people, were "enslaved." I prefer to use the term this way so that it denotes a condition rather than a description—a kind of shorthand. This use also puts the onus on the person who enslaved another person. Yes, people were born into enslavement, but no person was or is born a slave.

The dialogue between characters in Angels Make Their Hope Here *is inflected with the slang of the time, but the language also feels specific to the characters and their world. How much of it came out of your research, and how much was your creation?*

Again I'd say that I learned a lot from reading slave narratives and newspapers of the period. And because I had the freedom to imagine my characters' day-to-day lives, I gave myself the license to invent a few idiosyncratic terms. I consulted other works of fiction and dictionaries of period slang. Then, too, certain of the novel's very opinionated and eccentric characters seemed to be whispering phrases to me.

Are there historical events that you didn't include but wish people knew more about?

I wish there had been a way for me to include information about black immigration to Canada before and after the passage of the Fugitive Slave Act. In fact, I believe that there is fundamental ignorance of and misunderstanding about the travails faced by blacks after the passage of this law in 1850. The effects were profound upon free blacks north of the Mason-Dixon Line. In abject fear for their lives and their freedom, many crossed the Canadian border.

Questions and Topics for Discussion

1. *Angels Make Their Hope Here* is threaded through with events that surround the Civil War, like Dossie's passage via the Underground Railroad and the draft riots, but the story is separate from the war itself. How has the book expanded your knowledge of the period and opened your mind to different ideas about what life was like in the nineteenth century?

2. Russell's Knob is "a hide, a hush-up, a keep-quiet-about spot," its own hidden world within the greater surround. In what ways do its inhabitants hide from the outside world — and how are they very much present in it?

3. Would you consider Russell's Knob to be a utopian community? Why or why not?

4. Duncan is many things to Dossie — a man, a god, her savior, and her husband. In what ways does their relationship change over the course of the book? Why do you think she falls in love with him — and how does her perception of him change when she returns from New York? How did your perception of him change as his relationship with Dossie shifts?

5. Duncan's work is not always clear—though we know he is a smuggler of goods, a seller of cigars, a conductor on the Underground Railroad, and a protector of the People in Russell's Knob. Is he a good man or a bad man? Can he be both?

6. Duncan decides to call Dossie "Bird" when finalizing the papers at their wedding ceremony. What is the significance of birds in Dossie's life?

7. Duncan thinks to himself, "The pretty one is not responsible for her own prettiness. It is an accident of nature. She can't be credited or blamed for it" (page 41). Dossie's beauty both protects her and imperils her. In what ways does it bring events upon her that she does not ask for or deserve? In what ways does this create uniquely nineteenth-century problems for her, and in what ways do women in the twenty-first century still face the same problems?

8. Noelle and Duncan have an on-again, off-again relationship, and it is said that they would never fully commit to each other. Why do you think that is? How are Duncan's feelings for Dossie different than they are for Noelle?

9. How do Dossie's feelings for Jan change over the course of the book? How is her love for Jan different from her love for Duncan?

10. Early in the book Noelle tells Dossie that "all gods are welcome here." How would you define religion in Russell's

Knob? How does the people's belief in the Grandmothers, and the ancestors, define their lives?

11. Jan's name is not originally Jan. It is changed for him after his mother is killed. What meaning do names, and sweet names, have for the characters in *Angels Make Their Hope Here*?

12. Many point out that Pet could "pass" for white if he wanted to, but Duncan and Hat fight for him to stay in Russell's Knob and thus not be identified solely as his father's son. At the end of the book, Pet rejects his father's gift of a new birth certificate and states that he will never try to pass. Is it a difficult decision for him or one he had made long before his father's offer?

13. Though he is a purchaser of slaves, Ernst Wilhelm commits murder to protect the freedom of his unborn child and his mistress. He also sacrifices much of his wealth and gives up his home in Russell's Knob. Did his parental choices surprise you?

14. In the slang of Russell's Knob, a "dossie" is considered a found luck for a man, and a "jimmer" is a found luck for a woman. Is Dossie a found luck for Duncan?

15. Emil Branch's attack on Dossie makes it clear just how precarious the freedom of a black woman was before the Civil War. While she and Jan are ensconced in Five Points, Dossie asks herself, "Had she passed from Duncan's

pocket into Jan's then? It was a hazard to become the pocket floss of one man or another" (page 235). In what ways was the protection of a man both necessary and problematic for women—especially black women—in the nineteenth century? How is Dossie ultimately able to find her independence?

Also by BREENA CLARKE

Stand the Storm

"Deeply affecting.... An evocative, historically rich book that brings the turbulent Civil War period alive."　　*—Time*

"I loved this book. I loved these people.... Breena Clarke has written another striking work of historical fiction that weaves the passionate, dramatic, and uplifting story of the African American aspiration for true freedom into the great American tapestry.... *Stand the Storm* reads like a great nineteenth-century page-turner, like *Oliver Twist* or the masterful *Uncle Tom's Cabin*.... Breena Clarke writes about ordinary people who happen to be exceptional.... She writes in a deceptively simple and subtle style, with an almost perfect sense of period and history."　　*—*Gail Buckley, *Washington Post Book World*

"A gripping novel about a family's heart-wrenching journey out of slavery."　　*—*Felicia Pride, *Baltimore Sun*

"Breena Clarke again delivers a gripping story and seemingly effortlessly captures the bond between a mother and son and the price of freedom."　　*—Ebony*

Back Bay Books
Available wherever paperbacks are sold

Also by BREENA CLARKE

River, Cross My Heart

"An accomplished first novel....*River, Cross My Heart* flows quietly but carves deep channels in the reader's mind."
— Walter Kirn, *Time*

"A genuine masterpiece....Full of grace and beauty and profound insights....It bears traces of Eudora Welty's charm and Toni Morrison's passion." — Michael Shelden, *Baltimore Sun*

"A compelling novel....Inspired by tales her parents told her about growing up in the 1920s, Clarke brings to life a whole neighborhood of vivid personalities, writing blacks back into Georgetown's history." — Denise Kersten, *USA Today*

"Seldom do I find a novel that I can recommend to everyone. My aunt likes a book to be both sad and funny. My mother-in-law hates violence and sex. Friends like lyricism and depth of theme. Everyone wants a good story. I'm delighted to say that the debut novel by Breena Clarke fills the bill in all these respects." — Sandra Scofield, *Chicago Tribune*

Back Bay Books
Available wherever paperbacks are sold